The Rye Rooftop Club

Mother's Day

Mark Feakins

Books by Mark Feakins:

The Rye Series
#1 The Rye Rooftop Club
#2 The Rye Rooftop Club: Mother's Day

"We are all children of one great mother: nature."
Charles Dickens

For my mother,

the person who first took me to Rye, watched Blue Peter with me and still makes the best cheese scones.

CHAPTER 1

Three Years Ago

*The joy of Isopropyl alcohol, Eric,
Ernie and Karl Marx.*

Ruby crashed through her back door, slung the owl-shaped peg bag across the room and leant on the kitchen worktop gulping air into her lungs between sobs. She yanked open the fridge door, took out the half-empty bottle of Chardonnay, fumbled in the crowded sink for a cleanish glass and filled it with wine.

As she staggered to a chair, she knocked the imposing pine dresser and its muddle of china and glass wobbled precariously, "Go on, fall off! I dare you!" she hissed. However, the Birds of Britain mugs thought better of it, settling back into place, while the three china piggy banks in the shape of communist leaders steadfastly refused to leave their positions on the top shelf.

She wiped her face with the back of her hand and threw back a large slug of wine, then she sat with her eyes shut, holding on to the edge of her kitchen table, afraid she might lose whatever control remained. After a few minutes, Ruby opened her eyes, took a moment to focus and looked around the kitchen. The once bright blue walls were dull, the wooden cupboards faded and the pine dresser shabby.

Ruby peered at the distorted reflection of the woman in the glass of wine in front of her; drab hair loosely held in a rubber band at the back of a scrawny neck, tired red eyes smudged with day-old make-up, a pale face devoid of anything that might be described as life.

"Who are you?" she whispered.

Silence pulsed through the room in reply. She screwed her eyes shut as more questions swirled in front of her: When had she turned into a woman who had a meltdown because the washing line broke? Why had she trampled the clean washing into the muddy grass instead of picking it up? Why was she alone with two dead husbands behind her and no one to answer her questions?

Ruby took another sip of wine, acutely aware she had also become a woman who drank her first glass of wine before thinking about what she wanted for breakfast. But who was to blame? Who?

An image of her absent daughter, wild haired and angry, crept in from the corner of her mind. No, it wasn't Anna's fault, that wasn't right. Ruby shook her head and looked up to the very top of the dresser at the fat little piggy banks that she despised. Her memory was always clouded now, but she had a vague feeling Anna had a matching set - perhaps that's why she'd kept the miserable things. They sat there, day after day, watching and judging in their severe communist way.

Ruby felt the tang of wine chase across her tongue as she drank another mouthful, then she flipped her mousy ponytail over her shoulder, reached forward and slid a white envelope across the table. She let it sit, neat and clean in front of her for a few moments, enjoying the sight of something untainted and new. It had been there for three days, but she still thought of it as new. Every day since her birthday she had opened one of the cards that had arrived. Day one had been from her neighbour, who had written, *All the best from Claire and family*. No mention of it being her fiftieth, but how would Claire have known? Ruby couldn't remember the last time she'd sent her a card, maybe when the baby was born? Eric, was it? Or Ernie? On day two she had opened a card with spidery writing that spelled out, *Best Wishes from Auntie Beryl*. She knew she should give the old lady a call, but she also knew she wouldn't. Today was the third and final card. She had saved it for last as the familiar writing told her it was from her old school friend, Rebecca

Rebecca had been more of a Duran Duran girl than a Wham! fan when they met as children, but despite that they had still become friends. She tore open the flap and slid out the card, which was reassuringly solid and she gripped it tightly. She turned it over and brightly coloured words punched her in the face:

7

10,585 Days Since You Were 21!

She gasped, dropping the gaudy card onto the table. Her head spun as the numbers pulsed before her - 10,585 days. 10,585 days. Thousands and thousands of days gone. Ruby traced the embossed numbers with a trembling finger. She thought about how the girl who had loved Wham! so much had vanished, little by little, with each of those 10,585 days until *this* – this empty woman surrounded by ugly, useless things was all that remained. Ruby needed to get away from the numbers and as she stood up her chair knocked her bags-for-life off their neat little hook. She stared at them - were they really with her for the rest of her life? Did they have another 10,585 god-awful days to go through together?

"NO!" Ruby roared, grabbing the bags and flinging them at the dresser. "No, no, NO!"

She reached out and the next moment the sound of splintering glass echoed around the kitchen as the now empty bottle of wine hit the faded blue wall. She picked up the plastic recycling box, went to the back door and flung the jumble of empty wine bottles out into the garden. Kicking the box back into the room, Ruby picked up her glass from the table and threw it with all the force she could muster into the box, covering her eyes with her arm as it shattered satisfyingly. She grabbed another from the hated pine dresser and hurled it in, then another and another until they were all gone. Then she moved on to the neat little robin mug, then the blue tit, chaffinch and nuthatch until they too were no more.

Ruby's eyes landed on the wine rack at the end of the chipped kitchen counter. She loaded six pristine bottles of wine into her arms, strode down the hall and into the street. Starting with Claire next door, she put a bottle on her doorstep, rang the bell and moved on. The same at the next house and the next, until she had given them all away. As she walked back to the house, Claire was standing at her front door with baby Eric or Ernie on her hip, "Everything OK, Ruby?"

Ruby leant on the gate, catching her breath, "Fine. How's...?" she gestured at the puzzled looking child.

"Eric? He's good thanks, yeah."

Ruby's eyes suddenly lit up, "Does Eric have a piggy bank?"

"No, no, he doesn't..."

"Wait," Ruby said, disappearing into the house and quickly returning with her china pigs. "Karl Marx, Joseph Stalin or Chairman Mao? Take your pick," she held them out.

"Ruby, I..."

"Eric, won't care. Have Marx - he started it all, the bastard," she handed him over, dumped Stalin and Mao in her wheelie bin and went back inside, slamming the door behind her. She leant against the chipped wood, breathing heavily - when had she last slammed a door like that or used bad language? Too long ago.

As she pushed herself upright, something moved under her foot and she looked down to see a postcard lying on the doormat. It showed a glowing orange sunset behind the words: *Is there something missing from your life?* She picked it up and turned it over. On the back was a photo of a slim, tight-looking woman. This was Sharon, she read, who claimed to be an expert on negativity. Ruby grimaced, thinking she could give her a run for her money in that particular department, so Sharon got taken into the kitchen and shoved into the recycling box with the broken glass and porcelain.

Ruby stood in the square little room with her hands on her head, her heart pounding with exhilaration and anger in equal measure. Anger at herself, at her long-gone husbands, her overstuffed home that seemed constantly empty, the twenty-one-year-old Wham! fan she used to be who had deserted her. She began to turn slowly on the spot, round and round she went. Then, as quickly as the thought entered her head, she was off; the old garden shed was close to falling down, but still held her first husband's tools and it didn't take long to find an axe. Back in the kitchen she swung the rusty axe over her head and brought it down again and again on the pine dresser, without care for any collateral damage. The rage roared through her, the pain barely registering as the impact thudded through her hands and arms again and again.

Soon the dresser was in large chunks strewn across the floor and Ruby stood panting against the cooker. Suddenly a new thought came to her and she dropped the axe, stuffed her mobile phone in the pocket of her cardigan and scrabbled around in the kitchen drawers, eventually pulling out her mother's old bottle of rubbing alcohol and a box of matches. She grabbed an armful of dresser pieces and marched down the garden to the overgrown patio, deliberately walking over the abandoned washing. She piled the wood together and read the label on the bottle; *Isopropyl alcohol has a flammability range of between 2 and 12.7% in air. It should be kept away from heat and open flame.* "Too fucking right," she said, loudly, surprising herself with the pleasure of the sound of that word on her lips. The alcohol splashed on to the lumps of pine, swiftly followed by a burning match. Ruby stood back as it all went up with a roar of light and power.

Her hands shook, but she managed to get her phone out of her pocket and fumbled across the screen until she found what she was looking for - *The Greatest Hits of Wham!* Turning the volume up as far as it would go, she threw the phone behind her onto the grass and danced and danced to the soundtrack of her old self.

CHAPTER 2

Today

*The Queen's jigsaws, paper
hearts and a lazy daisy.*

Anna took a deep breath and wiped her face with the edge of her Magic Roundabout apron. She stood in the small triangle of kitchen at the back of The Cookery and counted to her favourite number - eleven. She looked down, but the box of eggs was still lying on the floor with yellow yokes oozing in all directions.

"What did you do that for?" Irene asked.

Anna bit her tongue, "To see if they'd bounce."

"They don't," Irene said as she leant over the wooden

counter. "Anyway, as I was saying, it was monstrous. All purple it was, puckered too. The doctor said he'd never seen anything like it – but, he said it as if that was a bad thing! I mean..."

Anna sighed, "Irene, you came in early to set up, didn't you? There's a lot to do," and she scooped the broken shells and eggs back into the soggy box.

Irene turned and sat at one of the pink gingham-covered café tables, which was piled with red paper napkins, "Fair enough, but my stuff is nearly done," she waved a bony hand indicating the red crepe-paper hearts that were stuck at odd angles all over the café. The shelves of random bric-a-brac that gave the place much of its charm looked even more chaotic than normal, as the stuffed owl sported a heart-shaped hat and Victorian dolls had bright red additions to their tiny hands and feet. The large glass windows onto the High Street had not escaped the crepe-paper onslaught either, with hearts liberally sprinkled across them like a bad case of measles.

Anna took another breath and turned up the pre-war Parisian café music she found comforting. She loved Valentine's Day, it was one of her favourite days of the year and she was determined to enjoy this one more than ever. Now she had decided to focus on herself and her career goals, she felt liberated from the seemingly endless search for the man of her dreams. She had gone all-out to prepare a menu for the café that would surpass all other years - it was going to be amazing, but she was already exhausted. She'd been up since five-thirty creating heart-shaped cherry scones, spiced cherub biscuits, several batches of her famous pies (today's special being oyster, bacon and horseradish) and two different lover's layer cakes, all featuring generous amounts of her new favourite ingredient, pomegranate seeds with chilli.

She slowly let out her breath, "I didn't think Valentine's Day was your thing, Irene - last year you said you'd rather eat sprouts for breakfast than take part."

Irene sniffed, "I think it's the side effects of these new tablets I'm on. I'm not sure they're doing me any good - they keep making me volunteer for things." She picked up a paper napkin and started to fold it carefully, "These are tricky bleeders. Her at the craft club is no more than four feet tall with her arms up, but she's got ever such nimble fingers. She made her what-nots into hearts in seconds, but it'll take me hours."

Anna quickly mopped the floor, blowing damp copper curls of hair off her face, "No pressure, but they need to be beautiful. We can't let standards drop, not this year, if I want to expand the business. Right, gravy next," she said. "I found a recipe packed with all sorts of ancient aphrodisiacs."

"You want to be careful with them aphro-wotnots, we don't want people keeling over who are on statins or have a pacemaker. And why you want another business is beyond me," Irene said as she attempted a particularly tricky origami manoeuvre. "I've told you before, that's why jigsaws were invented. When you miss a man, crack into a thousand-piece puzzle...I've done six of the Royal Family this year already and it's only the middle of February. Mind you, that lot are always changing, no sooner have you finished a nice wedding photo than they're up and divorced. I'm thinking of changing to Spitfires, they're much more reliable."

Anna started rummaging through some of the many

small cupboards in the old shop counter, gathering what she needed to make the gravy, "I want a new challenge. I love The Cookery, but I need to achieve something more – on my own - before I eventually get married and have a family..."

"...and ruin your sleep, your bosom and your life. It did me no good."

"Irene, that is not true! You have a huge family and you love them very much – despite what you say. For instance, how many Valentine's cards did you get from your grandchildren and great-grandchildren?"

Irene paused in her creative endeavours, "Nine - but I reckon they were forced to make them at school by teachers who wanted to watch Netflix for a couple of hours."

Anna smiled and returned to her ingredients just as the café door flew open, the little bell above it bouncing off the ceiling with shock. Rosie, the teenage, tooth-braced, weekend waitress stood dramatically in the doorway gasping for breath, "He's on the ground...he was dead...but he's not now...I called the ambliance... then he said to come...and find someone!"

Anna came around the counter into the café, "Rosie, you look nice," she said, still not used to her youngest staff member's overnight transformation from black-clad goth to boho hippy with plastic daisies in her hair.

Rosie looked down at the cream cotton maxi dress under her grey duffle coat, "Oh, thanks, being a goth was hard – I couldn't afford the hairspray."

Anna nodded, "Fair enough-ski. Now, what's going on? Who's not dead?"

Rosie flicked her sandy brown fringe, "Well, he was just lying in the road. I thought he was sleeping - people do on Sunday when they've had a skin-full on a Saturday night. Then I thought maybe he was dead, but he wasn't. He opened his eyes when I kicked his leg...I think that may have hurt a bit. He had a dog, it growled at me."

"Who, girl, who?" Irene shouted.

"Irene, wait, don't yell at Rosie."

"Well, honestly, she made more sense when she was a Klingon."

Anna sat Rosie in the nearest chair, "Rosie, focus on me - don't let Irene put you off. This man, he had a dog? Was it Ralph from next door? From The Bookery - the bookshop?"

"Yes, him."

"Blimey, and he ask you to call an ambulance?"

"Yes, I did that. The lady I spoke to had an accent from Scotland or Wales, I think, but that's a long way to come, isn't it? Sussex is right at the bottom of England."

"We'll let them worry about that, Rosie. Where is Ralph now?"

"Still in the gutter."

Irene opened her mouth, "Irene, don't," Anna warned. "But which gutter, sweetheart? Where in Rye is he?"

"Not far. Watch-thing Street, you know, the one with the Catholic church in it."

Anna started undoing her apron, "Well, done, Rosie," she said, quickly. "Right, Irene please will you go down the road to Let's Screw and see if Joe's in his shop. I need him to come and meet me at Watchbell Street. Rosie, you need to be really fast, I want you to run to Cinque..."

"Where?" Rosie said vaguely, fiddling with a rogue daisy that had come away from the others in her hair.

"Anna, go and find Ralph," Irene said. "Leave lazy

daisy to me."

"Thanks, Irene," Anna called as she ran out of the door.

Irene started to close in on Rosie who froze with fear to her chair, "Right, put on your listening ears, young lady - you need to go to the restaurant you worked at every day for a month over Christmas. Do you remember? It's called Cinque."

Rosie leapt to her feet and started for the door, "WAIT!" Irene yelled, stopping her in her tracks. "You don't know why you are going there yet!"

Rosie stepped back against the door, her cheeks burning red, "Oh yes..." she whispered.

"We need you to find Sam, the chef, and take him to where Ralph is. Now go."

Rosie didn't need to be yelled at twice and took off up the street.

"I swear those daisies are too tight round her head," Irene chuntered as she pulled the door too behind her and went in search of Joe.

❉ ❉ ❉

Anna was not a great runner. She was a woman who enjoyed her curves, but they were not necessarily conducive to speed. Also, her eclectic wardrobe of vintage clothes was proving less than helpful when travelling quickly over damp cobbled streets – of which the ancient town of Rye had plenty. Her traditional Dutch clogs with hand-painted tulips were making it hard work and today's heart-themed kimono over her Thunderbirds t-shirt was not much better, yards of silk flew around her as she pounded past the churchyard and across the square of old twisted houses.

A voice echoed off the buildings in front of her, "Stanley, sit down!"

"Ralph!" Anna called as she crested the top of the hill and, failing to control her speed with the wooden-soled clogs, shot down the steep slope towards him like a champion slalom skier. "Can't stop," she screamed as she hurtled closer.

Ralph was lying in the road, one hand holding tightly to Stanley's lead, the excitable beagle jumping and barking at Anna's sudden appearance.

"Stop!" Ralph shouted, his spare hand waving wildly at her.

Just as it looked like she would add to whatever injuries he had already sustained, Anna saw an old iron lamppost to her left and lunged for it, managing to grab it and haul herself to an undignified halt, collapsing in a heap.

"I couldn't...stop," she panted. "Dutch...clogs...no breaks. Have you been...run over?"

Ralph's face was very pale and he was shivering uncontrollably in his thin running clothes which were now soaked by the cold morning drizzle, "No, I f-fell."

"What?" Anna said, crawling towards him. "You fell off the pavement? How old are you, ninety-four?"

He shook his head, speaking with short shallow breaths, "Stanley took off ...s-suddenly...he saw a red balloon. It was heart-shaped...f-floating by. He pulled me round on his lead. My f-foot went into the gutter. I think I've...b-broken something...ah!" he yelped as another wave of white-hot pain hit him hard. He rested his head on the cool cobbles for a second, to make the stars of light dancing across his vision stop. As he heard more footsteps approaching, everything slowly went black.

CHAPTER 3

*The art of knitting, milky coffee
and Florence Nightingale.*

Ten minutes later Ralph was being laid gently on
the floor of The Cookery, while Anna tucked
a cushion under his head. Joe's well-sculpted
muscles had been developed primarily for viewing purposes, but today they had proved to be of great practical
use as the hardware shop owner had effortlessly carried
Ralph back through Rye. Anna had followed behind,
texting Sam and then calling the emergency services to
divert the ambulance to the café.

Ralph groaned as his leg settled on the hard floor,
"Sorry," Joe said, taking off his leather jacket and laying
it over his shivering friend. "But you're better here away
from the wet pavement and the rain."

Ralph grimaced, "I know. Sorry."

Irene leant over him, enunciating carefully, "Would-
you-like-a-milky-coffee?"

"Irene, he's in no state for a coffee," Anna snapped.

The bell tinkled as the door opened again, "Everyone alright?" The voice belonged to a tall man with distinguished features, who pulled a tatty tartan hat from his head to reveal grey hair tied back in a neat ponytail. He was wearing a long grey overcoat over a blue and white striped jumper, bright green corduroy trousers and a smart pair of leather brogues, "I thought I saw a dead body being carried in."

"Oh, Martin," Anna said. "It's Ralph, he's had an accident."

"Good heavens, what have you done, old thing?" Martin said, stepping inside.

Ralph grimaced, "I think I might have broken my leg."

"Ouch, is an ambulance on its way?"

"Yes," Anna said, kneeling beside Ralph.

"Nice jumper by the way," Joe said to Martin. "Is it new?"

"Thank you for noticing. For a change, it's not from the hostel's rainbow collection of lost and found items, I made it myself," Martin said with a proud smile. He was living in temporary accommodation for the homeless after an unhappy few weeks on the streets of Rye before Christmas. Years of a heavy drinking habit that didn't suit either him or his wife had led to an acrimonious parting of the ways and the loss of his home. Martin began to turn his life around when Anna and Ralph had supported him with some part-time work, but he had come in to his own when Sam had needed help in the kitchen of his restaurant, Cinque, over Christmas.

"You made it yourself?" Irene asked. "With knitting?"

"Indeed. It was suggested to me as a new skill to develop mindfulness. I've rather taken to it."

"Well, who knew men could knit? Not men like Ralph, you know, proper ones..."

"Irene!" Anna and Joe said together.

"What? Gay people are very creative; we all know that. Mr Mather at craft club - he's ever so nice, but an absolute screamer and can weave raffia like a demon...."

Anna stared at Irene, "Where did you hear the word *screamer*?"

Irene tutted, "I wasn't born on Thursday, you know. I've been around."

Martin interrupted, "Oh dear, our patient appears to have gone slightly green."

All heads turned to Ralph, who could see the floating stars again. Anna took his hand and squeezed it, "Ralph, talk to me...talk to me..."

"Please...don't break my fingers as well."

"Sorry, I thought you were going to faint again," she turned as she heard someone running down the High Street. "I think that's Sam. Ralph, Sam's here."

Ralph smiled and nodded as Sam skidded to a halt in the doorway. He was wearing chef's whites and his trademark baseball cap on backwards holding his hair back from his handsome face, which at this moment was flushed with exertion and concern, "Where is he?" he panted. "Rosie sent me up to St Anthony's church, then I saw your text saying he was here."

Ralph smiled as Sam knelt beside him, "Happy Valentine's Day," he said.

Sam took his hand, "What happened?"

Everyone started talking at once, giving him different elements of the story so far;

"Rosie found him on the pavement..."

"I carried him back when it started to rain..."

"He's very pale, thinks he's broken his leg..."

"The ambulance is on its way..."

"He doesn't want a milky coffee..."

Sam ignored them all, leaned closer to Ralph and whispered, "Hey, Mr Bookseller, what the hell have you done?"

Ralph smiled, speaking between deep breaths in order to keep the pain at bay, "I was on my morning run. Just fell over. Stanley pulled suddenly. Caught me off balance. Think I've broken something. I'll live."

"You'd bloody better or I'll kill you myself. Where's Stanley?" As Sam spoke, the little beagle's wet nose and wide concerned eyes poked their way under his arm. "Can someone take him away?" Sam snapped.

"It wasn't his fault. I wasn't concentrating," Ralph said.

Sam softened and scratched Stanley's ears, "Well, he needs to be kept away, we don't want him climbing all over you. Go on, Stan, clear off." He pushed him away and Anna took hold of his harness.

"I'll put him upstairs, Little House on The Prairie is on the telly, he likes that," Anna said leading him to the back of the café and through the door to her flat above.

"You could have chosen a better day," Irene said and all eyes turned to her as she sat at the table, her severe black bobbed hair hanging low over her painstakingly folded napkin hearts. "There's no one free to go to the hospital with you, not on Valentine's Day, we're all rushed off our feet."

"Irene," Joe said. "Give the guy a break. Hey, that's a joke, right? Break? His leg?"

"I'm going with him," Sam said, ignoring Joe.

Ralph frowned, "No. Full restaurant. Can't."

"I don't care - they can have salad."

"Sam," Ralph said, resting his hand on Sam's knee. "I'll be fine. Stay."

Anna appeared from the back of the café, "I'll go to the hospital with him."

Irene put her arm out and stopped Anna, "Just a minute, Florence Nightingale, who's going to cook forty pies and all that aphro-wotnot gravy for a café full of loved-up calorie counters? Not me and certainly not Rosie, the riveting, over there." She gestured towards Rosie who was now standing in the doorway chewing a plastic daisy she had plucked from her hair.

Ralph shook his head and groaned, "Anna, you can't. This is your busiest day for ages. I'll be OK."

"What about The Bookery?" Joe asked. "You said you've had a bad few weeks yourself, since Christmas. You needed the sales this weekend to make the books balance. Hey, that's another one...books balance...book-store? I'm on fire."

"Really?" groaned Ralph.

"Sorry," Joe said, leaning over him. "What I was going to say was, Let's Screw is going to be dead today. No one buys mouse traps on Valentine's. I'll close my place and open The Bookery for you."

Ralph shook his head again, "No. Not fair. Please."

"Look, the answer is obvious," Irene said, banging the table in front of her with a Bugs Bunny pepper pot. "I know the way round the hospital - I'm there so often they've practically named a wing after my kidneys. So, I will sacrifice myself and go with Ralph."

There was silence from the group as they looked at her and a small groan from Ralph, his desperate eyes trying to signal to Sam that this was the last thing he wanted.

Martin gently cleared his throat, "That is indeed an option. However, with a full café expected, how would this place function without you, Irene?"

"It'd be carnage."

"So," Martin continued. "May I make a suggestion? Anna, you cannot leave The Cookery until the lunch rush is over and the same is true for Irene. Sam, you need to be at Cinque." He held up his hand as Sam started to protest, "I am aware the charming Julia, who would normally deputise for you in the kitchen, is on a romantic break in Hastings. So, there is no-one available who is capable of running the restaurant at full stretch in your absence."

"Well," Sam said, sitting back on his heels beside Ralph. "I suppose."

"Exactly. Therefore, I propose the following: Joe closes Let's Screw, as it is right next to The Bookery. He can put a notice on the door and work between both shops relatively easily. I will accompany Ralph to the hospital and remain with him until lunch service is over at The Cookery, then Anna can come and relieve me. I will then return here and help Irene to serve the great and good of Rye with cake and scones for the quieter part of the day."

"It's like when Poirot explains who the murderer is on the telly…I never understand that bit either," Rosie said.

"It makes sense, but I still don't like it," Sam said, looking down into the pained face of his lover.

Ralph took his hand, "Clear off. I'm fine with Martin."

"True, true," Sam said, leaning down and gently kissing him on the lips. He rested his forehead briefly against Ralph's and whispered something no one could hear, then got up and made his way to the door.

Ralph sensed Sam hesitate behind him, "Someone tell the once second most eligible bachelor in England...to bugger off."

Sam pulled his cap tight on his head, "I hope they cut your leg off with a blunt bread knife. See you at home later." He turned away quickly, so they couldn't see the tears in his eyes as he was forced to leave Ralph in pain and go back to his restaurant. As he crossed the High Street the distant sound of an ambulance siren floated through the air.

CHAPTER 4

The trip to Christmas Eve, heroic
acts and tricky Paul Daniels.

Martin sat with a large plastic bag on his lap, from which extended a length of thick grey wool attached to two long metal needles he was using to knit a complex looking pattern. Lying next to him on a hospital trolley was Ralph.

"How long have we been here?"

"Oh, hello. Back with us, are you?" Martin said, his needles pausing. "Those painkillers sent you off for a little nap. Well, we've been in the hospital for a couple of hours, but we've been waiting for your x-ray for about half an hour, no more. Feeling any better?"

"Erm, yes, a bit, I think. The pain's not so bad, just feeling a bit woozy. I think I may be hallucinating."

"Excellent."

"I dreamt some mice were tap-dancing in my sink. I could hear their little feet tapping."

"Ah, that may have been the sound of my needles - I've been making good use of the time available."

Ralph turned to look, "Oh, yes, you're knitting."

"It was suggested to me as a kind of therapy to combat my desire for alcohol."

Ralph closed his eyes and began drifting off - a rowing boat containing two empty white picture frames floated across his vision. Pulling at the oars was a tiny old lady wearing an enormous sun hat and blue sunglasses.

Ralph shook his head, dismissing the images, and opened his eyes, "Sorry, what were you saying?"

"Those painkillers seem to be doing sterling work," Martin chuckled. "I was wondering if you had been inspired to paint anything recently? Your artwork around The Bookery is excellent."

Ralph shook his head, "No, not yet. I can't seem to...since Auntie B."

"Ah, yes, Mrs Bondolfi. I never got to meet her, but I knew her work, of course."

"Did you?"

"Oh, yes, quite beautiful. Do you still have many of her paintings to sell?"

"Yes, a few. Joe gave me most of them when she died, so they can live on in people's homes. She would have liked that."

"I'm sure she would," Martin pulled more wool from the bag. "Didn't she give you some of her empty frames to encourage you to pick up the brush and palate again?"

The pillow softly engulfed Ralph's head as visions started to swim in front of him. This time it was the image of a small iron table surrounded by a myriad of tiny white lights. He knew the table should be on their shared roof terrace above the shops, but here it seemed to be floating through space. Then a number of striped candy canes and a bottle of pink champagne danced around the table, while snowflakes began to fall in large silent waves. It was Christmas Eve again and they were all there; Anna and Joe sitting with him at the table, Auntie B in her usual seat smiling between sips of sherry and delicate puffs of her single daily cigarette. Then she looked directly at him under the brim of her ever-present sun hat and slowly began to fade away.

Ralph's head spun as he relived the shock of finding out she had died alone on the terrace a few hours later, apparently at peace with the world. She had been the beating heart of their family of friends, the Rooftop Club, and although the only one of them she was related to by blood was Joe, her death had hit them all hard. As Auntie B disappeared from his dream, he saw the table set sail again among the little white lights that slowly began to fizz and pop one by one. He watched the little pin pricks of light disappear in the darkness and could hear someone calling him from far away, "Ralph!"

Quietly, but insistently, "Ralph!"

"Ralph. Can you hear me, old thing?" Martin tapped Ralph's hand gently with a knitting needle until he opened his eyes. "Hello again. Where have you been this time? Anywhere nice?"

"Sorry, I was thinking about Auntie B. I'm not sure these painkillers are good for me," he shook his head to ensure the upsetting images were gone.

"They're doing their job, distracting your brain from the damage you've done to yourself. You kept saying, *I promise I will. I promise I will.*"

"Did I? I think I must have been talking to Auntie

B. Just before she died, she made me promise to start painting again, to fill the picture frames she gave me. But I haven't, I can't seem to face it. I mean, I suppose I don't feel ready or...brave enough."

Martin put his knitting back into his bag and laid it down beside him. He stood up, stretched and moved to the end of the bed, "Ralph, last year you made a courageous decision to leave everything you knew, your entire life in fact, and start again in Rye. You brought The Bookery back to life, made an excellent group of friends who would do anything for you, fell in love with a rather nice chap who is quite potty about you, coached a football team of marauding under-tens, helped an aging bum off the streets and to cap it all off you rescued a stray dog, called him Stanley and took him into your home - all in the space of a couple of months. Have I missed any other of your heroic acts?"

Ralph smiled, "I think you may have covered most of them."

"Excellent," Martin raised a bushy eyebrow. "Therefore, standing in front of a blank canvas should hold no fear for a swashbuckler such as yourself, should it?"

"I want to, I really do, but it feels too soon. After hiding for years from my friends, myself, my family...Helen...everything's happened so quickly, in a few months. I suppose the shadow of the shame of coming out doesn't go away overnight," Ralph shifted on the hard bed. "Once Helen and I have settled the divorce, I hope I will feel able to be completely me, then I'll paint something. I want to spend time with Sam too. Am I making any sense?"

Martin laid a hand on Ralph's good foot, "Perfect sense. I too went through a period of readjustment when I was young and had to start again from scratch. I loved painting but stopped for a long time, until I became an art teacher. Art needs a clear head, you'll get there. Trust me."

Ralph looked at the tall, gentle man in front of him, "Why did you have to start again?" he asked.

Martin looked around and ignored Ralph's question, "I think I need a coffee; I didn't have time this morning with all the excitement. There is a machine around the corner, I'll be two ticks."

Martin disappeared along the corridor and Ralph pulled the thin blanket up over his shoulders for warmth. He dozed until Martin returned and then did his best to focus, "That coffee smells good."

"I'm sorry, nil by mouth for you, old thing. However, you may indulge all you like in the aroma of the plastic cup and coffee-au-luke-warm-water" Martin said as he started to unravel more wool. "May I ask you a question, Ralph? And please, feel free not to answer if it is too personal."

"Of course."

"You mentioned the divorce from your wife. I too am going through the early stages of the process with my wife...which is not proving to be a pleasant or productive experience. Have you been given any indication of how long it generally takes?"

Ralph used his elbows to sit himself up slightly and let out a gasp as a shot of pain in his leg broke through the barrier created by the pain killers, "Ow! Bugger, that hurt."

Martin shook his head, "Sorry, this is not the time..."

"No, no," Ralph said. "It's fine. We have nothing else to do but talk, do we? The thing is, my divorce from Helen is going to be pretty straight forward. There is nothing to settle, as I left everything for her when I ran away. So, they reckon it could be done in a couple of months."

Martin sipped his coffee, "As long as that? I see."

"Is your wife proving to be tricky?"

"Tricky? Paul Daniels would look like an amateur next to her. Don't misunderstand me, living with a man who could polish off a bottle of brandy before elevenses can't have been easy, but she is now making a song and dance of what I had hoped would be an equitable arrangement, especially as she can quite clearly see my...erm...difficult circumstances."

"Martin, what can I do to help? Is it a question of money?"

"No, no, you have been generous enough providing temporary employment to get me off the streets. I am acutely aware neither you nor Anna can sustain an extra staff member now the busy festive period is behind us. Similarly, Sam is now only able to offer me the odd kitchen shift here and there. So, until the divorce is settled and the house sold, I need to find a proper job and my own accommodation. *Some painters transform the sun into a yellow spot, others transform a yellow spot into the sun,* so said Picasso. It is now time for my transformation. I believe they are looking for a new Ambassador to Paris, I may apply."

"Do you have to leave the hostel?"

"It's only designed as a temporary solution for those without shelter. The longer I stay the less room there is for those in greater need. But I have been given a few weeks to make other arrangements. Fear not, all will be well. Ah, I see an angel approaching..."

Ralph turned and saw a harassed looking porter bustling towards them, with a mini-Mars Bar disappearing into her mouth.

"Shorry, no jime for runch," she said, chewing cheerily as she flicked through Ralph's chart at the end of the bed. "Righ chen, ret's ger a priddy pickcha of ru," and she began dragging the trolley away and down the corridor.

CHAPTER 5

*The Haemorrhoid Islands, the Dr's
shoes and the wounded soldier.*

Joe was thinking about lunch when Anna appeared outside the window of The Bookery and waved a large sausage roll at him.

"You read my mind," he said as she came into the shop. "My stomach and I were having words about food."

"It's pork and pickle with a hint of fennel for crunch, oh, and a sprinkling of pomegranate seeds...with chilli, is that OK?" she said handing it over.

"Jeez, all that in one pastry?" Joe said, tucking an open book under the keyboard on the counter. "Aren't you supposed to be rushed off your feet?"

"It's been bonkers, but everyone has their meals now, so I can escape for a few minutes. Irene's in charge, so they should all behave. What are you reading?" Anna said, leaning over to take a look.

"Oh, just something I found to pass the time. It's been a bit slow."

Joe put his hand on the book, but Anna lifted the keyboard and was able to read the title, *Grow Roots From The Heart And Find Your True Self!*

"Really? I thought you'd be more of a Grow your Own Viagra sort of man," she said, laughing at her own joke until she saw Joe's embarrassed face. "Oh, sorry, that was unfair. I'm in a flap today, it's been so busy and then there's Ralph in hospital and I nearly forgot to collect some spare trousers for him so he doesn't flash the orthopaedic ward – they had to cut his running ones off. Sorry."

Joe shrugged, "It's fine. I've never read one of these self-help books before, I was looking around earlier and saw it. I guess I've been thinking a lot lately, what with Imogen and Auntie B...I mean, Grandma. Jeez, I still can't get used to calling her that."

Anna rubbed his arm gently, "But she only told you she was actually your grandmother a few days before she passed, you barely had time to process it. We all still miss her like crazy. Your girlfriend not being here can't be helping, either."

Joe slipped off the stool and returned the book to a shelf at the back of the shop, "I guess. For a while there with Imogen it felt like an achievement – it kind of felt good to be exclusive with someone. Not long before she died, Auntie B told me I was waiting to belong. Imogen wasn't really around long enough for me to be sure if she was right or not."

Anna looked at his tall figure, stepped up behind him and put her arms around his waist.

"Hey, what's that for?"

"I needed to do it," she said into the small of his strong, v-shaped back. "I always thought you were a *bloke*, you know? Like a proper blokey-bloke, who didn't really bother much about feelings. I never thought of you actually feeling anything."

"Great, thanks," he smiled, turning around to face her and returning the hug, which was awkward as her waist was somewhere down towards his thighs.

Anna looked up at Joe as if she were seeing him for the first time. She saw his handsome, beard-framed face and beautiful blue eyes, but she also noticed dark rings under them and some new, small crinkles around their edges. His positive outlook, rich Canadian accent and endless jokes had made him an irresistible force of nature, but Joe also had a considerable reputation throughout the town for his multitude of short-lived sexual conquests, strengthened by the name of his DIY shop, Let's Screw. All that had come to a halt before Christmas when he had met Imogen and had allowed himself, for probably the first time in his life, to let his emotions have free rein and it had started to seem like they belonged together. Then the local job she had lined-up for the new year had fallen through, and with the demand for trained wind power engineers being limited locally, she had accepted a job that took her up above Scotland to the remote Isle of Lewis.

"Are you still planning your trip up to see her? To the Outer Haemorrhoids," Anna asked.

Joe smiled, "Hebrides."

"That's them. You should go and see her."

"I know, she wants me to go, but it's not going to happen, is it?"

Anna was about to protest when the door to the shop

opened and a sweaty young man in a bomber jacket shot inside, "Can you help me?" he whispered with a furtive look over his shoulder.

Anna stepped away from Joe and whispered back, "Probably. What's wrong?"

"I need a book," the man hissed.

"Well, you're in the right place. Why are we whispering? Are you a spy?"

The man stepped towards them wiping his brow, but not before he had another quick look behind him, "It's Blythe, she thinks I haven't got her a present for Valentine's Day and is on the war path."

Anna crossed her arms and frowned at him, "Well, *have* you got her a present?"

The man looked from Anna to Joe and back again, "No!"

"Well, she's got a right to be after you then, hasn't she?" Anna said as she felt a hand on her shoulder pushing her sideways.

"Thanks, Anna, but I think this is a man-to-man thing," Joe said. "You need to get Ralph's trousers and head off, don't you?"

She huffed, "Hm, yes, I suppose." She made her way across the shop to the pass door that led up to Ralph's flat and turned back, "It'd better be a bloody good book!" she barked, then slammed the door behind her.

The moist young man yelped and looked at Joe, "Have you got one of those? You know, a bloody good book, like she said?"

"Plenty, my friend! Never fear, you are in good hands now."

* * *

As the light faded across Rye later that evening, a canopy of white fairy lights sparkled over the roof terrace that stretched behind the three shops, as if protecting those below. On the small iron table a single candle had been lit and the flame flickered in the evening breeze. When anyone gathered there now, the candle was always alight in memory of Auntie B.

Anna yawned from under a blanket in the depths of a deckchair, as she picked leaves off a bamboo plant in a pot beside her, "I preferred it when they gave you a proper plaster cast and people could write on it with felt tip pens. How long did they say it's got to stay on for? Eight months?"

"Eight weeks, it's only a minor fracture," Ralph laughed, looking down at the plastic boot encasing his leg which rested on a chair beside him at the little iron table. "Weren't you listening to the doctor?"

"I was distracted by his feet."

"His feet? Why were you looking at his feet?"

"I don't know, they were enormous. Didn't you see them? I meant to ask him what size shoes he took, I bet he has trouble getting a good fit."

Ralph shook his head, "For heaven's sake, you are so middle aged."

Anna ruffled her copper curls and flicked at the blonde streak she had recently added to the front of her hair, "It's true, I'm thirty-three – and the most excitement I've had recently is dying a hundred and fifty-three hairs blonde at the front of my head! I'm well past it! Luckily, I'm concentrating on my career at the moment rather than men, I don't seem to have got the hang of them at all, I always pick the rubbish ones. Talking of which, what are you up to tonight, Joe?"

"Charming! I'll probably speak to Imogen if she can get a signal from where she is on the island," Joe said as he leaned over the railing and looked out at the red roofs of the town falling away beneath him.

"Sorry, that must be tough."

"I'm fine. Don't bother about me, guys, it'll work itself out."

"Well, we do bother," Anna said, fiercely. "We bother a lot. We are the Rooftop Club, that's what we are here for - to bother and be bothered and bother each other...anyone need me to say bother again?"

"Don't bother," Ralph and Joe said at the same time.

"Well, as long as you've got the message. I know Auntie B's not here anymore, but we are here whenever you need us...and quite often when you don't. Right, now I have imparted my words of wisdom, I suppose I ought to take Stanley for his walk."

"Thanks," Ralph said. "I'll have to go down in a minute anyway, it'll take me at least half an hour to get sorted before Sam gets home."

"Ah, yes, your first Valentine's Day together!"

"You guys seem so settled," Joe said, turning from the railing.

Anna started squirming around under her blanket, "Hang on, incoming. Maybe it's my lucky Valentine!" She pulled out her phone, "It's a text...oh, shit-bags... sorry, language."

"What is it?" Ralph said.

Anna pulled a face, "Just my mother. She's decorated another cake for me and texted earlier to say it was ready, then she had a fit when I said I was at A&E - she thought I was a goner or something. Now, she's checking *you're* OK."

"Damn," Joe said. "I mean it's good your mum cares, but shame it wasn't a date."

"No," Ralph said. "Anna's decided to focus on herself and the business and not worry about finding a man, remember? Right, Anna?"

"I suppose."

"And you've reconnected with your mother after how long was it, six years? That's all positive, isn't it?"

"I suppose," Anna sighed. "It would have been nice to have at least had an opportunity for a date, so I could turn it down."

"OK, look, just to cheer you up..." Joe cleared his throat. "What do you call a small Valentine?"

Anna groaned, "Please, aren't I suffering enough? Not one of your jokes!"

Joe ignored her, "...A Valentiny!"

There was silence.

"I really do need to take Stanley for a walk," Anna said and started to untangle herself from the deckchair.

"Hang on," Ralph said. "We need to sort out arrangements for tomorrow."

"I suppose we have to go, don't we?" Joe said.

"Yup, we agreed," Ralph said, sternly. "It starts at eleven and because it's Dew-drop Dobson it'll be serious, so everyone will be in black, not like for Auntie B's funeral."

"Do you own anything black or serious?" Joe asked Anna, who was wrestling with her pink kimono sleeves that had become wrapped around the edge of the deckchair.

She looked down at her Dutch clogs, yellow 1950's pedal pushers and Thunderbirds T-shirt, "I'm sure I do, somewhere. I went through a kind of Victorian mourning period when Bowie died, so I should be fine. I can't believe we are going to Dew-drop's funeral so soon after Auntie B's."

"Let's meet in The Cookery at a quarter to eleven, then we can walk up to St Mary's together," Joe said. "I'm not coming to the wake, I'm not that heartbroken about the old guy."

Anna looked at him, "Trust me, none of us are weeping, but we need to be seen to be there." She took a breath and suddenly launched herself out of the deckchair, "Yes! She is free. She is also free of anyone remotely interested in a cheeky frolic in her knicker department on the most romantic day of the year, but I am in touch with my drunken mother who says she is sober now…so, according to Ralph, all is well with the world. Come on, Stanley, walk-time…walkies," and she disappeared into her flat hotly pursued by Stanley.

"I'm sure she snorts jelly tots or something to give her that much energy," Ralph said, leaning down to get his crutches. "Have you met Ruby yet? Her mother?"

"No, not yet. You?"

"Nope, she sounds like a bit of a monster, to be honest."

"Yeah, well, I wouldn't believe everything Anna says about her, you know how she likes to dramatise everything. You need a hand?" Joe asked.

"No, thanks, I need to practice," Ralph said as he struggled to his feet. "I'm like a spider with cramp at the moment. I've got ages until Sam gets back, so I don't need to rush."

As Ralph began to make his way back inside, Joe looked up to the stars as he always did at this moment, paused and blew out Auntie B's candle.

By the time the restaurant closed it was later than Sam had hoped. He'd been desperate to get back to Ralph, but he had refused to leave his staff to tidy up without him. Eventually, Dawa Singh, the imposingly dapper Maître d' brought him his coat, put it across his shoulders and forcibly evicted him from the premises, locking the door behind him.

"Did Dawa just throw you out of your own restaurant?" a voice said from the other side of the street. He looked up to see Anna standing under a lamppost with Stanley, who was enthusiastically inspecting the quality of the workmanship at its base.

"Oh, hi," Sam said. "What..?"

But before he could finish, the door behind him opened and knocked him sideways.

"Good evening, Anna," Dawa called in his deep voice from the top of the restaurant steps. "We haven't seen you for a while."

"Hi Dawa, sorry, I've been busy in the café."

"As long as all is well, that's the main thing," Dawa said, then glanced down at Sam. "Haven't you gone home to Ralph?"

"I was trying, then..."

"That colour suits you," Dawa said with a smile and a wave before he closed the door of the restaurant.

Sam looked confused, "What?"

Anna giggled, "I think he means me...my yellow coat."

"Oh, right, I don't know what's the matter with him - he smiled and he waved. I've never seen Dawa wave, ever. He doesn't break out a smile often either."

Anna pulled on Stanley's lead to get him away from the lamppost, "I can have that effect on people. You'd better skip home, Ralph's waiting for you for what's left of Valentine's Day."

"Yes, I'm on my way."

Anna hesitated, "How old is Dawa Singh, it's so hard to tell with that beard and everything?"

"I don't know, forty-ish. Why?"

Anna started to walk away along the High Street, "No reason, just thinking. He's got lovely shoes. Night."

Sam stood for a moment, after a long day the last thing he needed was a conversation that made no sense to him, so he did up his jacket and headed off.

As he approached the house, he noticed there were no lights in the windows. He had been in constant contact with Ralph by text all day to see how he was progressing, so he knew Anna had brought him back from the hospital hours ago. Sam dug out his phone and called him.

"Hey, where are you?" Ralph said as he answered the call.

"I'm here, where are you?"

"Where's here?"

"Home, of course," Sam said, trying to keep any sense of annoyance out of his voice at another confusing conversation.

"*Your* home? Your house?"

"Yes, I said I'd meet you at home."

"No! I'm at my flat. *My* home. I thought you meant here," Ralph sounded exhausted and emotional. "I'm so sorry, I never thought. I've ruined everything, breaking my leg, being in the wrong house. I'm such an..."

"Hey, don't say that word. You know it's banned," Sam was already turning and walking back up the road.

"I.D.I.O.T." Ralph spelt out defiantly.

"OK, that still counts. We had a big meeting about it and we all voted for you to stop calling yourself that."

Sam could sense Ralph smile down the phone, "Was I at that meeting?"

"I think you might have been in the toilet, but Stanley and I did a show of hands and it was unanimous. So, I'm afraid that means a forfeit."

"Damn, I'm not eating cauliflower again," Ralph moaned.

"Oh, I can think of something way more interesting than that," Sam laughed. "I'm on my way. Are you OK?"

"Tired, but I'll be better when you get here."

"OK, I'll be about fifteen minutes. Sit tight."

"Sorry."

"Idiot," Sam laughed and ended the call quickly before Ralph could respond.

As Sam walked into town, he thought of the first time they'd met during the chaos of the Rye bonfire night. The moment he had looked into Ralph's gentle brown eyes he knew he was lost. He had no idea the path to them actually acknowledging their feelings for each would be such a tortuous one, not helped by his own paranoia developed from disastrous previous relationships being splashed across the media due to the high profile of his parents and his associated celebrity status. But, somehow, their shared sense of imperfection and the long road each had travelled to reach the other had made their connection stronger and more special.

Sam let himself into the flat above the shop and was greeted at the top of the stairs by Stanley, "Hello, boy," he said as he scratched the little dog's ears. "Are you looking after the patient for me?"

Stanley gave a light woof and led Sam to the living room to show him Ralph was alive and well under his excellent care. Sam stood in the doorway, in front of him Ralph was fast asleep on the old sofa, snoring gently.

Sam shook his head and whispered, "My wounded soldier." He went through to the bedroom, where he undressed and collected the duvet and a pillow. Back in the living room he laid the cushions from an armchair in front of the sofa, then put the duvet carefully over Ralph, switched off the light and lay down on the floor beside him. Stanley quickly settled down next to him and Sam pulled the excess duvet over them.

"Happy Valentine's Day, Stanley," he whispered. As he lay on his back looking up at the ceiling, he couldn't help but smile. This wasn't the evening he had planned, but he knew there would be plenty more...or hoped there would be. His smile faded as his recent conflict of emotions returned: contentment, knowing with Ralph safely at his side he had everything he needed in the world, but a nervousness learnt from his previous experience - if things seemed too perfect, they surely couldn't last.

CHAPTER 6

The colour of positive energy, Yogini
Sharon and George Formby.

Ruby lifted the cake box carefully from the boot of her car, a shiny red VW Beetle she had bought as part of her new approach to life. Red was the colour that would fill her chakra with passion, excitement and energy according to smiling Yogini Sharon's laminated chart on her conservatory-cum-healing-studio wall.

It was a bright morning and she set off briskly for the short walk to The Cookery. It had been three years since she had set fire to her kitchen furniture and the woman she had seen in her glass of wine back then had undergone a long and often painful process of transformation. She had managed to stop drinking and with the help of life coach Sharon, whose postcard she had rescued from the recycling box, and tablets prescribed by her GP she was no longer hiding in the shadows, but living life in full colour...or trying to.

Passing the window of a linen shop, she paused as she saw her reflection in the glass. She saw a tall, slim, blonde, with a short, sophisticated haircut. Under her long cream coat, she wore a crisp white linen shirt and a pair of well-fitting jeans. Her classic flat shoes and cashmere scarf were red, like her car, to help promote positive energy.

She allowed herself a smile, slowly getting used to this new woman who she barely recognised. As she looked at herself in the window, she became aware of two large shapes inside the shop that seemed to be wrestling with each other, but on closer inspection she saw it was two women attempting to insert a duvet into its cover for a display. They sensed they were being watched and first one and then the other turned and smiled, each giving a friendly wave with a fat little hand. Ruby smiled back, blushing at being caught admiring her own reflection and quickly moved on.

Ruby opened the door of The Cookery cautiously, balancing the cake box in one hand, "Morning, Irene. How are you?"

Irene was flicking a feather duster over the wooden countertop with little enthusiasm, "It's Monday, I'm still breathing - sometimes that's all you can ask for, isn't it?" she said.

"Oh, dear, that doesn't sound very good," Ruby said, putting the cake down in the kitchen. "Didn't you have a good weekend?"

"Oh, it was fine. The grandchildren were eating me out of house and home, I'd made chocolate cornflake cakes, but they only wanted fruit. Fruit! I don't know what's wrong with them."

"This is the 50th birthday cake Anna asked me to do for one of her clients."

Irene waved her feather duster towards the ceiling, "Anna's upstairs if you want to go up."

Ruby paused, "I'll wait, if that's OK."

Irene put the duster away at the back of the kitchen, "Go up, she's decent...I say decent - she has some sort of black velvet thing on, so it's about as good as it gets with her."

"No, thanks, Irene, I won't. I haven't been invited into Anna's home yet and I don't think it's appropriate to be in her private space until she is comfortable with that," she sat at a table and removed her scarf.

Irene looked at her, "You're her mother, aren't you? Why do you need an invite?"

"Well, we are getting to know each other again after some time apart. Anna feels she needs to take things slowly, which I quite understand."

"Well, I never heard anything like it. I can't stand my lot, but I put newspapers on the furniture so they can come and go as they want."

For six years there had been silence between Ruby and Anna until Christmas Eve last year when, out of the blue, she had received a card from her. They had met on neutral territory half a dozen times since then, until Anna had built up enough trust to ask if Ruby would help out with celebration cakes when there were too many orders to cope with. Although it was Ruby who had taught her daughter to bake and decorate cakes, she was terrified of letting her down. It was a fragile, practical arrangement and Ruby was well aware it was Anna's way of testing her, but she didn't care. She was overjoyed they were connected again and was determined not to ruin it.

Anna came through the door from her flat and stopped when she saw her mother, "Oh, it's you. Hi."

Ruby turned on her chair, "Hello, darling. Oh, you look nice, is that new?"

Anna looked down at her long black velvet dress with dark green lace around the hem, sleeves and neck, "No, it's about a hundred years old - literally." Anna moved into the kitchen and began to wipe down the worktops.

"You know that's not what she meant - you normally look like you've just rolled around in a jumble sale. Tell her you are going to a funeral," Irene said to Anna, then turned to Ruby. "We're going to a funeral."

"Oh, I'm sorry. Was it someone you were close to?"

"No, I couldn't stand him. His name was Mr Dobson - he was my nemesis actually," Anna said, moving to the fridge and starting to move things about at the back of the shelves.

Irene stomped over to hiss at Anna, "Stop hiding in here and what's all this about you not letting her into your flat?"

Anna looked up, "Is that what she told you?"

Ruby rolled her new aromatherapy bracelet between her fingers, "I can hear you both, you know, you are only a few feet away."

Irene and Anna looked at each other, then Irene gave a sharp twitch of her head indicating Anna needed to join her mother, "I'll make myself scarce, I've got to de-bung some holes in the pepper pots before we go," Irene said, retiring to the back of the kitchen.

"Why did you tell her I wouldn't let you into the flat?" Anna said as she joined Ruby.

"Anna, I didn't. She told me you were upstairs and

couldn't understand why I preferred to wait for you down here, that's all. You haven't invited me into your flat and your home is your sacred space. Sharon says..."

"Not Sharon again! Why do you believe all her twaddle?" Anna picked at the edge of the tablecloth.

"Because her *twaddle* has been extremely helpful in getting my life in order," Ruby said, gently laying her hand over Anna's restless ones to prevent them fraying the fabric any further. "She's helping me and at the moment it's doing me good."

Anna resisted the urge to flinch or move her hand away at her mother's touch. Despite the anger she still held inside, she was pleased Ruby was looking so well and appeared to be a very different person to the sad depressive she had endured for long stretches of her childhood. However, she had witnessed periods when her mother had pulled herself together before, it had never lasted long and she always returned to the booze and left Anna floundering alone.

"Thanks for the birthday cake, by the way. It's the cricket one, isn't it? For Kevin?"

"Yes, it says Fifty Not Out on it, next to the stumps - which I had a few attempts at, but they look pretty good now."

"Great, his kids are picking it up at lunchtime," she got up and opened one of the many drawers behind the old haberdasher's counter and brought out an envelope, "Here's your money. I might need your help again next week, but I'll let you know."

"Of course," Ruby said. "I still feel bad you are paying me, I am just happy to help."

"No, it's a business arrangement. That's what we agreed," Anna said, putting the envelope down on the table.

Ruby looked at it and wanted to cry, but she took a breath and placed the envelope carefully in her coat pocket, "Thank you. So, tell me about Mr Dobson?"

Anna sat down at the table, nibbling on a cookie, "Dew-drop we called him, but his real name was Henry. He was vile and his nose was huge, it used to drip like a tap, great big globs of..."

"I get the picture."

"He was not a happy man," Irene chipped in from the kitchen. "Especially after Anna started her own café instead of just supplying him with her baking. His tearooms, The Copper Kettle, lost its pies and its customers as they trotted down the hill to this place."

"He had it in for me after that," Anna said with a shrug.

They turned as they heard a scrabbling noise at the door to the street and Anna leapt up to let Ralph in as he struggled with his crutches and the door handle, "Morning. I've closed the shop for the funeral and Sam is meeting us there," he said pulling out a chair and sitting down carefully.

"Oh, Ralph, how are you? I'm Anna's mother, she told me yesterday about your accident."

"It's good to finally meet you, Mrs Rose - the person responsible for Anna," he said with a grin.

"Please don't hold that against me," she said.

Anna flopped back into her chair, "You're both hilarious!"

"Call me Ruby, Ralph, Mrs Rose makes me sound ancient."

"She's fifty-three," Anna said, noticing her mother flinch, but not caring. "She had me when she was twenty, it's really young to have a child. Don't you think?"

Ruby clutched her scarf tightly in her hands and smiled at Anna, "Yes, it is. As young as I was, I made you and I am proud of that," she held her daughter's gaze for a second longer and then got to her feet, smoothing the front of her coat. "How are you feeling, Ralph? Is your leg very painful?"

"Oh, I'm fine, Mrs...Ruby," he said. "I'm more embarrassed than anything, causing so much fuss."

"You can't help accidents, Ralph. Well, I have to go, I have an appointment at the hairdressers," Ruby said, putting her scarf back around her neck.

"Are you two still OK to sort out the cake stall for the Rye Rovers' fair on Saturday?" Ralph asked.

"Yep," Anna said. "We're both making stuff, but Mum's looking after the stall on her own 'cos I need to stay here."

"I'm looking forward to it," Ruby said. "You are the coach aren't you, Ralph?"

"Yes, and Sam sponsors the team – well, his restaurant does. They're only little, all under ten, but they love it. We really need extra funds since the council started to charge us for using the football pitch, so this should help a bit. I'm really grateful."

"Oh, it's nothing. It'll remind me of the school fairs I used to help with when Anna was little."

"I'd love to see some photos of her when she was a kid. Have you got any?"

"Now hang on, we don't need to go through that ritual humiliation, thank you," Anna pouted. "If you've seen the film of Annie, then you've pretty much seen me as a kid, minus the dog and the bald fella."

Ruby headed for the door, "Right then, I'll be off. It's lovely to see you all," she said, without turning back and quickly disappeared.

Ralph leant towards Anna, "Why are you being so mean to your mum? She seems nice and I had no idea she was so glamorous, you made her sound like a monster."

"Glamorous? Well, she seems like that, but we've been through this before. Admittedly, she never looked this good, but she always lets me down. Always."

"Well, this time could be different. It must be hard for someone to start again, when she's alone, at her age..."

"I know, but you don't know her like I do. She may look fabulous now..."

"Who looks fabulous?" Joe said as he came through the door.

"Your timing never ceases to amaze me," Ralph said.

Joe winked at Ralph, "I've heard that many times before, my friend. Once in Bangkok..."

Before Joe could go any further Martin appeared in the doorway looking flushed, "I'm so sorry one and all, I lost all track of time sewing on my buttons." He was wearing a beautiful, well-fitting cardigan made from thick grey wool. The front was double breasted with six large leather buttons and the collar folded softly around his neck.

Ralph stared open mouthed, "Don't tell me that was what you were knitting yesterday at the hospital? You'd only just started it."

"Ah, merely an illusion, old thing. That was a sleeve, the rest was already complete back at base camp. I spent most of the night finishing it off and joining it all together."

Anna moved to him and felt the soft wool between her fingers, "It's beautiful."

"Well, I seem to have taken to the craft rather well. It has certainly enhanced my mindfulness, which was the purpose of the activity in the first place," Martin said with a shy smile.

"Everything's ready for you and all set up," Irene said, looking suitably funereal in a dark blue raincoat and tightly tied navy scarf over her severe black hair. "I'm not staying for the tea afterwards, so I shouldn't be long."

"All is in hand, Chief. Now, it is nearly eleven and as George Formby used to say, *It's not the coughing that carries you off, it's the coffin they carry you off in.* So, be on your way all."

CHAPTER 7

*The secret life of a twitcher, Miss Marple
and nice biscuits.*

The tower of St Mary's Church had stood on the hill at the top of Rye for more than nine-hundred years and Anna looked up as the brightly coloured figures that flanked its sixteenth century clock struck the quarter hour.

"Well, that was short and not very sweet," she whispered as the coffin was carried out of the church.

"I'm surprised this many people came, to be honest," Ralph said, leaning against the lychgate in the churchyard to take the weight off his leg. "He didn't go out of his way to make himself popular."

Sam looked around the meagre group of mourners, "I think most of them are from the council or the independent trader's association, aren't they?"

"He wasn't always unpopular, you know," Irene said as she stepped forward to see what was happening.

Joe laughed, "That I find hard to believe."

Irene's angular frame twisted and she faced him, her eyes flaring, "I know that you just see us as old people, but we were all your age once. Flighty pieces, giddy things at parties and picnics. I didn't have my kidneys then, so I played tennis and swam in the sea all the time, went to dances. We were just like you."

"Sorry, Irene," Joe said. "He may have been different when he was young, but he was plain mean when he was old and you can't get away from that."

"I know, but life happens to people sometimes," Irene said, turning back to watch the action at the graveside before continuing, speaking as much to herself as the others. "We went to school together, he was a good runner, ever so speedy. I was too, we both won the hundred-yard dash one year. We had our picture in the local paper. The day we won that race Henry had big red welts across his back, you could see them either side of his vest. He'd been beaten by his father for something or other. The other boys teased him about it, they were rotten to him, so he kept himself to himself. I liked him though, he was quiet and serious, not like the other boys. They were dashing about here and there, flashing their doo-dahs at the girls. Silly devils."

Anna moved to Irene's side, "I didn't realise you knew him so well. You never said."

Irene shrugged, pulling her scarf tighter around her head as Henry Dobson's coffin was slowly lowered into the cold earth, "People change, like I say. We went to a few dances, but his dad didn't approve of me, so it never really went anywhere. Then I met my Fred and he took against Henry from the start, he didn't think it was possible for boys and girls to be just friends. I suppose he was right, it was touch and go for a while my eldest wasn't Henry's...'til the baby was born and had bloody great ears like Fred, thank the lord. So, that solved that question."

Joe looked at Sam then back at Irene, "You mean, you and Dobson? While you were married to your husband, you..?"

"Sex wasn't invented by your generation, you know. You didn't all pop out of eggs, we'd been doing it for years before you lot started in at it," Irene said with a sniff. "I told Henry I couldn't see him after that, it could have got a bit tricky. So, that was it. He met his wife eventually, nice woman. Flat feet, big teeth. That's his daughter," she pointed at a thin woman with long brown hair tied back in a neat plait, standing stiffly by the graveside. "Fiona, they call her. She hasn't got her mother's teeth, thank goodness." They all looked at Dew-drop's daughter, as Irene got lost in her thoughts.

＊ ＊ ＊

Half an hour later, Anna shimmied around the portly vicar bringing two cups of tea in pale green cups and saucers to Ralph, who was sitting at a table in the window of The Copper Kettle Tearoom.

She put the tea down on the table, "Can you believe it, there are only rich tea biscuits and those long thin ones? You know, nice ones. Are they *Niece*, as in your sister's daughter, or *Nice*, as in lovely? I never have known. The very least you expect at a wake is a nice bit of cake...or is it, a niece bit of cake?"

Ralph, shook his head, "I'm sorry the catering has spoilt your enjoyment of this otherwise delightful event."

"Oh, that's alright," Anna said, not appreciating Ralph's irony. "We're not staying long anyway. Irene's gone back to help Martin, but I don't want to leave them alone for too long. I wanted a quick gawp at Dew-drop's family, I didn't get a proper look at them at the church."

"Well, here's your chance, his daughter's coming over."

"Oh damn, is she?" Anna quickly picked up her tea, taking a big slurp, which was far hotter than she had anticipated and immediately spat it back out into the cup. "Christ....Oh, hello!" she whispered hoarsely as Dew-drop Dobson's daughter appeared at her side. "Sorry about that, just a bit on the warmer side than I was expecting."

The woman was slim and tall, like her father, but had pretty features and dark eyes. She looked pale and tired, her hands clasped tightly in front of her, "I'm Fiona. Henry Dobson was my father."

"I'm Ralph," he tried to juggle his crutches and stand up, but Fiona waved him back down.

"Please, don't get up. How did you hurt your leg?"

"Oh, well, I just fell over, really."

"I see, that gravity business can be quite hard to get to grips with, can't it?"

Ralph frowned looking at Fiona's drawn face, but saw the corner of her mouth twitch slightly, "Yes, it can," he laughed.

"Sorry, I forget people don't expect me to have a sense of humour because of Dad. Hello, it's nice to meet you at last, Anna."

Anna had just taken another sip of her tea to try and sooth her burnt lips and looked up at Fiona with it still held in her mouth, "Mmmm."

"I'm afraid I haven't been into The Cookery yet."

"Nnnnn?" Anna mumbled, trying to swallow the hot liquid.

"I once had a piece of your preserved lemon and rosemary cake, though. It was lovely."

"Fanks," Anna slurred, finally emptying her mouth. "I haven't made that in ages. I'm not surprised you haven't been in The Cookery, though, as Dew...I mean, your dad, wasn't very keen on me setting up on my own."

"He made it very clear we shouldn't darken your door - family loyalty and all that nonsense. I had the cake here, when you used to supply them to The Copper Kettle," Fiona gave a thin smile and looked over her shoulder in a quick nervous movement. She leant down and whispered, "You're not dashing off, are you? I need to speak with you."

A loud voice cut through the hushed chatter, "Fi! Oy, over here!" Fiona gave the quick look over her shoulder again at a small, round man, with pale hair spread thinly and unevenly over his pink head.

"Please, stay a few more minutes," she said as she turned and hurried away.

"What's that all about?" Ralph said, watching her go.

"No idea," Anna shrugged. "Who's the angry little man?"

"Well, I think he might be her husband. See that small round boy standing beside him?"

"Oh, yes, with the ears?"

"Yes, well that's Dew-drop Dobson's grandson, George. He's in the football team."

They watched for a few moments as Fiona joined her husband and a group of men who were talking animatedly and examining the back of the tearooms, making notes and taking photos on their phones.

"Perhaps they're the ones going to take over the café," Anna said. "He was trying to sell it before he died, wasn't he? It's pretty run down, so they'll have some work to do."

Ralph looked around him at the roughly plastered walls and heavy wooden beams, beneath his feet the dark red carpet with swirls of gold and black was stained and thin. Everywhere looked tired, as if the whole place had simply run out of energy some time ago and given up the fight against cobwebs and cleanliness.

"It's in a prime location, right next to the church and the old marketplace. It should be a little gold-mine really," he said.

"Well, it was once," Anna said, checking the table under the stained cloth. "You had to queue to get in here. It was really sweet and traditional, a proper 'ye old-e English-e tea shopp-e'. When I was doing catering from my kitchen, I used to do dozens of pies and cakes for him each week. When I stopped to open The Cookery a lot of his customers abandoned this place. He threatened to sue me, you know? Honestly, he was horrible, he kept reporting me to environmental health, for no reason, even the police sometimes."

They continued to watch Fiona, who stood next to her husband but seemed ill at ease. Her arms were folded tightly across her chest as she nodded stiffly, shifting uncomfortably from foot to foot.

"What do you think she wants?" Ralph asked.

"No idea. Maybe Dew-drop's left me the whole place in his will, to say sorry."

"I really need to stretch my legs, I'm starting to get

cramp," Ralph said as he stood up unsteadily.

"We can't go," Anna said, holding his crutches while he got his balance.

"I know, but she's been with her husband for ages. Let's take a jog round the room, we can take our teacups back," Ralph set off slowly towards the side of the room where no one was standing, most people were gathered towards the door hoping for an excuse to slip away.

Anna followed with the teacups, "Did you see the vicar's shoes? They had tassels."

"You are obsessed with people's shoes, first the doctor at the hospital, now the vicar. I'm beginning to worry."

"Well, it's not right for a funeral is it, tassels under his dress?"

"I'm not sure they call it a dress, officially," he stopped as his crutch caught on a chair and he lost his balance falling sideways into the wall, where he dislodged a framed picture which crashed noisily to the floor. Everything fell silent as all heads turned in their direction. "Sorry, my fault, bad crutch control," he said, blushing and waving a crutch in the air as Anna bent to put the teacups on the table. His crutch hooked a cup and saucer out of her hand and sent them flying down on to the swirly carpet.

"Bollocks," Anna yelled, then quickly looked across the room. "Sorry, language, Vicar."

Ralph turned towards the wall as he started to laugh, "I can't believe you said that."

"What? Bollocks?" she whispered.

Ralph was trying hard to control his laughter, "No, 'Language, Vicar', it's like an old Agatha Christie film."

"Stop it, you'll set me off," Anna picked up the crockery, which had miraculously remained intact. She waved the cup and saucer at Ralph, "Shall I offer him more tea?"

Ralph snorted with laughter and Anna bent double as she giggled, trying to keep quiet.

"Is everything OK?"

"Sugar!" Anna gasped as she stood up to face Fiona who had quietly joined them, the rest of the mourners having returned to their strained conversations. "You made me jump. I'm so sorry, we seem to be a little bit hysterical."

Fiona's mouth twitched, "I don't blame you; funerals can do that to people. They're ridiculous, don't you think?"

Ralph had managed to compose himself, "Oh no, this is lovely. A good send off for your dad."

"That is kind of you, but the truth is - it's miserable. I know that, but I wasn't allowed to make anything of it really."

"Oh dear, the glass seems to have broken in this picture," Anna picked it up from the floor. "It's still held in the frame, so none has actually fallen out."

"I'm really sorry, that was my fault. I tripped over, I can't get the hang of these crutches," Ralph said.

"It's fine, don't worry. Here, I'll take it," Fiona took the picture from Anna. "It's a cuckoo - the European cuckoo."

"Is it? It's beautiful," Ralph turned and looked at the wall beside him that displayed three more detailed pen and ink drawings of birds. "They all are."

"I know, he was very good," Fiona said. "Would you like to see some more?"

"More? Well..."

"Please," Fiona whispered, shooting a look at her

husband who was deep in conversation with the same group of men. "Just come with me and pretend you are interested."

She turned and crossed the room, speaking more loudly than before, "Yes, there are plenty more. I'm happy to show you them." As she passed her husband she said, "I'm showing these people some of Dad's pictures, Andy, I won't be long." The round, pink faced man looked at her briefly, then went back to his conversation.

Ralph shrugged at Anna, "Let's go look at some pictures."

They made their way to Fiona, who was waiting for them at the bottom of a set of narrow stairs holding back a rope which usually stretched across the first step to keep customers out, "After you," she said.

Ralph hopped his way up to the floor above, which wasn't easy as the stairs weren't even or straight. Anna followed and Fiona hooked the rope back in place and came up behind them.

"Did you say your dad drew them? The birds?" Anna said as they crowded onto the small landing.

"Yes, didn't you know? He was a twitcher - a bird watcher. He'd go out for hours across the marshes, take photos, then come back and draw what he'd seen."

"I had no idea. He didn't seem the type...sorry."

Fiona shrugged, "I know exactly what you mean. Come in here," she stepped past them and opened a badly chipped door that led into a small sitting room. There was little furniture, just a couple of high-backed chairs that had seen better days, an old wonky sideboard and a small gas fire, but at the back of the room was a large drawing board, surrounded by neat rows of pots containing pens and pencils of all shades and colours. On the board was a large sheet of paper neatly taped around the edges, with a partially drawn image of a bird in flight.

Anna stepped forward to take a closer look, "This is amazing, so much detail. I can't believe he could do this."

"He was a very talented artist. I think he wanted to do it professionally once, but his father wasn't keen. But they were his passions, birds and drawing. I suppose it was only right he died doing what he loved," Fiona said, emotion sounding in her voice for the first time.

Anna stepped away from the drawing board, "He didn't die here, though?"

"No, out on the marshes. We think he'd gone to look for birds," she lowered herself into one of the chairs, suddenly looking tired. "I'm sure you've heard all the rumours. I know he wasn't well liked and could be... difficult, but I can assure you he did *not* commit suicide. He wouldn't. He just wouldn't," she sat very still and straight staring into the unlit fire.

Ralph looked at Anna, then moved over to sit in the other chair beside Fiona, "We had heard something."

"Yes, because the authorities weren't really sure if he killed himself or whether it was an accident, so everyone started gossiping and speculating. He was found floating in the military canal, out in the Romney Marshes. The doctors said he'd had a heart attack, but they couldn't be sure if that was before or after he went into the water. He had sandbags in the pockets of his coat, you see, which held him down."

"Bloody hell," Anna said, coming to stand behind Ralph's chair. "Had he put them in there and jumped in

64

the canal?"

"No, no, that's what people don't understand. He always took them with him. He used to lay for hours in the marshes, waiting for the right birds, and he'd rest his binoculars or his camera on the sandbags to keep them steady in the wind. So, it was quite natural he had them with him. When they found him in the water, he still had his camera around his neck. He would never have gone into the water deliberately with the camera, it was his pride and joy. No, he must have had the heart attack at the side of the canal and fallen in. With the weight of the camera and the sandbags he wouldn't have been able to get out again," Fiona spoke calmly and quietly, but wiped a tear from her cheek.

"Fiona, I am so sorry. He may have been a git, but he didn't deserve that."

"Anna!" Ralph hissed.

"No, she's right. He could be a bit of a git," Fiona smiled lightly. "He was not a pleasant man. He didn't like people, not really. After Mum died, he got worse. Locked himself away in here, neglected the business and focused on the birds. I think that was why he was so angry when you stopped supplying the café, because it meant he would have to spend time finding new suppliers and rebuilding things. He resented being taken away from his birds," she waved her hands at the half-finished painting.

"FIONA!", they all turned at the loud cry from what was undoubtedly her husband down below. "People are going. Where the hell are you?"

Suddenly she leant forward, looking earnestly at Anna, "Can I come and see you? I can't talk now, but I need your help."

"Yes, of course. Come to The Cookery."

"Friday, I can come then. In the afternoon."

There was another fierce cry from downstairs, "FI, COME ON!"

Fiona touched Anna's arm briefly then stood up quickly, "I have to go," and she hurried back downstairs.

Ralph looked at Anna, "Blimey, what's going on? I keep expecting Miss Marple to pop out of a cupboard at any minute."

"I have no idea, but she is very, very scared of something and I have a nasty feeling he has a big pink head and a loud, shouty voice."

CHAPTER 8

*The new friend, bad habits and
raspberry netting.*

After the funeral, Joe had walked back down the
hill towards the High Street with Sam, "What
do you think the offspring of Irene and Dobson
might actually have looked like? It was a narrow escape
for some poor kid..."

He was looking at Sam, so didn't see the door of the
hairdresser's open and a slim blonde woman step out in
front of him until it was too late. As they collided Joe
threw his arms out and ended up hugging her in an attempt to stop them both losing their balance.

"I wasn't watching..." Joe apologised as he gripped the
woman to help steady her. "Did I hurt you?"

"No, I don't think so. Nothing broken," she smiled at
him, tucking a strand of blow-dried hair behind her ear.

Sam patted Joe on the back, "I'll see you later, I need
to get back to prep for lunch service. Glad no one was in-

jured," and he set off down the hill.

Joe didn't seem to hear him as he clutched the elegant woman, acutely aware of her soft creamy skin, the smell of newly washed hair and a tempting perfume he recognised as Chanel No. 5, "You look familiar, have we met?"

"Well, I've bought a few things in your shop," she said, flustered as Joe's piercing blue eyes held her gaze from close quarters. She stepped back, adjusting the red scarf at her neck, "A trowel and some slug killer, I think."

Joe didn't move back, she was older than him, but something about the flush his gaze was bringing to her cheeks was appealing, "Yes, that must be it," he said, smiling at her.

"Actually, I was going to see if you have any netting for my raspberry canes this week," she said, regaining her composure.

"Sure, I was heading back to Let's Screw, if you want to come now."

"I imagine you have great fun with that name, don't you?" she smiled as they started down the street and Joe's hand brushed the back of Ruby's cream coat.

* * *

Ruby could feel her hand shaking slightly, so she placed it firmly on the shop counter to steady it while she waited for Joe to find the garden netting. She thought she had seen the last of the tremors when she gave up alcohol, but since bumping into Joe they seemed to have returned.

"Here you go," Joe said as he came back down the long aisle with a roll of green netting.

Ruby laughed, blushing as she realised she was behaving like a schoolgirl, "Thanks. I ripped out my old garden about two years ago, it was just a large patch of mud and a slightly charred patio. I turned it into a space where I could grow lovely fresh fruit and veg. I am very much a beginner, but I love it. I suppose falling in love with your garden comes with getting older."

"Well, you must be the exception to the rule," Joe said with a smile.

"Do all Canadian's come with a flirt mechanism or is it just you?"

"Most of us have one, it develops when we are about six or seven. I'm impressed you can tell the difference between a Canadian and a US accent, most people don't have a clue."

Ruby looked down and tucked some hair back behind her ear, unwilling to admit her inside knowledge from Anna just yet. She was also enjoying the attention and her first proper conversation with a man, apart from 'hello' and 'how do you do', for more than ten years.

She watched him take off his jacket, fold it up and put it under the counter, revealing his trademark uniform of tweed waistcoat and white shirt pulled tight over his impressive chest. She felt herself flush again and quickly asked, "So, how much do I owe you, Joe?"

"Let me check...wait, how did you know my name was Joe?"

"Oh, your grandmother told me, she was very proud of you."

"Grandmother? She only told me I was her grandson a few days before she died, how did you...?"

Ruby dug her hands deep into her coat pockets, knowing the game was up, "Actually, I knew Auntie B when I was a child and we kept in touch. But I also know Anna, so she has told me a little about you and the rest of the Rooftop Club."

"Right," Joe said, looking suspicious. "So, how long have you known Anna? You're not from the tax people, are you?"

Ruby laughed, "Do I look like a tax inspector?"

Joe gave her an exaggerated look from top to toe, "Not like any I've ever met."

"I'll take that as a compliment. I'm Ruby, Anna is my daughter," she held her breath as she waited to see Joe's behaviour change towards her.

Joe let out a whistle and looked at Ruby, trying to see something of Anna's wild red hair, curvy frame and freckled face in this slim, fragile looking woman with soft skin and vulnerable eyes, "Well, of all the things I imagined Anna's mom would be, it was not you."

"Thank you...I think. As I'm sure you know, Anna and I were estranged for a while and Auntie B kept me informed of how she was doing - please don't tell Anna I told you that. I wouldn't want her to think I was spying."

"No, of course, not," Joe said. He clicked his fingers, "I've got it now, I saw you on bonfire night. Anna thought you were a ghost and we followed you."

"Yes, I remember that, I was trying to pluck up the courage to speak to her. I came into town so many times, but never went through with it. I didn't want to upset her life and, if I'm honest, I wasn't sure I was strong enough to take it if she didn't want anything to do with me. Sorry, this is far too much information."

"I'm really glad you and Anna have made up."

Ruby looked up into his face and smiled, "Well, it's

early days and we have a way to go yet, but it's OK."

"I'm desperate for a coffee, can I make you one?"

"That's very kind, but you have to work and I should get going."

"Do you have anywhere you need to be?" Joe asked.

"Well, no, not really..."

"Then, how do you take your coffee?"

She smiled, "Just black, thank you."

Joe flicked the switch on the filter machine and set off down one of the aisles to the back of the shop, "I'll only be a minute, I need a fresh pack of coffee."

Ruby watched him disappear through a door to what she assumed was his stock room and undid her scarf. Joe wasn't at all what she had expected from his reputation and the little Anna had told her about him. He was certainly as attractive as people said he was – but gentler, with the most extraordinary eyes. It wasn't only the intensity of their blue colour, there was a kindness in them that made her feel both safe and confident at the same time. She shook herself - she was being ridiculous. She picked up her raspberry netting and tried to focus on reading the label until she heard Joe returning.

"Here we go," he said, pushing a stool from behind the counter towards her and began to prepare the coffee. "So, you have nowhere special to be today? I can't imagine a woman like you being at a loose end."

Ruby laughed, "You'd be surprised, Joe. Days can be very long when you are on your own - you can develop all sorts of bad habits. I'm trying to replace them with good habits, like growing raspberries."

"We all have bad habits. I know you'll find this hard to believe – but even I have them."

"I'm sure you do," she said with a grin.

"You shouldn't believe everything Anna tells you. I'm not such a bad boy," he smiled. "Just really, really misunderstood."

"Is that so?"

The coffee started to burble and drip through the filter, "Absolutely. Tell me one of your bad habits and I'll tell you one of mine."

"Oh, no, I don't think so."

"Why not? Go on, look I'll start. OK, I bite my nails instead of cutting them."

"Really, let me see. Hmm, yes, you need a manicure."

"Your turn."

"Me? Well, I...I've started to enjoy swearing," she blushed as she said it.

"Really?"

"Oh yes, quite loudly too. But only in the house."

"You? No, you don't look like a swearer."

"I bloody am," Ruby said with enthusiasm.

Joe threw his head back and laughed, "Is that the best you can do? That's not proper swearing. You can do better than bloody!"

"Tosser," Ruby said quickly, turning away from him on her stool laughing.

Joe chortled, "That's more like it," he slapped his hand on the counter and looked at Ruby giggling joyfully. "You are making my day - even though you called me a tosser! So, what else?"

Ruby's hand went instinctively to the bracelet around her wrist, "Well, I have an awful habit of negative thinking, which can spiral. This is my new tool for self-improvement – an aromatherapy bracelet. Isn't it ridiculous?" She fiddled with it and smiled to herself.

"Not if it helps," he poured coffee into a mug and

handed it to her.

"That smells wonderful, thank you," she took it and read the words on the side. "*Suck it up?*"

"Sorry, that's not...it's a joke. Here have mine," he held out his mug and Ruby giggled. He looked at it and read, *Keep Calm and Snog Me.* "Damn, sorry, I didn't mean anything..."

"Joe it's fine. I know you're not flirting with me."

"Really? I must be slipping."

Ruby blushed, then looked him in the eye, "Tosser."

"Bullseye!" he shouted, laughing. "But now you need to up your game, you can't stick with that one."

"If your mugs are better at flirting than you are then I think it might be you that needs to up your game," she said with a wink. Then blushed again, did she really just wink at him? She grabbed her bracelet and tried to calm herself by rubbing the soft, lavender scented beads against her wrist.

"Good point," Joe said. "OK, look, I owe you one more bad habit, then we can move on to good things. So, as we're being honest, something I've been thinking about lately is that I make too many excuses."

"Like what?"

"Well, excuses to avoid people or a decision or to get out of something I don't want to do. Like, for years I've kept making excuses not to move on from here or go back to Canada. I think it's become a habit."

"Well, that doesn't seem so bad, if you feel you belong here."

"I'm not sure I know where I belong," he said, surprised he was comfortable enough to share so much with a woman he had only just met. "Anyway, let's move on. Tell me two of the good things in your life."

"Well, being in touch with Anna is great and I'm making cakes again, which I love. What about you?"

"Well, I tell the best jokes in the world and I made a new friend."

"Really? Who?"

"You."

"Oh, thank you. I don't have too many friends."

"Well, you have one more now. What do you call a sad raspberry?"

"I'm sorry?"

"It's today's joke. What do you call a sad raspberry?"

She smiled as his eyes shone like a child's, "I have no idea."

"A blueberry!" Joe said with glee.

Ruby groaned and shook her head, "Are you sure your jokes don't count as one of your bad habits?"

"Some may say so, but secretly they love them."

Ruby sipped her coffee, thinking carefully about what she wanted to say next, "Joe, I need some advice and I really don't have many people to ask. You don't know me and your loyalty is absolutely to Anna, she is your friend..."

Joe put his hand gently on her shoulder, "And so are you, now. Look, I love Anna and I don't get what the issue was between you and her, but I know Auntie B...I mean, Grandma...was convinced you two should reconcile, so if I can carry on her work then I'll try."

They both felt the heat of his hand warming her skin through her coat, but she didn't dare look up into his eyes, "Thank you, Joe. I suppose the first thing I should do is be honest with you about the issue between Anna and I. I let her down many times because I used to drink. A lot, wine mostly. I shan't bore you with the reasons for my drinking, that is not important, but the result was she felt I let her down after her father died. As she grew up, she tried to help me, but at the time I was beyond help. Eventually she had to leave to make her own life without her mother holding her back," she stopped and looked at Joe, who had withdrawn his hand from her shoulder. "Do you want me to continue or would you like me to leave?"

"Why would I want you to leave? It sounds like you were both suffering."

"I suppose we were, I never really thought of it like that. Anyway, I have not drunk any alcohol for nearly three years. I won't say it's easy, but I believe I have it under control and my life is so much better. Being back in touch with Anna has meant everything to me. I wish I could talk to her properly, tell her how sorry I am, but she keeps me at arm's length. What should I do? Things are fragile and I don't want to spoil them."

Joe leant against the counter and took a swig of his coffee. There was silence until Ruby slid off the stool and started to tie her scarf, "I'm sorry, I shouldn't have asked you. I've embarrassed you."

"No, not at all. That was my thinking face, not my embarrassed face - it's new, I probably haven't got it right yet. I can see Anna wants to protect herself, I understand that now."

"So, what should I do? Should I do anything or accept that this is how it will be?"

"Well...why don't you try a blind date?"

"What?"

"Hear me out. She was moaning about not having a date for Valentine's, so I'll say I've found someone for her - she is really bad at choosing men for herself. She'll come for dinner and it'll be you - you'll be her blind date! She can't avoid you then and you get to say whatever it is you need to say to her."

"Oh, Joe, it's a lovely idea, but she'll turn around and leave. Then you'll be in trouble too."

"I'm always in trouble with Anna, I can handle it. Anyway, if we do it at Cinque, Dawa Singh, the Maître d' will make sure she stays. Trust me, she wouldn't argue with him."

Ruby thought for a moment, "I suppose it could work. It would be good to have some time alone together to really talk. There is so much we both need to say."

"It'll be great! I'm so pleased we bumped into each other today, I feel like I'm carrying on my grandma's work," Joe smiled, the lines around his blue eyes crinkling as he took Ruby into a hug that surprised them both.

After the initial shock of such intimate contact with another human body, Ruby's resistance softened and she submitted herself to his powerful touch for the second time that day, her hands remarkably steady as they settled on his back.

CHAPTER 9

*The only chance, Donald Duck
and debtors' prison.*

L ate on Friday afternoon, when the lunch time
rush had faded away, Anna finished tidying up
the kitchen at the back of The Cookery. Suddenly
she was aware of a presence beside her, "She's here,"
Irene whispered from behind Anna's left ear. The baking tray she had been holding landed on the floor like
a cymbal crash, sending Irene flailing back against the
coffee machine.

"Are you trying to do me in?" she said, clutching her
chest. "My kidneys nearly made a public appearance
then. What's the matter with you? Flinging stuff about."

"You crept up behind me! You don't normally do that,
I'm used to hearing you coming," Anna said.

"I was being considerate to Fiona; she's lost her
father. She won't want people charging about shouting,
will she? God knows what she'll think about you jug-

gling pots and pans in her moment of grief. You need to be more respectful," Irene then turned and started preparing a tray, banging teapots and saucers about.

Anna went through to the café, where Fiona was sitting at a table in the corner with her back to the window.

"Hi, how are you?"

"I'm fine thanks, Anna. Thank you for seeing me," Fiona said with a smile.

"I think we might get some tea in a minute, Irene's just taking things out on the cups and saucers. If they survive, we might be all right."

"That's lovely, thank you. I'm afraid I can't stay long though," she shifted in her chair, glancing over her shoulder at the street outside.

"No problem," Anna said, looking at the pale woman in front of her. Fiona slid her simple grey woollen coat off her shoulders and laid it across the back of the chair next to her. Underneath, she was wearing a high neck ribbed jumper in a warm camel colour, over a pair of slim grey trousers. Despite the simplicity of her clothes, which Anna could tell were not expensive, Fiona looked elegant and stylish.

Anna pulled her lilac and green kimono across her Donald Duck t-shirt and folded her arms, "So, this is your first visit to The Cookery."

"Yes, I'm sorry I haven't been in before. It's so lovely. All those...things, on the shelves, where did you get them?"

"All over, really. Anytime I see something odd or unusual I'm drawn to it."

"The tea is strong, I've put three bags in," Irene said as she put the tray of tea things on the table. "You need it strong when you're dealing with death."

"See what I mean," Anna whispered. "Thanks, Irene. Perhaps we could have a pot of hot water too, just in case."

"Please yourselves, it's your funeral...if you see what I mean," and Irene marched back to the kitchen.

"Sorry about that," Anna said as she started to pour the tea.

"It's fine, I know she means well," Fiona paused for a moment, then sat forward. "Would you like to buy The Copper Kettle?"

"What?" Anna said, the teapot frozen in mid-air. "Me?"

"Yes, I thought maybe you might think about expanding and take on another venture."

"Yes, well, I am thinking about growing the business, but don't you want to keep it in the family?"

Fiona looked over her shoulder in the familiar gesture Anna had first seen on the day of Dew-drop Dobson's funeral. "Oh, no! Sorry, I mean...it's a bit tricky. I thought you would be the best person to take it on, that's all," Fiona said, but stopped as tears formed in her eyes. "I'm sorry...it's so hard."

"Now what have you done?" Irene said to Anna as she placed a pot of hot water on the table. "If it was her throwing stuff about, she didn't mean to upset you. She's always dropping things. It was eggs the other day, then a big load of mince..."

Anna glared at Irene, "Thanks, Irene, that'll be all."

"Alright, Lady Mary," Irene said, muttering to herself as she left them alone.

"It's really soon after your dad passed, maybe you need some time..." Anna started to say.

"No! Time is exactly what I don't have," Fiona said, fiercely, wiping the tears away with the back of her hand. Anna passed her a paper napkin, "Thank you. I didn't know whether you felt so badly toward Dad that you would never consider taking on The Copper Kettle, but when you came to his funeral I had to try."

"Well, I'll definitely think about it, but why don't you have time? What's the rush?"

Fiona took a deep breath, "I need to sell the tearoom as quickly as possible or it'll be too late," she flashed another look out into the street.

"Are you afraid of something? Tell me what's going on and I might be able to help," Anna said, gently laying her hand on Fiona's arm.

Fiona stiffened and gazed at Anna's hand, "Of course, why would you want to buy the place if I make a mystery of it all? I'm so stupid," she said.

"I doubt that very much."

"Thank you, but when you hear the mess I'm in you might change your mind."

"It sounds like you have a story to tell and that needs cake, hang on," Anna got up and brought the remains of a large two-tiered chocolate cake to the table. She went back and took two pastry forks from a drawer, giving one to Fiona, "Right, that's better. No need for polite slices, hack it off in chunks."

Fiona hesitated, "Go on, dive in," Anna said and dug her fork deep into the chocolate icing. Fiona watched her, then the small twitch of a smile came to her lips and she took a small corner from the cake.

"Mmm," Fiona said. "That's lovely, what's the flavour in with the icing?"

"Lime marmalade. It's my secret ingredient, oh, now

I've told you I might have to kill you."

Fiona laughed, "I'm not usually allowed cake, so I can't tell you how good this feels."

"*Allowed*? Why aren't you allowed cake? Are you a diabetic?"

Fiona shook her head, "No, nothing like that. Anna, I've never spoken about this to anyone, so I don't really know where to start, but please understand this cannot go any further than the two of us."

"Of course," Anna said, spearing another dollop of icing with her fork. "I won't tell a soul."

* * *

"So, you cannot tell a soul," Anna whispered to Ralph, Sam and Joe as they sat around the small iron table on the roof terrace later that night.

Joe whistled under his breath then banged the table with his fist making Auntie B's candle jump and flicker, "What a bastard! I mean, a complete bastard."

"Now I can see why he was behaving like that after Dobson's funeral," Ralph said. "Wait, did I hear somebody's doorbell?"

"I think it was yours," Sam said and got to his feet, "I'll go, back in a sec." He jogged across the terrace and disappeared into Ralph's flat.

Anna wound a piece of her hair tightly around one of her fingers, "I've spent most of the afternoon thinking about ways to get revenge on men…"

"Don't look at me," Joe said. "Actually, that reminds me, Ralph, when I looked after The Bookery last Sunday a bloke came in and chose a book about revenge. When he brought it to the counter, I said, *You'll pay for that!*

Revenge – You'll pay for that! Do you get it? It's a joke."

Ralph groaned, "No wonder Imogen moved to a remote Scottish island."

"Good evening all, sorry to interrupt, I was returning the shop keys to Ralph," Martin said, as he appeared around a potted conifer. "But Sam tells me there is a bit of a situation brewing and thought I might be of some use?"

Anna pulled up the remaining iron chair and patted the seat, "Come and sit, Martin...oh, is that alright Joe? This is Auntie B's seat."

Joe paused, no one had used that chair since Christmas Eve when Auntie B had sat in it for the last time, "Sure, of course. We can't leave the chair empty for ever."

"No, I suppose not," Anna said.

"I can quite easily stand or pull up a deckchair..." Martin said.

"Absolutely not, sit, Martin, sit," Joe said, standing and moving Martin into the chair.

"Can we get you a drink?" Anna asked.

"Nothing for me, thanks, that ship has sailed, I'm afraid."

"Bugger, I forgot. Language too, sorry."

"We have some lemonade, I think," Ralph said, reaching for his crutches.

"Let me, we don't need you doing your Spiderman impression again," Joe said, heading for the makeshift bar at the far end of the terrace.

"That is very generous, thank you," Martin said. "As the great Sherlock Holmes possibly once said, what is a-foot?"

Everyone looked at Anna, "So, Fiona – she's Dew-drop

Dobson's daughter – told me this afternoon about her husband, Andy. How he was lovely and made a fuss of her when they met, wining and dining her – all that stuff. He was a dealer in antiques, had a nice car and always plenty of cash. So, they got married and had George."

"We know George a bit, he's in our under-ten's football team," Sam added.

"Anyway, Fiona took time off work when he was born and when it came for her to go back, Andy said he wanted her to stay at home to take care of George. He said it wouldn't look good if she worked, people might think they needed the money and he couldn't provide for his family. So she agreed to take a few more months off. Well, that was nine years ago and she hasn't been to work since. She's lost her friends and has to make excuses to leave the house, like shopping or hair appointments."

Joe returned with Martin's drink, "She should definitely go to the police, there are laws now to help people like her."

"She is absolutely adamant she won't, I couldn't persuade her," Anna picked up her glass of red wine and sat back in her chair. "She's more or less a prisoner in that house unless he approves where she goes. I mean, I know it happens, but it makes my eyeballs bounce when you actually see people like him. She doesn't even have her own bank account, he made her close it and now she has to rely on him. So when Dew-drop died she saw the chance to get some money of her own and get away. He left the café to her in his will, you see, so the husband can't get his hands on it. Although, he is trying."

Martin sipped his lemonade then said, "Surely if the

tearoom was left to this lady in her father's will it is entirely up to her to decide what to do with it?"

Anna sniffed, "You'd think so wouldn't you, but Andy has told her he is going to deal with it. He's got this idea to turn The Copper Kettle into an antiques shop. He's a crook, selling knocked off goods from burglaries mostly, Fiona thinks. Apparently, he reckons it'll seem more legit if he has a shop in a nice town like Rye. Fiona has heard him talking about making it easier to launder money through a shop too. He's a proper rogue. It took quite a bit of persuading from Fiona for me not to walk round there and pierce his scrotum with a pastry fork right there and then, I can tell you."

"I can see Fiona's point, there are subtler ways to deal with him," Ralph said, rubbing Anna's shoulder. "But I would have liked to have heard his screams if you'd done it."

"Well, it sounds to me like Fiona is an incredibly brave woman to have the strength to tell you and plan her escape," Martin said.

Anna nodded, "I wish she would see it like that. She thinks she has failed somehow, that she shouldn't have got herself into this situation. Her son is why she won't go to the police, she doesn't want to put him through it all. She just wants to leave and start again. That's why she needs me to buy The Copper Kettle, as quickly as possible. With the money she will be able to set up on her own. She reckons it's her only chance."

Martin put his drink carefully on the table and turned to Anna, "Therefore, the question is yours, dear girl. Do you wish to buy The Copper Kettle Tearooms? Forget Fiona's predicament for a moment, is it something you would have considered before you heard of the good lady's plight?"

"Yes, definitely. When Dew-drop first put it up for sale I thought about it then, but he would never have sold it to me. I'd love another business, but…"

"Here we go," Ralph said.

Anna straightened her back, "What?"

"This is the part where you say you can't do it, you don't know how, you haven't got the skills to run two businesses," he said, crossing his arms.

"No. Well, maybe…it's a massive thing! Just because I've done it once doesn't mean I can do it again."

"Of course, you can," Sam said. "Despite the somewhat blunt approach of my other half, he does have a point - you are your own worst enemy. You need to have more faith in yourself."

"But if I had someone with me, as a partner, it would be easier," Anna protested.

"Not necessarily," Sam said. "Every decision would be a compromise - you wouldn't always get your own way."

"Listen, old thing," Martin said, rubbing his hands together against the chill of the evening. "Although he was a little bit on the giddy side of sanity, as witnessed by the loss of a perfectly good ear, it was Van Gogh who said, *What would life be if we had no courage to attempt anything?* This is your moment to find your courage. If the opportunity is one you have dreamt of, then you should take it."

Anna looked at Martin and his kind, tired eyes. Then she looked around the faces of the other members of her rooftop family, "You really think I can do it?"

"Yes," they said as one.

"But none of you want to come in and do it with me?"

"No," they said, again in unison.

"Bastards," Anna grumbled, but she was smiling. "OK, fine, I'll think about it."

"Anna..." Ralph began.

"No, I mean, I'll think about it *properly*. I'll need to sort out finance, Fiona's not asking the full commercial value 'cos she wants to get rid of it quickly, but I don't have that much cash lying about, plus it's very run down with no real existing customer base. It will need its own unique selling point as the town is already full of cafes and I certainly don't want to compete with myself in The Cookery."

"You see, you know exactly what you're doing," Ralph said, smugly.

At that moment Joe's phone began to play the Raider's March from Indiana Jones, he took it out of his pocket and stepped away from the group.

"On that positive note, I shall love you and leave you," Martin said, getting to his feet. "Many thanks for the lemon fizz."

Sam was checking his own phone, which had been vibrating on the table, "I need to take Stanley out for a quick trot round the block and pop into Cinque. Dawa's just texted to say he needs me there pronto, so I'll come down with you Martin," he said.

"Anything wrong?" Ralph asked.

"No, idea, but he said to come over straight away. Probably that dodgy freezer again, I won't be long," he kissed Ralph and ruffled his hair. "See you all later."

"I should get going too," Joe said, finishing his beer. "That was Imogen, I said I'd call her back when I got home to the beach house. Don't forget, Ralph, you promised to talk about that *thing* to Anna."

"Did I? What thing?"

"You know, the *thing*," Joe said with a wink.

"You winked, there was a wink, why did you wink?" Anna said, suspiciously.

"Oh, right, that thing," Ralph said with a groan. "Yes, of course."

Anna looked at them both, "What thing? What are you two up to?"

"Nothing, nothing," Joe said, heading towards Auntie B's flat.

Anna scowled, "Don't try and be mysterious, it doesn't suit you."

Joe stopped and looked back, "How many mystery writers does it take to change a lightbulb?"

"See what you've done?" Ralph said to Anna.

"Two. One to screw it in nearly all the way and then another one to give it a surprising twist at the end." Joe held his hands out, "Now, that's a classic, right there."

"Clear off," Anna said, picking up her drink.

"Every one's a critic," Joe said as he left the terrace through the empty flat.

"Another drink?" Ralph asked Anna pleasantly.

"Spit it out. What are you up to?"

"Me? Nothing, I don't know what you mean."

"You know exactly what I mean," Anna said. "Blimey, you'd have never been any good as a spy. The Gestapo would have taken about four seconds to work you out."

"Why?"

"It's written all over your face, you can't hide any-thing."

"It took you long enough to work out I was gay," Ralph said, huffily.

"That was different, I was put off by your wife and the fact you loved football. You weren't a straightforward gay, but don't try and change the subject. Spill!"

"Alright, alright," Ralph shifted his bad foot, which was propped up on the edge of a canvas deckchair, and lent over and took both of Anna's hands in his.

"Are you going to ask me to marry you?" Anna asked.

"No."

"I'm quite a catch you know."

"I know, but you are also a woman and that creates a bit of a problem, doesn't it?"

"Fair point."

"Look, you know this blind date Joe has arranged for you? I think you should go."

Anna drew her hands back from Ralph's, "No way, I have told him a hundred times this week I won't go. I'm not going out with anyone Joe has chosen."

"I thought you'd come to terms with him having a sensitive side? He's gone to a lot of effort for this date. If it's any help, I know who it is and I like them."

"Really?"

"Yes."

Anna sat back in her chair and sighed, "Alright, fine, I'll go."

"Blimey, that was easy."

"Well, if I'm going to have to deal with some sort of abusive husband criminal mastermind to get a new business and maybe go bankrupt and go to debtors' prison in the process, I might as well go on a blind date and meet a serial killer. Get it all over and done with in one weekend."

"They don't have debtors' prison anymore, you're not in a Dickens novel," but he was cut off by the sound of a text arriving from Sam. He checked his phone and saw the words, "GET HERE NOW!"

CHAPTER 10

*The celebrity mother, Love Island
and Joan of Arc.*

The lights were still blazing in the windows of
Cinque as Ralph carefully made his way across
the cobbles towards it, his heart pounding. He
hopped up the steps and pushed the door as the familiar
face of Dawa Singh appeared inside and held it back for
him.

Dawa, immaculately dressed as always in a well-cut
suit, pocket handkerchief and precise turban, held out a
well-manicured hand and placed it gently under Ralph's
elbow to steady him as he made his ungainly entrance,
"Good evening, Ralph. Can I assist?"

"Thanks, Dawa. What's the emergency? What's going
on?" Ralph said looking around for Sam.

"We appear to be hosting an impromptu celebrity
event," Dawa said, rubbing his beard distractedly.

"Really? Who's the celebrity?"

"Jane Scott," Dawa said without the slightest hint of enthusiasm.

Ralph looked at him, "Seriously? International film star, Jane Scott?"

"Yes."

"Wife of the late could-have-been James Bond actor, Damien Ross? Mother of Sam Ross? My Sam?"

"The very same."

"Wow! I had visions of the place being on fire or something really bad happening."

"Indeed? I think this may qualify as either of those options. Would you like a drink?"

"Do I need one?"

"Almost certainly, follow me," Dawa turned and moved effortlessly through the crowded bar as the large throng of people laughed and applauded. He brought out a bottle of beer and opened it for Ralph.

"Thanks, where is he?"

Dawa adjusted his tie, stepped back and looked down onto the floor behind the bar, "Sam, Ralph is here."

Ralph leaned over the bar to see Sam sitting cross-legged on the floor next to Dawa's feet, the peak of his baseball cap pulled low over his face, "Erm, what are you doing?"

"I like Dawa's shoes, I'm having a closer look at them, Anna said he had nice shoes." Sam let out a groan, "Everywhere my mother goes it becomes some damned circus."

Ralph looked at the crowd behind him, but couldn't see the famous film star at their centre, "What is she doing here?"

"We're not entirely sure," Dawa said. "She made her entrance earlier and has been holding court ever since.

Ah, one moment," he slipped from behind the bar and discretely waved at a dark shadow outside the door to the street. He then coughed loudly, "Ahem, ladies and gentlemen, a point of information. It appears the local police are carrying out checks on cars parked along the road for tax and insurance purposes. I thought you should know." He then stepped back and casually started to polish a glass, as a stampede of diners headed for the door or demanded to pay their bills as quickly as possible.

"How did you manage that?" Sam whispered.

"I texted Sergeant Phil, my neighbour, who happened to be on duty close by and is now walking up and down outside. You will owe him and his wife a free meal."

"You are a genius, Dawa..."

"Sam?" A cut-glass voice at an opera singer's pitch shot through the room. "Is that you?"

"Good luck people," Dawa said with a sigh as he helped Sam to his feet and whispered to Ralph, "Don't look her in the eyes. Never look in her eyes."

"Sweetheart! I thought I heard your voice, come give your mother a hug."

Sam grunted and pulled the cap tight onto his head, "Don't leave my side," he hissed to Ralph as he came out from his hiding place.

Ralph kept his back to Jane Scott, "You've got me scared now, I'll stay here with Dawa and clean something."

Sam thumped Ralph on the shoulder, took hold of his hand and dragged him with him, "Hi, Mum."

Jane Scott was perched on a bar stool in the centre of the empty bar, the perfect position to be hit by soft lighting from above. She was swathed entirely in black, her high heeled shoes sharp, her long legs crossed, her thigh length silk dress tight and her fiery red hair sleek. She had the blood-coloured nails of one hand wrapped around a martini glass and with the other she reached forward, diamond rings sending shards of light bouncing across the room, and took hold of Sam's chin. "Darling, take off that awful hat, let me see you."

"Mum, you know what I look like."

"I do. You look like me, with a hint of your father. That's why I love to look at your face. Are you going to deny me that in my grief?"

"He's been dead eight years, look at a photo," Sam said coldly, but when he felt Ralph squeeze his hand he rolled his eyes and slowly took off his cap. "Is that better?"

Jane pursed her well-glossed lips, "Look at my beautiful boy, I forget how tall you have grown and...you seem to be attached to a person with a plastic leg."

Ralph limped from his position behind Sam to stand in front of the great actress in the full glare of her famous glass green eyes.

"Now, who are you? Do I take it my son has fallen for your slender beauty, rich chocolate eyes and innocent..."

"Bloody hell, Mum, pack it in." Sam turned to Ralph, "She does this a lot, she tries to frighten people."

"She's good at it, it works," Ralph said with a weak grin.

Jane Scott let out a whooping laugh, "He knows I'm only joking. Look at you, like an injured bird. Come give me a kiss, it took me a considerable time and a large gentleman with noxious breath to get me up on this stool, so I do not intend to come down unless I have to." She flung out her diamond encrusted hand again and turned her cheek slightly to allow Ralph to step in and be embraced.

"It's great to meet you. I've seen some of your films, I...I...liked them," Ralph managed to stammer as he was released from her grip.

"Did you darling? Only some? How kind," Jane said, sipping her cocktail. "Now tell me, is my son holding your hand to ensure you stay upright or has he been withholding information of a romantic nature from his mother?"

"Mum, this is Ralph. Ralph this is my mother, Jane Scott. Ralph and I are together - so, that sorts that out. Why are you here?"

She ignored Sam's question and flashed a high watt-age smile instead, "Ralph? What a charming name? So unusual these days, boys are always Keanu or Conan or Cognac, aren't they? Well, it's lovely to meet you, Ralph. We must have a proper heart-to-heart, so I can find out all about you and you can tell me all about my son, be-cause, quite frankly, he is a mystery to me. He has disap-peared down here to the ends of the earth, hiding away, abandoning his mother..."

"Where are you staying? Have you got a hotel?" Sam interrupted.

"No, darling, I thought I would stay with you."

"Well, OK," Sam said. "But wouldn't you be more com-fortable in a hotel?"

"Probably, but your little place is so charming. Small, but charming. Oh, who's this?" She squealed as she saw Stanley bounce round the corner and begin to circle Sam and Ralph.

"This is Stanley, he's with me," Ralph said, fussing Stanley's long floppy ears. "Sam took him out for a walk earlier, it's a bit hard for me to handle both him and the cobbles at the moment."

"Does he slobber? These shoes are not meant for liquids."

"Not unless provoked," Sam said, menacingly. "Do you want a drink, Ralph?"

"Dawa already got me a beer. It's on the bar."

"Right, I'll get myself a strychnine and coke," Sam said and headed off followed by Stanley, who was not convinced the new stick-like woman was going to be much fun.

"Come, sit, sit," Jane Scott said, patting a stool next to her until Ralph hopped up on to it. She leant in close and in a loud stage-whisper said, "How *is* Sam, is he happy?"

"Yes, I think so."

"He tells me so little and I worry about him. Stuck down here, nothing to do, no excitement."

"He's hardly stuck here, he chose Rye. He created Cinque, which is one of the best restaurants in the area. He..."

"Oh, yes, yes," Jane Scott waved her martini glass vaguely through the air. "It's nice and I'm very proud, but it's not going to set the world on fire is it."

"I don't really think Sam is the sort of person who wants that," Ralph said.

"Who wants what?" Sam asked, returning to them with a glass of Scotch and handing Ralph his beer.

"You, darling. Ralph was saying that you don't really want much from life."

Ralph choked, "Erm...wait...that's not what I said."

Sam looked at Ralph with a raise of his eyebrows, signalling this was a familiar scenario for him, "Well, I'm sorry to have disappointed you, but I'm happy. I had hoped that might be enough."

Jane pouted, "I suppose it could be, but when you come from a family of high achievers to settle for being happy seems a little unambitious, don't you think, Ralph?"

"Leave Ralph out of this, if you have something to say to me spit it out,"

"I don't know what you mean, darling. I was simply asking after your well-being."

Sam looked at her from under the edge of his loose hair, now it was free from the cap. Jane Scott took a sip of her drink, savouring the taste and then swallowing delicately, "Well..."

"I knew it!" Sam said, triumphantly. "Come on, out with it."

"I think you have so many opportunities to really go places. You are a restauranteur and a cook." She turned to Ralph, "For instance, Ralph, last week I was talking to a lovely lady called Angharad, who is from Wales but surprisingly sweet. She works for the BBC on a programme called MasterChef..."

"No," Sam said, shaking his head.

"...and I thought what an excellent opportunity it is for talented people to get into the spotlight."

"No, no, no."

Ralph looked at Sam who had gone red in the face, then back to Jane Scott, "I don't think Sam is a spotlight sort of person, Mrs Scott."

"Ralph, darling, don't be so formal. Call me Jane, everyone does. Mrs Scott makes me sound like somebody's mother."

"Holy crap, you are somebody's mother!" Sam shouted, leaning heavily on the back of a chair.

Jane was unperturbed and kept her laser like eyes on

Ralph, "Sam was making a name for himself a few years ago as something of a celebrity. He was voted the country's most eligible bachelor; did you know that?"

"Erm, wasn't he the second most…"

Jane Scott waved her hand dismissing Ralph, "My point is he could make a real splash. If MasterChef is not quite right, what about Love Island?"

"Kill me," Sam muttered.

"He'd be a sensation on Love Island!"

Ralph was beginning to get a tension headache, "I think him being gay might be a problem…"

But Jane Scott was not really listening, her famous green eyes were shining with excitement, "Imagine him in a little pair of swim shorts, with those cheek bones, not to mention my eyes. Things would really take off for us then, don't you think, Ralph?"

"Us?" Ralph said with a frown. "You said, us. I thought this was about Sam?"

"Ah ha," Sam swung around and pointed at his mother.

"I meant us as a family, darling. Sam, you…me."

"There it is," Sam hopped about the bar, kicking chairs and banging tables. "I knew you were up to something and it had to be about you, it's always about you. What's happened? Offers from LA slowing down, are they? Only being offered 'woman behind bar' or ageing tart parts?"

Ralph tried to calm things down, "Sam, hang on…"

"I knew it," Sam raged, returning to the bar as the large figure of Dawa Singh appeared behind it.

"Ladies and gentleman, I think we really need to remain calm," he said.

Jane Scott smiled coldly, "Dawa, always the voice

of reason, especially when Sam had one of his tantrums...or your father had one of his..."

"Jane," Dawa warned.

"It's late, we are all tired," she slipped elegantly from her stool, finished her drink and set the glass on the bar. She brushed down her sleek black dress, "I need the little girl's room, if someone would point me in the right direction."

"I will show you, Jane. I'd like the opportunity for a quick word," Dawa said with enforced politeness. Jane hesitated, smiled tightly and let him lead her out of the bar.

Sam was pacing backwards and forwards, "Did you see that? Her face when Dawa said he'd like a word? He was the only one who could cut through the bullshit and tell her the truth. Dad said Dawa was his bodyguard against nutty fans, but mostly against Mum. She tried to sack him loads of times, but Dad ignored her."

"She's quite something, I'll give her that," Ralph said as he got off his stool and put his now empty beer bottle back on the bar.

"I knew she had an ulterior motive, her career has stalled so she is looking for some sort of media hook to get her profile up."

"Yes, but she wouldn't really use her own son for that, would she?"

"If it got her career back on track, of course she would."

"I'm sorry, but no mother would do that to her child. Especially when she has seen how painful it was for you before, to have people sell stories about you and expose your love life..."

"Trust me, you don't know her. She is like a guided

missile when it's about her career, nothing will stop her. Nothing," Sam had forgotten how vulnerable his mother made him feel and reached for his cap in a reflex action, putting it back on and pulling the peak down to hide his face.

Ralph put his arms round him, "It is not going to happen again. You are safe here, with me, with Dawa."

"I know, I know."

"Ow!" Ralph felt something bang into his leg and looked down to see Stanley nudging up against hum. "Hello, boy. We forgot all about you with all the excitement of film stars and Sam in speedos on national telly, didn't we?"

Sam gave Ralph's leg a gentle kick as Stanley danced around them, "Sorry, that must have been Stanley. Take care you don't fall again."

Ralph pointed at Sam, "Kill! Go on Stan, kill!" But Stanley was too busy trying to open the front door of the restaurant with his nose and get out into the fresh air.

A moment later Dawa reappeared wrapping a long black scarf around his neck, "Well, gentlemen, I believe it is time for me to be off. As enjoyable as this evening has been, I need to go and do my best to pretend none of it actually happened. Goodnight." Before they could stop him, he had slipped out into the night.

Jane Scott quietly returned to the bar holding a deep red coat over her arm. She stood for a moment not saying anything or meeting the eyes of either Sam or Ralph. Sam picked the label off the empty beer bottle and Ralph stood between them with his leg and head throbbing from the tension.

Eventually, Ralph couldn't bear the silence anymore

and launched into an overly jolly report on the weather from his phone, "It's going to be nice in the morning. A bit of sunshine, with some cloud and a little bit of rain. Something for everyone."

"What did you talk to Dawa about?" Sam said, sulkily, to his mother.

Jane touched a finger delicately to her eyebrow, "He has lost none of his straightforwardness, but his charm seems to have evaporated as he's grown older."

"As long as the rain holds off until lunch time it'll be fine," Ralph continued to cling to the weather for safety.

"Why lunch time, darling? What are we doing in the morning?" Jane Scott said to Ralph with exaggerated charm.

"Well..." Ralph began.

"We, as in Ralph and I, are organising a fundraising fair. We need good weather to make sure people turn out. Aren't you going home tomorrow?"

Ralph edged towards Sam, "Sam? Perhaps your mother would like to come and help out."

"Well, there's always the stall where you bash the rat over the head with a baseball bat as it comes down the drainpipe," Sam mumbled.

"I would love to help, what is it for?"

"We run a football team for local children and the council have started charging us to use the pitch for matches and practice, so we've got to raise some money to cover the costs," Ralph pulled a photocopied leaflet from the wall and handed it to Jane. "There's all sorts of stalls and games, the parents are doing most of it, but we need to be there."

"Oh, aren't you clever. Now, would you like me to open the event? Say a few words? I'm sure my publicist could arrange..."

"We don't need your publicist," Sam snapped. "It's been in the Rye paper and there are leaflets in all the shops and the library."

"But surely a little boost would help raise the profile," she was already delving into her bag to bring out her phone. "I'll text her now."

"Mum, this is a charity event it is not about you."

"For goodness' sake, darling, I want to help. Get the kiddies their baseball pitch."

"Football," Ralph and Sam said together.

"Look, boys, trust me. I know about charity events; I am the face of Pelvic Inflammatory Disease for the whole of the northern hemisphere and an ambassador for Help the New Forest Ponies. A little sprinkle of celebrity dust will bring in a lot more money, trust me," she began typing into her phone.

"But..."

Ralph put his hand on Sam's shoulder and whispered, "Let her help if she wants to. What harm can it do?"

"They said that about Joan of Arc when she was put in charge of the bonfire and look what happened to her."

CHAPTER 11

*The longest hug, sporrans and
cheese and onion crisps.*

The following morning the weather was as predicted, as Ralph prepared The Bookery for opening. Despite the bright sunshine, his continuing tension headache warned him a storm may be brewing close to home.

He had reluctantly left Sam to finish a silent breakfast with his mother, but not before she had insisted on organising a book signing event at the shop for her long ago released autobiography, "I do so want to help you boys make a success of your little businesses," she had purred. Ralph had to admit that a little bit of star power would not be a bad thing to help his sluggish new year sales, as his ability to stay in Rye was entirely dependent on The Bookery remaining afloat.

Jane Scott's memoir was not something he was familiar with and he'd just found *Whatever Happened to Jane,*

Baby? in a publisher's catalogue, when the shop door jangled.

Before he got a chance to say The Bookery wasn't actually open yet, a familiar voice cried, "Crisps! Do you sell crisps? Cheese and Onion. Do you sell them?"

Ralph looked up, "Bloody hell, what are you doing here?" He leapt from his high stool behind the counter, but had forgotten about his bad leg and promptly thundered to the floor, "Oof, bugger!"

"Ralph!" yelped the woman in the doorway.

"I'm fine, fine," he said, quickly pulling himself upright with the aid of a shelf of biographies. "You might need to come to me though."

The slim woman, with light brown skin, beautiful oval eyes and a cascade of thick, dark braids, crossed the shop quickly and threw her arms around him. They stood holding each other tightly, the woman refusing to let go as she felt Ralph's shoulders silently rise and fall in time with the gentle sobs that escaped him.

"Helen," he whispered into her neck.

"I was only joking about the crisps," she whispered back. "I'll take smoky bacon if you don't have cheese and onion."

"But you love cheese and onion," he managed to say, slowly regaining control of himself, while still not letting her go.

"I know, but things change," she said.

"I'm so sorry," he said.

"Now, don't start that," Helen said, sharply, but not unkindly. "We're not doing that all over again," and she released her tight hold of him and stepped back.

Ralph pulled up the bottom of his green shop apron and wiped his eyes, "But I am...*really* sorry."

"So you've said a hundred times on the phone and in your letter. I believe you, Ralph," she smiled at him, a smile he had seen so many times before. Although they had only been married for a few years, they had been best friends for much, much longer.

"I've missed you," he said. "I hadn't realised how much, until now."

Helen turned away, unravelling the woollen scarf around her neck, "So, this is The Bookery. Where's Stanley? I've driven two hundred and fifty miles to meet this dog of yours and he's not even here."

"He's with Sam…" Ralph blushed. "Sam is…"

"Your boyfriend, you told me," Helen turned to face him. "Ralph, I know about your life, we've talked loads of times on the phone after…well, after Jim found you and I knew you weren't dead. He sends his love by the way."

"How is he?"

"Still my brother. Still a pain in the arse. Still married to Carol – just," Helen started to wander around the shop, running her fingers along the books and stopping occasionally to look more closely at the scenes Ralph had painted on and around the shelves.

"This place is amazing, I love these paintings of the sea," she removed a couple of travel books, behind which was a painting that looked like a window overlooking a sandy beach and inviting azure sea.

"Thanks, making over this place was great therapy for me, I loved it. How long has it been since either of us painted or drew anything?"

Helen shrugged, "A long time. It feels like another life…like we were other people. I'm so pleased you've started again."

"What about you? Have you done any sketching lately?"

"Not yet, no. I haven't really had the...you know..." she fell silent, smoothing her hands down the front of her blue wool coat.

Ralph took a step towards her then stopped, "Damn, I'm not sure what's appropriate between best friends who were married and are now getting divorced because I got my first boyfriend...I wish I had some crisps; things are less awkward with crisps."

Helen laughed, "Too right, I could murder some Monster Munch. Look, we're still friends, I've made that clear. I don't blame you for wanting to be yourself, I understand it. So we need to get used to being friends again." She adjusted an earring then suddenly punched him on the arm, "Breakfast! I'm starving."

"Ouch!" Ralph rubbed his bicep. "I'd forgotten how deadly accurate you could be with a single knuckle."

Helen feigned another punch, which he saw coming and dodged away, remembering how they had done this a hundred times before, "Your reactions are sluggish," she said. "You've lost it."

"I'm sure I'll get plenty of practice while you're here... how long are you staying?"

"It depends," Helen said moving towards the painted castle that surrounded the shelves of children's books. "Right now, I'm starving. Last night I stopped at a B&B just this side of London, the car still has a mind of its own about long distances, so I didn't want to risk doing it all in one go. It was nice, but I couldn't face more than some toast this morning. Shall we get some breakfast?"

"Ah, well..." Ralph started to say, as the door opened again and Martin stepped in.

"Morning, old thing…oh, we have a customer. My apologies, am I late?" He asked.

"No, Martin, not at all. This is not a customer, this is Helen. My wife," Ralph said.

Ignoring any potential for embarrassment, Martin held out his hand to Helen, "Well, what a treat. Dear lady, it is a pleasure to meet you."

Helen took his hand, which was firm and strong, "Martin, it's good to meet you too. It will be good to put faces to all the people Ralph has told me about."

"Likewise, although I have to say Ralph missed out one important piece of information about you," Martin said, looking sternly back at Ralph.

Helen withdrew her hand, "Really?" she said, pushing some of her braids back over her shoulder.

"Yes, indeed," Martin said. "That you are stunningly beautiful. We have all heard of your kindness, humour, ability to forgive this unhappy young sinner…but never has he once mentioned that you looked like *this*."

Helen laughed and dropped a brief curtsey, "And he never told me you were such an old phoney."

Martin rubbed his hands together and moved to the back of the shop, "I am going to like her, Ralph. I hope she is staying a while."

Ralph stuffed his hands into his apron pocket, "Are you? I mean, it's really nice and everything, but why are you here?"

"I'd hoped to stay for a few days if that's alright. It's a sort of holiday. I had lots of time owing from work and nowhere really to go, so I thought I'd come and see what was so marvellous about Rye." She too put her hands in her pockets, "Plus, I need your help with something… but we can talk about it later. I should have warned you about turning up, but it was all a bit spur of the moment. You know what that's like," she said and aimed another deadly punch at his arm.

Ralph leant sideways at the last moment and she missed him, "And I shall apologise for the rest of my life for running off without talking to you. So, despite your violent streak, you are really welcome. I have a spare room upstairs, I'll give you a key and you can come and go as you want," he said.

She quickly jabbed a knuckle at Ralph's shoulder, "Fab!"

"Bugger, you are too good at that."

"You snooze you lose, bozo," she sang, triumphantly. "Right, I'll go and get my bag and then we can get something to eat. I assume they cater for vegetarians in these wild southern lowlands?"

"Yup, they keep big bags of frozen sprouts in the freezer for people like you," Ralph said. "I'll give you a hand."

Martin had pulled out a stepladder and was setting it up in the middle of the shop, "Ralph, haven't you forgotten something?" he said as he unhooked a feather duster from his back pocket. "The small matter of the football team fair? That is why I am here after all."

"What? Of course, yes, how could I forget? Sorry, Helen, Martin's here to look after the shop for me because I have to go to this fundraising fair. We're raising money for the kid's football team."

"It's fine, I didn't expect you to drop everything because your traumatised, abandoned wife turns up on your doorstep...kidding. I'm only kidding," she grinned.

Ralph smiled sheepishly, "Right, good."

"Too soon?" she asked. "For jokes?"

"Maybe a bit," he said.

"Fair enough," Helen said, swinging another winning punch at his shoulder, but at the last-minute stopping and stroking his arm gently. "I'll stay here with Martin until you get back. It's great you have someone reliable to take over if you had to go away."

"What do you mean?"

"You need to get going, Ralph," Martin said from the top of the ladder, as he flicked dust off a scale model of the Starship Enterprise. "Helen, I shall introduce you to the delightful Anna at The Cookery next door and she will provide you with anything your heart desires, food-wise."

Helen looked up at the ceiling, "What's all this stuff?"

"Ah," Martin said. "This was Anna's idea. It's The Ceiling of Curious Things. People are drawn in to view all of the weird and wonderful objects hanging here. Very few leave without buying something else from the shop while they are here. The kids love it and we try and update it every so often, so people keep coming back. It's ingenious, don't you think?"

"It's great," she said, moving around looking at all the different items hung with clear fishing wire from the ceiling, the Victorian baby boots, a stuffed skunk's tail and sewing bobbins in the shape of the Two Ronnies.

"This is our latest acquisition," Martin said, pointing with his duster to a small green purse. "It is a genuine old kilt sporran, which Anna has on good authority, from Jumble Jim at the antiques market, is made from children's hair."

"Really?" Helen said with disgust.

"Well, Anna believed him," Ralph shrugged. "Are you sure you're OK to stay here? The fair finishes at two, so

I'll be back as soon as I can."

"It's fine," she said, undoing the top buttons of her coat. "I'll have some breakfast, then I'll probably have a snooze. Catch up on some sleep."

"OK, I could leave Sam to it, only it's a bit complicated with his mother suddenly arriving last night. I don't like to leave him alone with her."

"Would that be the delectable Jane Scott?" Martin asked with interest.

"Yes, it would. Do you know her?"

"Not personally, obviously, but she's jolly famous. Do you know her, Helen?"

"Of course, doesn't everyone. Is she really Sam's mother? I didn't realise you were dating celebrity royalty!"

"Blimey, don't let him hear you say that," Ralph said.

Martin was leaning on the top of the ladder, "She was a fine stage actress. Before she was lured to the silver screen I saw her in The Taming of the Shrew and she was quite magnificent. Vicious, artful, mean and manipulative."

"Yep, that's pretty much what Sam says about her," Ralph sighed as he folded his apron. "I'm hoping it's a flying visit. It was pretty tense at Sam's house this morning."

"Oh dear, I do hope she is not going to cause any unrest between you two. After the disastrous end to my marriage, I was pinning all my hopes on you and young Sam for romantic longevity." Martin gasped and threw a look at Helen, "Dear girl, I must apologise that was crass and insensitive..."

Helen waved a hand, "Martin, it's fine. Blimey, this is going to be really hard if everyone is walking on eggshells around me." She took a deep breath, "Look, for the record, I was devastated when Ralph disappeared, then I was mad as hell he'd run off leaving me only a crap little note on a packet of Jaffa Cakes...I mean, I don't even like Jaffa Cakes. But he was my friend before he was my husband and I couldn't bear to see him so unhappy. I had no idea why, but now I know, I'm happy for him. We never should have married if we are honest, we were... are, much better as friends. And I hope we will still be there for each other."

There was silence for a moment, then a car rumbled past on the cobbles outside and Martin let out a low whistle, "If I were a hundred and twenty-three years younger and my divorce had been finalised, I'd ask for your hand in marriage, I really would. Beauty and the wisdom of Cleopatra."

"I don't know about that, but thank you," Helen laughed, then she turned to Ralph. "So, Sam and his mother don't get on?"

"She is pretty...what's the word...self-obsessed, I suppose. She used revelations in the press about Sam when he was young to her own advantage, so he hates all that celebrity child nonsense. He's afraid she's here to try and use him again to revive her career, which seems to be flagging a bit. I don't know what to believe, she seems so nice on the surface, but underneath it feels like the sharks are circling."

Martin looked at Ralph from under his exuberant eyebrows, "*Happy is he who causes a scandal,* according to Salvador Dali. Sam's mother will need watching carefully, but please, don't let the tension affect you and Sam - it can often spread like wildfire. Be united."

Helen nodded, "I agree, when animals are hunting

they try and separate off their prey and go for the one left alone."

"Well, that's a cheerful thought," Ralph said.

Helen smiled, "My pleasure," and settled down on the step in the middle of the shop. "Right, clear off to your fair then, I need time alone with Martin to share stories about our ex's."

"Fine, I know when I'm not wanted," Ralph said and picked up his jacket and headed for the door.

"And don't you dare come back without any crisps or Stanley, you know I really came all this way just to meet him, don't you?" Helen called after him.

Ralph laughed and turned in the doorway, but she and Martin were already deep in conversation.

CHAPTER 12

*The little pink man, megawatt
smiles and beaver tails.*

As Ralph approached the Victorian architecture of St Mary's parish halls, his mind whirred around the arrival of Helen and all she stood for in his not-so-distant past. Apart from the times they had spoken on the phone, for the last three months he had put her from his mind and focused on his new life. She had been such a big part of his old life, as a source of both pain and great friendship, and he had missed her. Yet he had experienced an incredible freedom being away from her – a conflict that had become all too real as she had stood in front of him.

She had hinted she needed help from him and he was pleased, not that she still needed him, but that he might be able to repay her and assuage some of the guilt he felt for his sudden destruction of her life when he ran away. He knew he would do anything for her to try and make up for it, then perhaps he and Helen could go back to being the friends they were before they stumbled into marriage.

His thoughts were broken by the frantic activity in and out of the halls. Along the front of the building was a long banner that had been made by the team of little players to advertise the fundraising fair. It was covered with brightly coloured pictures of footballs, goal posts, football boots, cakes, books, quite a few portraits of Stanley and even a pirate flag with the words *GIVE US YOUR MONEY!* scrawled underneath. Many of the small players were wearing their football shirts and racing in and out of the doors, trying to help where they could.

In the cream-coloured hall, with high ceilings and tall windows, there were a lot of stalls already set up, a tombola, a book stall, knitted toys and baby clothes, bric-a-brac, home-made jams and someone's grandmother preparing to look mysterious while telling fortunes over the steam from a flask of hot tomato soup. Then there was little Elliot, the team's blue-plastic-spectacled goalkeeper, proudly wearing a sign around his neck asking people to *Guess The Weight of The Goalie.* For some reason he was dressed as Pocahontas, which, when asked, he simply declared was his favourite superhero.

Ralph couldn't see Sam, so abandoned his crutches to help Ruby carry a pile of plastic boxes from her car, "Thank you so much for doing this. These cakes look amazing," he said.

"You are more than welcome," she puffed, putting the boxes down next to another pile under a long trestle table. "I hope we've made enough. Cakes are usually the first thing to go."

"Morning all," Joe said as he came up behind them with a length of grey drainpipe over his shoulder. "Where would you like this? Sam asked me to bring it down, something to do with bashing rats over the head. Sounds a bit medieval to me, but I am learning not to be surprised by your English traditions."

"It's quite straightforward, you drop a pretend rat down the pipe and people have to try and bash it on the head when it shoots out of the bottom before it goes into a bucket...actually, I suppose that does seem a bit odd when you describe it."

"Didn't you have it in Canada?" Ruby asked Joe, tucking a piece of hair behind her ear. Although they hadn't seen each other since the day of the funeral, they had kept up a jokey text conversation across the week and she had been excited and nervous about seeing him again.

"No, ma'am, we are a civilised nation – except for eating Beaver tails."

"No! Really?"

"Nope, they're a type of doughnut!" Joe laughed in a way that made her stomach flip. She quickly turned and busied herself throwing a gingham cloth over the wooden table. He took hold of the other end and helped straighten it, "I sure hope you've made plenty of cakes with all the extra publicity from Jane Scott being here, there could be crowds of people coming."

"She only found out last night," Ralph shrugged. "So I doubt anyone will really know about her until they get here."

"You haven't seen the fuss on the internet then?" Joe said, pulling his phone from his back pocket. "It's all over Facebook and Insta-thing and Twitter. There's a cute photo of you. Look," he held out the phone and Ralph scrolled through the different photographs and posts.

Jane Scott's publicist certainly knew her stuff; wherever he looked there were pictures of Jane alongside images of the team taken from their website. His heart sank as he looked through a different string of posts featuring a photo of him and Sam she must have had taken secretly in the bar the previous night. No wonder Sam was keeping a low profile.

"Sam's not going to be happy, it'd better pay off and we earn plenty of money for the team," Ralph said, handing Joe back his phone.

"Oh, Ralph, Sam was here earlier," Ruby said. "He told me to tell you he had to go back to the house to collect his mother, apparently she hadn't got her face on by the time he left this morning."

"Thanks, I wondered where he was. I thought he might be hiding."

"Poor thing, the curse of famous parents, I suppose. Still, it must have some advantages."

"Probably, but I'm not sure he's actually found many yet," he said as he took the drainpipe from Joe and went off to look for Mr Ringrose, who was in charge of the bash the rat stall as well as his headstrong daughter, Joanne, the team's defender.

Joe stood with Ruby as she started to lay out carrot cakes and chocolate brownies on the table, "Do you need a hand?"

"That would be great if you have time. That box down there has some of Anna's new experiments, chocolate eclairs with a cream and Horlicks filling."

Joe picked up the box, "What's Horlicks?"

"Is that another British thing? It's an old-fashioned powdered drink, you make it with hot milk. It's a mix of chocolate and malt really."

Joe laid them out on a large plate, "Well, they look great. Anna always makes things I'm sure should be disgusting, but somehow they always work."

Ruby smiled, "I know, she is a miracle worker when it comes to baking."

"How's the swearing going?"

"Bugger knows," Ruby said, looking round to make sure no children were nearby. She giggled, "It still feels so naughty and it's your fault for encouraging me!"

"Hey, you wanted to become a better swearer – it's your new hobby, not mine."

"I never said it was a hobby..."

Joe grinned at her, "Anyhow, are you ready for your blind date tonight?" he whispered conspiratorially. "I had to enlist Ralph to persuade Anna, but she will be there."

Ruby looked worried, "Oh dear, does everyone know about it except Anna? She won't like that."

"She'll be fine, honestly. I know she really wants to spend time with you, she needs a bit of encouragement sometimes."

"Well, I hope you're right," she smiled at him. "You have been very kind to organise it, thank you."

He smiled back, "It's my pleasure."

Ralph appeared at the side of the table, "Well, things are hotting up!"

Ruby took a step back, "What do you mean?"

"Little Jilly-bean, one of our strikers, has brought her mother's belly dancing class to do a demonstration. That should liven things up, don't you think?"

"It sounds too wild for me, I'm off back to the shop," Joe laughed. He leant in and kissed Ruby on the cheek, "Good luck tonight." He hesitated, as if not quite sure he had done the right thing, then saw her smile at him and he smiled back. What was it about this woman that made him feel so...so...damn happy? Disconcerted, he quickly set off for the door, "Hey, Ralph, I think your guest of honour has arrived. Sam's car has just pulled up."

As Ralph turned, a short man with a large camera swinging round his neck stepped in front of him, "Are you Ralph?" the photographer said through a set of teeth the colour of custard. "I'm from the Rye Observer, when's the great lady arriving then?"

"Oh, hi, well, actually..."

"I had no idea we had a celebrity in our midst, I wish I'd known before. Could have got some great stuff for the paper and maybe sold some to the nationals," the man said, scratching his unshaven chin.

"Well, she doesn't live here, she's visiting," Ralph said, stepping back slightly out of range of his breath.

"Not her, her son. He'd make me a few quid, they like a delinquent celebrity kid..."

Ralph's fists clenched, but before he could say anything the photographer was haring off towards the car park, his socked feet gripping the edge of his sandals as he ran, getting there in time to see a long pair of film star legs emerge slowly from Sam's car. Ralph followed as quickly as he could, but by the time he got outside there was already a large crowd and at its centre was Jane Scott. She had shed her classic black outfit from last night and was wearing a blue vintage summer dress, entirely out of place for a chilly February morning, high white heels and a pair of 1950's inspired cats-eye sunglasses in a leopard-print design. As she posed and preened for the photographer and phone cameras surrounding her, she looked every inch the international film star she was.

"Suddenly, it's all about her," a voice said from behind him. Then Sam's chin appeared and rested on Ralph's shoulder, their faces cheek to cheek.

"Well, they say, all publicity is good publicity," Ralph said with a weak smile. "If it helps us make more money, then it's a good thing. Right?"

"Maybe. Come on, I need to keep on the move or she'll try and drag me into it," Sam stepped away and they headed inside, reclaiming Stanley who Sam had left with some of the little footballers and their parents.

After nearly fifteen minutes with the photographers, Jane Scott led the crowd like the Pied Piper of Hamlyn into the large hall. As if drawn by some mystic call of star quality, everyone drifted towards her and gathered around in a large circle. Then the performance really began.

Jane threw both arms in the air and called for quiet with a loud, "Hush, my darlings, huuussssshhhh!"

Once silence had fallen, she continued, "You are all so kind, it's lovely to be here with you all today. Thank you for inviting me." A ripple of applause spread through the growing crowd, as more and more people seemed to appear from nowhere.

"Now, we are not here because of me, but to help these children to continue to enjoy their football in this fabulous corner of England you all call home. I can understand why my son has settled here in Rye, it is so pretty and everyone is so damn friendly," she paused to give them all a winning smile and a chance to applaud, which they eagerly did.

She began to turn around and look amongst the crowd, "Samuel? Sam, where are you?" she called, a cry which was taken up by some of the parents as they tried to find him. However, he had known what was coming and had disappeared back to his car, where he was quietly laying on the back seat, out of sight.

When he couldn't be found, Jane's beady eyes landed on Ralph, "Ralph! Ralph, come here," she laughed her loud hyena-laugh as he shook his head, but he was soon being ushered through the crowd to stand beside her. "We can't seem to find Sam, but this is Ralph who, along with my son, has put this whole thing together for the Rye Rangers."

"Rovers. They're the Rye Rovers," Ralph said through clenched teeth.

"Of course, they are," she said without pausing. "So, all that is left for me to do is to say, please do *not* spend wisely..." she waited expertly for a murmur of laughter, "...and declare this lovely fair well and truly open!" She finished with a flourish and the crowd cheered.

Ralph was able to move quickly away as they closed in on her to seek selfies and autographs. He saw the top of Sam's head in the back window of the car and beckoned him over.

"All over and done with," he said as Sam approached, the peak of his cap pulled low over his face. "I can't believe how many people have turned up."

"Well, maybe it's worth it then" Sam said, gloomily.

"Your mum was brilliant, such a pro. I know she's tricky, but she's helped us, hasn't she? She's got some publicity for herself as well, so maybe she'll leave you alone now."

Sam laughed, "I love your wide-eyed innocence, like Bambi facing a crossbow."

"What do you mean?"

"This is small fry for her, a temporary massage of her ego. She's got her eyes on something bigger than this, take my word for it," Sam's normally handsome face was set like stone and his shoulders hunched with tension.

Ralph remembered Martin's words of caution and remained positive, "Well, we'll deal with that when it happens...together. For now, we need to mingle - no hiding, remember? We agreed to face the world openly."

"Fine, but I'm keeping the cap on," Sam grumbled.

"Good, because you've got a face like a smacked arse and we don't want to put people off their indiscriminate spending, do we?"

Sam stretched his shoulders, "You're right, let's try and win some athlete's foot powder in the raffle and see if we can guess the weight of the world's cutest cross-dressing goalkeeper. Come on."

Sam and Ralph worked their way around the various stalls, which were heaving with locals all putting their hands in their pockets and donating to the good cause. As they approached the cake stall, which looked like a rugby scrum with a flushed Ruby at its centre, Ralph saw a familiar face.

"Hey, George," he said to Dew-drop Dobson's small round grandson. Behind him came Fiona, who looked pale and Ralph could see the shadow of dark circles under her eyes. He smiled at her, "Hello, again. How are you? Sam, you remember Fiona, from the...er, funeral."

"Of course, how are things?" Sam said, shaking her

hand.

"Good, thank you. I've never seen the halls so full, it's amazing."

"I want cake. A chocolate one," George demanded from somewhere down near Ralph's hip.

Fiona frowned at him, "I've told you, until your Dad gets here we don't have any money. You'll have to wait." She smiled at Sam and Ralph, "I left my purse at home. So, I'm waiting for Andy, my husband."

Fiona took George by the hand and led him away, "He's not given her any cash, has he?" Sam whispered.

"Doesn't look like it," Ralph said. "I hope Anna really can buy Dobson's place so she's got the money to get away from him."

With a whiff of expensive perfume and a hooting laugh Jane Scott engulfed them from behind in an elaborate embrace, "There you are, boys. Such a lovely turn out. You see how they still love me?" Her voice dropped to a deep whisper, "I wish the fucking producers could see this in LA, that'd get them moving."

She turned as a nervous young man approached with his phone held out and asked if he could take her photo, "Of course, darling. How about one with my son, too? Two for the price of one, eh? Sam, come along let's have a family photo. Hop over there, Ralph, darling, out of shot, would you?"

"Mum, no," Sam hissed. "Absolutely not," and he turned away to help Ruby on the busy cake stall.

"He's shy," Jane said to her fan.

Ralph also managed to get away and set off to see if he could locate Stanley. He squeezed his way between the long queue for the fake fortune teller and the even longer line of dads waiting to try to throw a hoop over a bottle of booze. As he came through the other side, he found himself looking at the pink, oval face of Andy, George's father, "Oh, hello, Mr...erm?"

"Hawkins, mate. Andy Hawkins, the missus says she's met you before. Is that right?"

Ralph looked over Andy's shoulder to see Fiona standing behind him holding one of George's hands, while his other one manoeuvred a large piece of chocolate cake into his mouth, "Yes, I was at Mr Dobson's funeral. Fiona showed us some of his bird drawings, actually, they were beautiful..."

"Yeah, yeah, whatever. Look, she seems to think you know Jane Scott. Do you?"

"Well, yes, sort of. She's..."

"Good, I need a photo with her. Let's go," he turned as if he was going to find Jane and expected Ralph to follow.

"Hang on, I've no idea where she is," Ralph said, refusing to be bullied by this man who seemed to expect everyone to do his bidding. "Perhaps George could see if he can find her?"

Fiona quickly stepped forward, "That's a good idea, then Ralph doesn't need to fight his way through all the people with his bad leg. Off you go, George, you know who we mean, don't you? The lady from the films on TV. See if you can find her then come and tell us where she is."

"Alright, but don't eat my cake," George said, handing his mother the sticky remains.

Andy leaned in to Ralph, "His cake is safe with her, she don't eat cake, she has to watch her figure. She's still got cracking legs, though, don't you think? Don't want them getting spoilt." He chuckled, turning even pinker than before.

Ralph threw an embarrassed smile to Fiona, who turned away.

"Is this her?" Fiona said, pointing to the flame red hair of Jane Scott as she moved through the crowd towards them.

"There you are, Ralph, have you been hiding? I need Sam," she said, ignoring Fiona and Andy.

Ralph smiled sweetly, "He's busy, but this is Andy and he is one of your biggest fans. He'd like a photo with you."

To her credit Jane didn't flinch as she saw the rotund, rosy pink man and turned on her film star smile, "How precious, of course. Would you like one with your wife?"

Andy shook his head, rummaging through his inside jacket pocket, "No, she'll take it." He produced his phone and then his hand shot out and grabbed the collar of the passing photographer from the local paper, "Oy, mate, get one for the paper too. It'll be good publicity for the new shop."

Despite being jostled by Andy and the photographer Jane kept her megawatt smile in place, "Oh, are you a shop owner too, like Ralph?"

"I will be soon, gonna open an antiques shop. Lovely stuff it'll be, from all over the country," he said, putting a pudgy arm around her waist.

"How nice for you," she said, without enthusiasm.

Fiona quickly took a photo of them with Andy's phone and then her own, "Check 'em, Fi," he snapped. "Make sure you haven't cut our heads off. Right, come on then, fella, make it a good one, you're supposed to be the pro."

Jane allowed the photographer to take two very

quick shots, before she expertly extricated herself from Andy's grasp and disappeared seamlessly into the crowd.

"Nice woman. Hot - even at her age," Andy said to no one in particular as he wandered off, followed at a short distance by Fiona.

Ralph breathed out as he watched the two of them move away to find George, wishing he could have done something to help Fiona, but he was not supposed to know about her secrets and this was certainly not the time or the place to discuss them.

The crowd was almost gone from the cake stall as he returned with Stanley a little while later. Ruby took a long drink from a bottle of water, "Thank you, Sam, I was drowning until you arrived."

Sam swept crumbs from the table into his hand and emptied them into a box at his feet, "You're welcome. Oh, Ralph, Ruby's saved you some cake, she's hidden it under my jacket over there."

Ralph and Stanley joined them behind the table, "Brilliant, I could do with some sugar."

"What's happened? Not my bloody mother again?"

"No, she's been great. I've just met Fiona's husband, Andy. Oh, and there's someone I need you to meet back at the shop. It's a surprise, well, sort of..." he said as Stanley wedged himself into a large Tupperware box and started to lick chocolate icing from around the edge.

CHAPTER 13

The blind date, lovely teeth and moving cutlery.

Ruby sat at a quiet table tucked in a corner of the restaurant far from the noise of Cinque's bar. She nervously sipped a glass of Perrier and tried not to play with the sweet-smelling beads at her wrist. Her new shoes were pinching, her ankles were puffy after a morning behind the cake stall and around her people were enjoying large glasses of wonderful looking wine. If this was not some sort of test, she thought, then she didn't know what was.

She had arrived early to be greeted by the charming Dawa Singh, who was waiting for her and quickly settled her at the table and made her feel as comfortable as he could in the circumstances.

"As soon as Anna arrives, I'll bring her through the long way round. Then it will be more of a surprise for her," he'd said.

"I doubt she'll want the surprise to be any bigger really, but the later she sees me the less chance there is of her bolting, I suppose."

Dawa had made an understanding noise, smiled and left without comment. Ruby had prepared so much to say to Anna; explanations, apologies, regrets, but as her nerves took hold the words seemed to get jumbled in her head. Perhaps a small glass of wine would calm her and she would be able to remember everything properly?

"Oh, you're joking," Ruby heard from behind her. "Mum? Dawa, what's going on?"

Dawa pulled out the chair opposite Ruby without a word and waited for Anna to sit, forcing her to move in front of her mother and take the seat.

"You look lovely as always, Anna," he said, calmly. "Would you like a drink? With Joe's compliments."

"I'll have a Rioja…a whole bottle, please, as he's paying," she said, reaching out and pulling a wine glass towards her.

Ruby leaned forward, her mind suddenly clear, "I'll have another Perrier, please…and can you take this glass away, Dawa? I won't be needing it," she handed him the wine glass that was sitting in front of her.

Anna blushed, "Oh, I didn't mean…I wasn't…sorry, it was the shock. I thought I was meeting a man, I was ready for a man…if you see what I mean," she sank into her chair, a green velvet carpet bag held tight to her chest. She looked up into the friendly eyes of Dawa, who smiled at her in a way that made her feel calmer.

"I'll be back with some menus in a moment," Dawa's deep voice seemed to bring a soothing balm to the table as he turned and glided away.

Ruby sipped her water, "I'm sure you're disappointed not to be here with a proper date, so a glass of wine is a good idea."

Anna started to rummage in her large bag, "I'm going to kill Joe! Honestly, I've got all dressed up and have been worrying about meeting a man all day. I'm not good with men as a rule, you see. I suppose he thinks this is some sort of joke."

"He was trying to help," Ruby said. "I've been keen to have a good chat for a while, but we never seem to get a chance to be alone." She looked at her daughter, Anna's bottom lip protruding just as it had done as a girl when she didn't get her way. She looked more human, less of the unfamiliar adult Ruby knew so little about and more of the child she remembered, "I thought it might be good for us."

Anna looked up, "Why didn't you ask me?"

"Would you have said yes?"

"Of course," Anna ran her hands through her hair, twisting her curls around her finger – another throwback to her childhood self. "Maybe not. What do we need to talk about?"

"Anything you like, Anna, but it would be good to talk, wouldn't it? Properly, after nearly six years of silence."

Closing her bag Anna nodded, "I suppose it would."

Dawa returned with Anna's bottle of wine and two menus.

"Thanks, Dawa," Anna blushed as she took one of the menus. "Sorry if I was rude."

Dawa poured the deep red wine into her glass, "You didn't seem rude to me." He gave her another attractive smile and moved on to seat another table.

Anna watched him go, "He's got lovely teeth, I never noticed them before. Very straight and white. And his shoes are a normal size."

"He was right - you do look lovely."

"Oh, thanks," Anna fiddled with her yellow and purple outfit. "It's a Punjabi Salwar Kameez, I got it this week."

"It's beautiful, the embroidery and gold beading are so detailed. I love your style, I wish I was as creative as you," Ruby looked down at her cream linen jacket and burgundy silk blouse.

"You've got your own style. I mean you've smartened your act up, haven't you? Everything is much more, well...tailored now. Shall we choose?" Anna opened the menu and disappeared behind it.

After they had ordered, Ruby filled Anna in on the busy morning with the cake stall and the success of the fair thanks to the presence of Jane Scott. This gave her time to get her thoughts in order, and as they started to chat more easily she was ready to say what she had been wanting to say for a long time.

"Anna, this is difficult for both of us. So much happened...and didn't happen as you were growing up. I think we need to talk about it. It would be good for us to be honest with one another."

Anna cradled her glass of wine in both hands and looked deeply into it, "I'm not sure I'm ready. I don't want to fight."

"But I want to apologise, not fight. Please let me say how sorry I am."

Anna looked up, her eyes wide, "Apologise? To me?" She had not expected this, she had thought her mother would trot out her usual list of excuses and people to blame. More gently, she said, "You don't have to."

"Oh, but I do! I let you down, Anna, again and again. You needed me and I wasn't there for you. I was so wrapped up in myself that..." Ruby halted as their starters arrived and were placed in front of them. "Thank you," she said to the waiter.

"It's fine," Anna said. "I survived, didn't I?"

"Surviving is not enough for a child," Ruby said, vehemently. "You should have flourished and had a proper childhood. You lost your father, then you as good as lost your mother too."

Anna hesitated then held her hand out towards her mother, "Look, it was hard for both of us, but we're back together now. We can't change what happened, let's just agree to make a fresh start."

Ruby took Anna's hand, savouring the rare touch, "I have so much more I want to say, though. I prepared it all, to explain why I started drinking, why I couldn't cope, why I married Derek after your father. I understand it now."

"Well, that's great. As long as it helps you that's brilliant, but I don't need to know it all. I blamed myself for Dad's death for years..."

Ruby looking horrified, "Oh, Anna."

"Then I blamed you for not telling me it wasn't my fault...which is crazy, 'cos as an adult I know he just had a heart attack. The fact I was angry with him before it happened had nothing to do with it."

"Anna, of course it didn't. I had no idea. After he died you seemed unreachable, like you had gone somewhere I couldn't go. I was so lonely..."

"*You* were lonely?" Anna hissed snatching her hand away, but then Dawa passed the table and gave her a brief look with his warm dark eyes and she was able to release her tense breath. "Look, I don't really want to go over it all. Neither of us are the people we were then. So, let's move on. Besides, this soufflé is sinking fast," she turned her attention to the food.

"Fine, let's talk about something else. Let's talk about you, tell me about The Cookery."

"I think I've burst it," Anna looked into her dish at the pile of soft egg and cheese at the bottom. "The soufflé - not the café. Well, the thing is with The Cookery I have an opportunity to expand the business, to take on another place."

"Really? How exciting."

"The new one is The Copper Kettle, up beside the church. The daughter of the old owner, we went to his funeral, he was vile - but I can't say that now he's dead... although, I just did - never mind. Fiona wants to sell it quickly and she's given me first refusal."

Ruby sat back dabbing her lips with her napkin, "But that's amazing, The Copper Kettle used to be the best place in town for tea and lunch. I used to go in there with your father and I'm pretty sure I used to take you in as a child, do you remember?"

Anna picked up her wine glass, "Not really, was it before Dad died? We didn't really go anywhere after that."

Ruby hesitated for a moment, her throat dry, "Yes, I think it probably was," she took a sip of water. "No wonder you can't remember; it was an awfully long time ago." They both sat for a moment, Ruby realising her relationship with her daughter had been so different before Alan went. Anna had only been ten, but after his sudden death it was a blur of half remembered images and muddled memories.

"Still," Anna said, brightly. "It's a great opportunity. I've been thinking for a while about expanding, so this might be the way to do it. I'm nervous though, it's a big decision."

"Of course it is, but what an opportunity. If you don't buy it, I will!" Ruby laughed.

Anna smiled back, "Can you imagine that? Honestly, it would be a disaster," she didn't notice the light dim slightly in her mother's eyes as her casual comment stung. "Seriously, there is so much to think about, my head's been spinning for days, but Fiona needs an answer soon."

Ruby drank some more water as the waiter removed their empty plates, knowing Anna was probably right - she was not a person who could do something like that. She had failed at so much in her life and it was Anna's turn to shine, "Well, tell me how it would work?" Ruby said, tucking a stray piece of hair behind her ear. "Would you sell the same things in both places?"

"No, they'd have to be quite different, with a distinct offer in each. I was thinking The Copper Kettle should be more traditional and The Cookery could be more experimental - different fusions and flavours, like the naughty little sister down the road from the classic tea shop."

Ruby loved the excitement shining in Anna's face, "Of course, that makes sense. It seems like you know exactly what to say to Fiona - you must buy it!"

"Do you think so? I don't know, it feels such a humungous thing. Besides, there's the money, I'd need to get a loan and I'm not sure the bank would lend it to me, even if Fiona could wait that long."

"Why wouldn't they? You have one successful business, why couldn't you run two? It makes absolute sense."

"I don't think the banks give out money too easily these days. I don't know what the terms would be, I'd be in debt...I could lose everything if it goes wrong," Anna took a large slug of wine and filled her glass again.

"Well, with that attitude you won't get anywhere," Ruby said. "Look, if it's just a question of money let me give it to you. Obviously, I don't know how much you need, but I have money from two husbands. Your father and Derek both left me substantial amounts..."

Anna thumped the wine bottle back on the table, "No! Absolutely not. No."

"Why not? It would be so much easier..."

"I am not going to borrow money from you," Anna shook her head, trying to clear some of the fog created by the many glasses of wine she had drunk too rapidly. "Look, Mum, firstly, you got me here under false pretences and now you are trying to tie yourself to me with your money. I have managed everything perfectly well up to now without your help and I will not be beholden to you. That ship has sailed, up the creek and past the paddle...no, that's not right. The ship has sailed and will not spring a leak now....damn, the more I think about The Copper Kettle the more I sound like barmy old Dewdrop Dobson," Anna took another mouthful of wine.

"Anna, I wasn't trying to do anything except help," Ruby's shoes were pinching badly now under the table and her head was starting to ache. "Don't forget that your father's money from his life insurance helped you before. You wouldn't have been able to buy The Cookery if I hadn't given it to you, so why not..."

Anna brought her wine glass down on the table with

such force the wine sloshed up and over the side, "Careful, Anna, the wine!" Ruby said, putting her hand to her temple where the blood was now throbbing painfully.

"It's not me that needs to be careful with wine, remember?" Anna mumbled, scrabbling under her chair for her carpet bag. "I do not want your money, even if it was Dad's. If this happens, it will happen because of *me*, not you," she rose swiftly and tried to step away, but some of the cutlery and her wine glass started to move with her. She paused and found her linen napkin and a large chunk of the tablecloth tucked into the fabric belt around her waist. With as much dignity as she could muster, she detached herself from the table, "Thank you for the offer, but my answer is no. I'm not feeling very hungry now, so...well, good night."

Anna knew she was being dramatic, Ruby's hurt, confused face told her she had over-reacted, but she couldn't stop herself. She realised she still didn't trust her mother; she had learnt not to need her and she was not about to be forced into a relationship with her that she did not want.

She collected her coat from Dawa without a word, the tears burning at the back of her eyes, but she kept herself together as he held the door open for her.

"Good night, Anna. I'm sorry your evening has not worked out as well as was hoped," he said, gently.

She looked at Dawa Singh, his kind eyes and those lovely white teeth, "Me too," she said, as the pent-up tears from so many years of missing her mother started to fall and she disappeared into the night.

CHAPTER 14

*The immaculate conception, good old
Uncle Joe and being shouty.*

J oe walked past Cinque just after eight o'clock and caught a glimpse of Ruby and Anna through the window, "Mission accomplished," he said proudly to Stanley who was pulling on his lead, eager to investigate a carrier bag that was waving in the wind outside the bank. He was beginning to enjoy his occasional walks at the end of the day with Stanley, while Ralph rested his leg and Sam worked, it meant good old Uncle Joe could deputise and accompany the small beagle on his evening stroll around the town's quiet streets.

Joe squared his broad shoulders as Stanley pulled him away from the restaurant, it was great to have helped Ruby and Anna. He'd always felt on the periphery of his group of friends, through his own choice not to fully commit to anyone or anywhere, but after nearly ten years in Rye he was aware the excuse that he was passing through no longer worked. Maybe it was time to grow up a little and engage properly with his life here. He shivered at the thought of it.

Was it such a bad thing to commit? The option to go to Scotland and be with Imogen would mean leaving his rooftop family, so by committing to her he would have to leave them. Feeling more than a casual connection with people was new to him, either as a lover or as a friend. Stanley was straining on the lead, keen to move on again now the carrier bag had been dealt with, "Come on my four-legged friend, let's pick up the pace," Joe said and started to walk quickly down the street. "I'm not sure this thinking stuff is really my scene."

* * *

Up on the terrace above the shops, Ralph and Helen sat together in silence at Auntie B's small iron table, the candle unlit. Helen wore her blue woollen coat and had a large tartan rug wrapped tightly around her shoulders against the evening cold, while Ralph had on thick gloves and a blanket over his knees.

Helen sighed and took a sip of the peppermint tea that was rapidly cooling in the night air, "I imagined this is what we would be like when we were eighty - two old wrinklies on a park bench at Whitby, but we're not even thirty yet!" she managed a weak smile, but it didn't reach her eyes. "Look, I didn't mean to be so blunt, I had thought of all sorts of ways to tell you, but in the end I needed to get it out and say it."

Ralph stared past her through the canopy of sparkling lights and out to the bruised, deep-blue night sky beyond. His face was very pale and his jaw slowly worked up and down, but he couldn't seem to find a way to say anything.

"Yup, that was pretty much my first reaction too," Helen said, watching him silently taking in the news she had shared with him.

"How long?" Ralph said, in a low whisper.

"About five months, roughly."

Ralph's scared eyes came down from the sky to rest on Helen, his leg was starting to shake and he laid his gloved hand on it, "But you don't look any…"

"Different? I know."

"And you're sure it's…"

"A baby? Yep, it's definitely a baby. At first I thought I'd been hitting the crisps a bit hard and put on weight, but nope, I am definitely pregnant," again Helen tried to smile.

"But five months means it happened back in September."

"Yes, I know…oh, bugger, sorry! Wait, back up…in my carefully planned speech that bit was the most important part and I forgot it when I blurted it out…It's not yours, Ralph! The baby is…someone else's."

Ralph grabbed the edge of the table with both hands, "But…but…how?"

"Well, I'm not going to start riding around on a donkey with a tea cloth on my head and call it immaculate conception - I had sex! With someone else…while we were married. Sorry."

Ralph looked at the small, white candle and began to fiddle with the lighter that lay beside it, but his gloves were too thick and his hands were shaking too much to make it work.

"Here, let me," Helen said, reaching across and taking

the lighter from him. She lit Auntie B's candle and sat back, "This is a lovely thing to do for your friend, keeping her flame alive on the roof terrace."

"I wish she was here now; she always knew what to say." They sat in silence for a few minutes, then Ralph looked at her, "What are you going to do?"

"Well, that's the million-dollar question. Ralph, this is where I hoped you might come in. I know it's a lot… it's not like…" she wiped her face, noticing her hands had started to shake like Ralph's. "Boy, this is hard, but… I really need you."

Helen turned as she heard footsteps and saw Joe step onto the terrace, "Hey, only me," he said. "Stanley has emptied his bladder all over the better parts of town and I'm ready for the first beer of the day. What about you guys?"

Joe had met Helen earlier when she was having breakfast in The Cookery, but she had looked a lot calmer then than she did now, "Have I come at a bad moment?"

"No," Helen said with a tight smile.

"Actually, yes," Ralph said.

"OK, well, while you decide I'll be over here getting a beer," Joe said, sidling away from them to the rickety bar.

"What can I do?" Ralph said to Helen. "I'll do whatever I can. I swore to myself I'd never let you down again if you needed me."

Helen looked at him, her arms crossed tightly over her chest, "Do you mean it?

"I do."

"Thank you, I hoped you would say that. I mean, it's not like you've been here long enough to put down proper roots, is it? What is it, twelve weeks or something since you left?"

"Anyone want a drink while I'm pretending to be busy over here?" Joe called.

"Look, we can't talk now. Besides you need time to take all this in. I'll see you in the morning," she crossed the terrace towards Ralph's flat. "Goodnight, Joe. It was nice to meet you today."

"What do you mean *proper roots*? How can I…?" Ralph said to her disappearing back.

Joe waved at her as she passed him, "Sleep tight." He quickly snapped the top off a bottle of beer and headed towards Ralph, "I think you two have got this thing sorted."

"Hardly, she hasn't told me what she wants yet."

"What do you mean?"

"What do *you* mean? What have we got sorted?" Ralph shook his head, trying to clear the confusion that was making it spin.

"Splitting up. Being civilised about it. I mean things have got a bit messy with some of the women I've had in the past, you know what I mean?"

"No, not really," Ralph said. "Helen wants my help, but I've no idea what I'm supposed to do."

They both jumped as the doors to Anna's flat were flung open with a crash and she charged onto the terrace, a bottle of red wine in her hand, "Oh, you're both here, thank the little baby Jesus. I have had the worst night EVER! Well, it started OK, Dawa liked my frock… thing. He's nice, isn't he? Smashing teeth. Then Mum wasn't really what I thought she was, which was nice. Then she was, which wasn't."

"How much have you had to drink?" Ralph said, wearily.

"Oooh, ever such a little bit of a lot of red wine. This is bottle numero tres, so two-ish," she said as she swayed towards them.

Joe smiled, "Good evening, Anna, how was your date?"

"Ah, here he is, the betrayer-in-chief! I hope you are proud of yourself? What were you thinking, Joe? Setting me up with my mother? It was a disaster. It's so obvious you know nothing about relationships. I feel so sorry for Imogen. Did I say 'Imo-gin' then? Or did I say 'Imogen'? I didn't mean the drink, the tonicy drink, I meant that poor girl who ran all the way to Scotland..."

Ralph groaned, "Anna, please stop."

Anna ignored him and pointed the bottle at Joe, with its wine sloshing violently inside, "She tried to buy me, you know that? Her own DAUGHTER! Tried to PAY me for all the years she abandoned me..."

Joe called up an image of Ruby as she had been in his shop on the day they had first met, looking vulnerable and beautiful and he heard his voice rise to match Anna's drunken fury, "ENOUGH!". He was as surprised as Anna and Ralph looked, but he was mad, very mad.

"Ruby did NOT abandon you, Anna, she was always there. She was struggling with the death of the man she loved and, yes, with a problem with alcohol, but she was trying her best. Tell me honestly – did your mom really offer you money to buy you back?" Joe had no idea where the calm, good old boy had gone, but for a fleeting second he liked this new guy with his emotions fully on display, "Well?"

"She didn't actually...I mean, she did offer me money."

"What for?" Joe demanded.

Anna suddenly felt dizzy, "Erm...she...well, to help me buy The Copper Kettle."

Joe nodded not taking his eyes off Anna, "So, she was trying to *help* you, not buy you."

Anna turned away from him, "You weren't there. It was awful. I was so angry with her, I stormed off...after I'd taken the table cloth out of my dress – no, my shammy kaweez. It's Pakistrani, it was stuck. I don't know how it got there. Look, p'rhaps I wasn't angry about the money, p'rhaps it was other things," Anna's shoulders slumped.

Joe's anger too had started to subside and he moved to her side, taking the wine bottle from her and handing it to Ralph, "Go on," he said, guiding her to a deckchair.

"I felt ambushed, it was confusing, she was so nice, so...ordinary. All of a sudden she was the mother I had always wanted...but it's too late," she fell into the chair. "I needed her before, when I was a kid."

Joe put a hand on her shoulder and knelt beside her to look in her eyes, "I get it, but does that mean she can't be here for you now?" he asked.

"I suppose not," she said. "But, Joe, what will she want in return?"

"I don't know, maybe to see you succeed? Ruby is a good woman, Anna."

"How would you know?"

"We talked and she's lost a lot of her life to grief and booze, but she is working real hard to turn it all around. I admire her...and I like her."

"What are you going to do, Anna?" Ralph asked. "You want to buy the other café, right?"

She nodded.

"You need money to do it, right?"

She nodded again.

"Your mum can help you with that, so where's the problem?"

Anna shook her head, "No, it's never that simple. I don't want the money to come with any strings. We get on OK, or we did until tonight…but it's fragile." She shivered, "It could get complicated if we are tied together financionally, no, functionancially, damn, financiatedly…with money!"

Joe sat at the table, "Anna, you have a mother who wants to help you build your life, take it from someone who never appreciated what his Mom really did for him - grab it with both hands while you can."

"Didn't you get on with your mum?" Ralph asked, realising that apart from knowing his mother was Auntie B's daughter, she was called Ginger and had died in Canada, Joe had told them nothing about her.

"Oh, yeah, she was amazing. She'd been through a lot in her life, so she was tough," Joe tipped the beer bottle up to get the last few drops. "She wanted me to go off and see the world, to travel. Get away and move on, she said over and over. As a teen I was mad with her, because I thought she was pushing me away. She'd had me late in life, at forty, and I got it in my head she wanted rid of me because she wanted her life back. My Pop worked so hard that I didn't really see him much and he left us kids to Mom to deal with most of the time. I got into smoking pot and she threw me out – I don't blame her, to be honest, I was a pain in the ass. So, I took off as soon as I could and shot around the world trying anywhere and anything I could to show them I didn't need them. It was crazy.

Pop died in a traffic accident in my first year away

and Mom told me not to come home, to carry on seeing the world. In my head that meant she didn't want me back. Eventually I ran out of money and steam, until Auntie B bailed me out and paid for me to come to the UK. When Mom died, I realised I'd got it all wrong and by then I'd missed my opportunity to make things right with her...Hey, this is not about me. Bottom line – Anna, I think you should take the money from Ruby."

Anna shivered in her striped deckchair, "I hoped you'd forgotten about me," she said. "I've been rotten and shouty and fighty, haven't I?"

"Yes," both men said.

"Couldn't one of you have said no?"

"No," they said, but with grins this time.

"Take the money," Joe said.

"What do you think, Ralph?"

"It solves a problem, doesn't it?" he said with a shrug.

She looked hard at the wine bottle on the table, picked it up and took a glug from the neck, "I mean, Fiona...isn't she lovely? Fiona? She needs money quickly and going through the bank takes time. This is cash and I s'ppose it's the best way to help her."

"Too right," Joe said.

She groaned, "OK, so now I have to say sorry to my mother for being a complete poop tonight AND I have to grovel to see if she'll still help me with the money. Cheers ev'ryone!"

Joe grabbed the wine bottle from her and slammed it onto the table top with a loud crack, "Jeez, woman, this is madness. She's your *mom*, damn it, just ask her! What's so hard about that?"

Anna stiffened, "You have no idea what I went through with her."

"Oh, get over it," he snapped.

"What? Listen, Mr Canadiania-man, like you know anything about emotions or feelings! I mean, you haven't felt anything for anyone in years, 'cept Imogin...gen! And she's got as far away from you as she can at the arse end of Scotland. Right, Ralph? I mean, you can't even make up your mind if you can be bothered with her now or not, just the same as always!"

"Hang on, you two..." Ralph said.

"Really? Is that what you think?" Joe thundered as he leapt to his feet. "Is that how you see me? Dead from the waist up?" He turned to Ralph, "Is that what you think too? What everyone thinks? I'm a walking dick?"

Ralph had not expected the evening to get as complicated as it had and he had lost his way a bit, "Joe, look... not everyone...I mean...we all...you're just you."

"Which is what? Hmm? You know what? Forget it, I'm out of here," Joe yelled as he stormed off the terrace.

Ralph struggled to his feet, "Anna, why do you have to lash out at someone who loves you every time you feel threatened or out of your depth? Sometimes it is really, really hard to be your friend! How Ruby is supposed to work out how to be your bloody mother I have no idea," and he limped into his flat and slammed the door, leaving her alone, cold and feeling sick.

Joe raced through Ralph's flat, down the steep stairs and on to the street so fast that Ralph stood no chance of catching up with him. He fought to get his keys from the pocket of his tight jeans, swearing under his breath, then unlocked Let's Screw and went straight to the storeroom at the back, grabbed his bike and practically ran through the shop with it, oblivious to the things he was knocking off the well-ordered shelves. His head was spinning with confusion. He was always so sure, so in control – happy keeping everyone at arm's length. So why had he reacted so strongly to Ruby being wronged? Was he really able to commit to someone like Imogen? Was he capable of feeling anything that strongly for anyone?

He locked-up the shop, his breathing hard and fast, then threw himself on the bike and peddled for all he was worth, away from the centre of Rye, away from the rooftop and the emotions he cursed himself for showing. As his legs propelled the bike forward, his mind echoed with the words of his mother, *get away and move on, get away and move on, get away and move on.*

CHAPTER 15

The lecherous gnome, pork pies
and speaking Italian.

Sunday morning was quiet for Rye's independent shops, as a biting wind and cold rain kept people locked in the comfort of their homes for a day of slippers and squabbles over roast potatoes.

"Perhaps we've been a bit premature with our 'get out in your garden' display," Joe said as he sat in a garden chair in the window of Let's Screw watching the rain lashing against the glass.

Next to him, Ruby dusted a lecherous looking gnome with either a cheeky wink or a dirty squint, she couldn't decide, "Maybe a bit, but it will cheer people up. This time of year can be so depressing."

They had spent the last couple of hours cleaning out the window display and creating a summer scene with outdoor furniture, fake grass, garden tools, painted birds, bees and butterflies, not to mention a small army of gnomes.

"I was so pleased to get your text asking me to help, I've loved it," she said. "Thank you, it was just what I needed after last night."

"I had a feeling you might need a distraction; I know I did," Joe stretched, revealing his flat stomach beneath his shirt.

Ruby had to drag her eyes away from the smooth tanned skin and readjust a blue tit that was dangling near her left ear, "Stop it!" she said to herself, feeling like a love-sick schoolgirl again.

"Pardon me?"

"Oh, just this little bird bouncing around," she kept her back to him. She told herself she was being ridiculous; he was one of her daughter's friends and Auntie B's grandson! He was trying to help, that was all.

"I guess the evening didn't go as planned for either of us," Joe said, shaking his head. "What happened between you and Anna in the past has gone in deep, and she will not let it go."

"I know, but she won't even talk about it. There was a point last night when I thought we were really getting somewhere, but then she closed down."

"She'll come round eventually; she always does. Don't give up on her. If you want my advice...no, sorry, what do I know?" He rubbed his hands over his tired eyes.

She left the bouncing blue tit alone and turned to him, "Please, I'd love your advice. I'm pretty sure you know Anna better than me. What should I do?"

Joe smiled at her, finding her delicate features and soft eyes soothing, "Well, I'm not any good at this stuff, but if she does come and ask you for the money, insist it's a bridging loan, not a gift. Give it to her on the understanding that if she gets finance from a bank in due course then she can pay you back, or you can set up some sort of repayment plan from the café's profits. That way it's a proper deal, not just her mum bailing her out."

"Brilliant, that is much better - a proper professional arrangement," she said squeezing his arm. "My goodness, you must spend hours in the gym, your arm is rock solid...oh, I'm so sorry, how inappropriate..." she swiftly removed her hand, her cheeks flushing.

Joe laughed, "Ruby, it's fine...actually, I was tensing deliberately to show off."

Ruby straightened a little fishing rod on a particularly dodgy looking gnome, "Were you? Oh, dear..."

"There must be a law against interfering with a garden little person in a shop window," a voice said from the door behind them.

Ruby turned, "Anna, hi...no, yes...I was saying to Joe...well, it was...oh, dear."

"I think you'd better put him and his rod down before you make things worse," Anna said, smiling nervously.

Ruby looked down at the fishing rod that was now gripped tightly in one hand while she held the brightly coloured gnome around the neck with the other, "Shit...I mean, sorry, I don't normally swear," she said as she hurriedly replaced it in the display.

"You're great at swearing," Joe said, firmly.

"Well, I am working on it," Ruby grinned at him.

They both turned and looked at Anna, who was standing sheepishly half in and half out of the shop doorway, "Well, either come in or go out, but don't let the rain in," Joe snapped.

"Yes, sorry," Anna said, stepping inside and shutting

the door behind her. As they looked at her in silence, she stood awkwardly brushing the rain from her plastic poncho, which had images of Minnie Mouse dancing across it with an umbrella. She produced a small paper bag from inside the wide sleeve of her pink and black kimono under the poncho and took a step towards them, "I…ah! What the…?" she had come to a sudden halt, unable to go any further. She tried again, but it was like an invisible force-field was preventing her moving forward, "I think I'm having a stroke…"

"For the love of mike," Joe said under his breath. He got out of the deckchair, moved past Anna and released her and her voluminous Minnie Mouse plastic cape from the door in which she had trapped herself.

Anna stepped forward and looked behind her, "Well, as if I wasn't embarrassed enough this morning, that's dropped a big old gherkin on the blanket."

Joe stared at her, "That's put a what on the what?"

"You know what I mean, it's a thing…a proverb."

"But it makes no sense…"

Anna frowned, "I didn't come here to argue. Irene said she'd seen you both in here so I came to bring peace offerings," she held the paper bag out. "Pork pies with walnuts and mango. They're nice, I promise."

"I'm sure they are, they sound delicious," Ruby said taking the bag. "Mango? Who'd have thought? Thank you."

Joe just nodded.

"The window looks great, very summery," Anna did her best to sound cheerful, but was met with silence. She fiddled with her hair, wrapping it around her fingers, "OK, right, this is awkward, isn't it? So, here's the thing - I'm really sorry. To both of you. *Really* sorry. I was so mean last night, I blame the shock of the blind date and the wine - it must have been off, I think, because it had a really funny effect on me. My head's been all over the place thinking about The Copper Kettle and then Fiona's awful situation with her husband and you being around again, Mum, and last night Joe wasn't just a lump, no offence, you normally wouldn't get involved but you stepped in and made some sense and I'm not used to that and...well...then, I was a bit of a tit to be honest...oh, that rhymes – bit and tit – anyway...will one of you say something so I can stop talking, please..."

Joe sighed, "Did you know that the average height of a gnome is 27.5 cm?"

Anna tried hard not to roll her eyes, "No, I didn't know that."

"It's a little gnome fact!" Joe said, before moving back to the window and resuming his position in the deckchair.

Anna tipped her head to one side, letting her curls bounce in what she hoped was a look of contrition, "Does that mean you forgive me?"

"Maybe. The pork pie is a good start."

"I am genuinely sorry, Joe. I didn't mean any of it, I don't know why I say those things. Ralph gave me a right telling off. I know you are sensitive and have feelings and emotions, I know that. I was being a cow."

"Yes, you were," he said without smiling.

"Oh, right, blimey, excellent honesty. Good. Sorry, Joe."

Joe nodded towards Ruby, "And?"

"I know, I know," she turned to her mother and took a deep breath. "I'm sorry, Mum. You were trying to help me, I can see that. I didn't handle it well."

"It's fine. Let's forget it," Ruby said.

"Good, thank you. It was nice to spend a bit of time together...maybe, we should, erm, do it again some time? If you'd like to."

Ruby smiled, "I would love that."

Anna looked down at her rainbow-coloured welling-ton boots, "Great, I was wondering whether you wanted to go shopping together? I could maybe do with a few new clothes for the business, you know, up my game a bit...clothes-wise."

"Yes, let's do that, it would be lovely," she stepped around the gnomes and gave Anna a hug, pulling away when her daughter tensed rather than hugged her back. "Let me know when."

"Great. I've got to get back, I've left Irene and Rosie alone for too long as it is, they need a referee most of the time when they're together. Mum, can I ask..." Anna paused, twisting the edge of her rain cape. "That offer you made, of the money for the café..."

"Oh, yes, I was going to mention that. My offer was a bit clumsy last night, what I forgot to say was that I would see it as a loan. Until you get proper finance from a bank perhaps or are able to pay me back. A business ar-rangement that allows you to move swiftly for the sake of Fiona. I should have said that last night, so I'm sorry too."

Anna looked stunned, "Well, that's great! A business arrangement, wow! Shall I email you the figures and stuff then?"

"That sounds like an excellent idea. I can look at it and then get the money into your account in a couple of days," Ruby said, trying to sound professional. "I think you will make a huge success of The Copper Kettle,

Anna, I really do."

"Thanks, so, I'll see you both later. I'll let you know about the shopping date. Enjoy your pies," she waved as she opened the shop door and headed back to The Cookery.

Ruby and Joe looked at each other, "Well, that went well," he said.

"Yes, I think it did, but *A little gnome fact*? Really?" she laughed.

"I thought that was one of my best jokes, I've been working on it all morning."

"Well, if that's the best you can do, I pity poor Imogen stuck on a remote island with you night and day," Ruby checked through her bag for her car keys waiting for Joe's come back, but he remained quiet and looked out of the window. "Sorry, have I said something wrong? I've been insensitive."

"No, no, not at all," Joe said, shifting in his chair. "It's just that I haven't made a decision about moving to Scotland and it's not fair. The problem is, I'm not sure I know how I feel."

"Oh dear, what are you not sure about? Going to Scotland or being with Imogen?"

"Both, if I'm honest," he leant forward, putting his head in his hands. "Being with Imogen was great, she really made me think about another person for a change and I thought maybe I could put down some roots with someone for the first time. After the fight with Anna and Ralph last night I was convinced I really didn't belong here, so the best thing would be to give it a go with Imogen. I barely slept going over what I'd be giving up and what I'd be gaining - it fried my brain to be honest. But now, talking to you and then sorting Anna out -

it's like I've actually made a difference here."

"Oh, Joe, you have – never underestimate what a decent man you are."

Joe shook his head, "That's not a word that has been used about me for a long time...for ever, maybe. I mean, if I can make a difference to my friend's lives then perhaps I do belong here."

"Belonging is important."

"I know, but where? If I belong here, then I have to let Imogen go."

"It sounds like you have some more thinking to do, Joe," Ruby said.

He smiled, "I guess so, but it helps to talk. Perhaps I'm more of a talker than I thought I was - at least, I am with you. Would you like to go for a drink sometime?"

Ruby hesitated as she put on her coat, "Gosh, that's very kind, but I don't drink. Besides, don't you want to talk to someone closer to your age, more..."

"No, I'm happy talking to you and you're not that much older than me."

"Joe, I'm fifty-three."

"Great, I'm thirty-five."

"I'm a widow – twice."

"Yeah, like I don't have a history either."

"I'm a mother."

"I love mothers, I had one myself."

"I'm not good with alcohol."

"Have an orange juice."

"You have an answer for everything, don't you?"

"Pretty much," Joe stepped out of the window garden and gently helped settle her coat on her shoulders, "Ruby, you are way more than you think you are and I'd like to find out who that person is."

Ruby swallowed, her entire mind focused on Joe's eyes locked on hers, "I'd quite like to know that too."

"Great, then we have something in common. It's just a drink – a soft drink - as friends."

"Friends?" Ruby nodded slowly. "Of course, as friends. Right, then let's do it. How about Friday evening?"

"Perfect, I'll text you."

"Great, I'm looking forward to it. Well, thanks for letting me help you. See you on Friday, ciao!" With that she found the strength to turn away from Joe and leave the shop. She walked away flustered by Joe, pleased to have made a breakthrough with Anna and mortified she had said *ciao!* for the first time in her life.

CHAPTER 16

Home Wormeries, Mr Bump and
doing the right thing.

Sam said "Hi" to Ruby as she passed him outside The Bookery, "Ciao!" she chirruped back, then muttered, "Not again, what's the matter with me?" and hurried off up the road through the rain. Sam watched her go then went back inside, "I'm beginning to see some of Anna in her mother, I think she may be a tiny bit bonkers."

"Were the daisies straight?" Ralph said, distractedly. "You went outside to check."

Sam folded his arms, "Yes, your daisies are fine. What's got into you, you seem on edge?"

"Me? No, nothing," Ralph said, wiping a paintbrush on an old rag. He had created a series of crazy doodle-style flowers cut out of heavy cardboard to go into a new window display to welcome the spring. "As long as the daisies are straight, the daffodils can have a bit of a tilt, but I think the daisies should be straight - or is it the other way round?"

"Now you are freaking me out. Helen, what's the matter with him?"

Helen looked up from the counter where she was sorting through a pile of books, "Is it a full moon? It could be that."

Ralph picked up a paint tin and took it down into the basement, "I'm fine, I don't know what you are on about."

Sam whispered to Helen, "Is it the fight with Anna last night? He's barely spoken since he told me about it."

Helen looked behind her to make sure Ralph had gone then turned back to Sam, "Possibly, but he and I had a chat on the roof terrace too."

"Ah, right, if that terrace could talk it would have some tales to tell!"

Helen leaned over the counter towards him, "Listen, Sam, did he tell you..?"

There was a thud as Ralph started to make his way back up the stairs from below, "Ow, bloody hell!"

Sam shot to the back of the shop, "Are you OK? What have you done?"

"Banged my head," Ralph said from the bottom of the stairs.

"Any blood?"

"No."

"Brain damage?"

"Nothing to damage."

"True, true. Right, Mr Bump, I've got to get to the restaurant to check everything is underway for lunch service. Do you think you can stay in one piece for a few hours?"

"Can't promise," came Ralph's depressed voice up the stairs.

"Well, I've seen some bubble wrap down there, Helen can wrap you in that until I get back," he shook his head and grinned at Helen.

"Do you have to go?" Ralph said as his head appeared at the top of the stairs. "We always seem to be rushing past each other at the moment."

"I know, but now I've managed to get my mother off to a spa for a few days we can spend a bit more time together," Sam looked at Helen. "With Helen of course. It'll be great to get to know you better."

"Absolutely," she said.

"Right, gotta go. Try and keep him alive for me Helen," and he headed out the door and off to Cinque.

"So," Helen said. "I've picked out some stuff to display that might be good for Mother's Day presents. I think we should include more than cookbooks and romance novels and go for books like these; *How To Build Your Own Spa, Home Wormery and Wine Cellar*, and this looks good, *Raise your Children: The SAS Way*. What do you think?"

Ralph looked at her, "You're the only mother here, so I bow to your knowledge."

Helen dropped the books down on the counter and ran to the front door, she turned the key in the lock and the sign to closed.

"What are you doing? I can't afford to close," Ralph said.

"You can for ten minutes while we finish our talk, I can't bear it any more. We have to sort this out."

Ralph sat on the step in the middle of the shop, as Stanley settled down for a snooze on his bed in the window with a paw over his face, as if anticipating a tricky conversation.

Helen returned to the counter and reached underneath; pulling out two packets of crisps she threw one at Ralph, kept the other for herself and sat down beside him, "I know we don't have a great record for talking things through, but now seems like a bloody good time to start. And you need crisps for this sort of talk, crisps are important," she ripped open the packet and stuck her fingers inside.

Ralph fiddled with his packet, "Can I ask who the father is? Are you absolutely sure it's not mine?"

"Ralph, we barely spoke for the last six months, let alone...you know, bounced around the bedroom. It was a guy from work, it was a one-night thing. I'm really sorry I betrayed our marriage, but under the circumstances, with you being gay and everything, I hope it isn't going to be an issue."

"No...no, why should it?" he opened his packet of crisps. "Does he know? I mean are you two...?"

With a mouthful of crisps Helen shook her head, "No, we are definitely not together and he doesn't know. Not yet, but I will tell him. I don't want anything from him and I certainly don't want him in my life, but he has a right to know his child."

"OK, so where do I come in?"

Helen sat forward staring out of the shop window, "I'm frightened, Ralph. What do I know about raising a baby? I mean, how the hell am I supposed to keep a baby alive, when I can't even spot I've married a gay bloke?!" She punched him gently on the arm.

"I didn't fully understand I was gay myself, so you hardly stood a chance. I was damn good at hiding it too, even when I did work it all out."

"I know and it's not really about that or you. When I first found out I was pregnant I was in shock, I just kept going, ignoring it. Luckily it doesn't really show yet, so I didn't have to tell anyone. You are the only person who knows."

"Wow, not even Jim or the rest of your family?"

"Nope, no one. It's so complicated, our marriage ending, going through a divorce and then – wallop! - I bring a brand-new baby into it all. My family already think I'm a galloping great failure and now this! I can't tell them, not yet," she began to fold the crisp packet up into tiny triangles. "Shit, everything's changed, Ralph. My friends were all over me when you vanished, but as soon as you were found it was less exciting and they all slowly faded away. Nothing's the same and I don't know what to do," her voice cracked, but she could not stop talking now she had started. "I can't do this alone, I can't. It could be fun, couldn't it? Deciding names, shopping for teeny tiny clothes, prams and toys, decorating the spare room, painting pictures of rabbits or dinosaurs on the wall? We'd have a proper laugh, wouldn't we? Imagine the ante-natal classes - all that breathing and puffing and trying not to fart. I mean, Sam could come and visit sometimes, if you wanted. Please, Ralph, I need you. Don't make me do this alone. Just six months, until it's here, maybe twelve at the most. Wouldn't it be fun? It would, wouldn't it?"

Ralph took the tiny triangle of plastic from her tense fingers, "Wait, wait, slow down. What are you saying?"

She looked at him, tears spilling onto her cheeks, "I'm terrified, but I think everything will be alright if you are with me. I have palpitations just reading the words scan or ante-natal and who the hell even knows what breast pumps are? I came down here to ask you to come back with me, to see me through it all - then I saw Martin and I thought, great! He's perfect to run the shop while you're away - he needs the work, he told me..."

Ralph got to his feet, "Stop, stop! That's crazy, Hels. This is my home. My friends. My *boyfriend*. My business." He swept his arms around the shop, taking in the street outside, "This is me now."

"I know, but you haven't been here long, have you? They're all really nice, but how attached can you get to each other in a couple of months? Besides, they'll all still be here if you come back..."

"What do you mean, *if*? You don't understand what I've been through, what this place has given me. Hels, you can't ask me this. You can't," Ralph started to move up and down across the front of the shop. Stanley, sensing his distress, got up and trotted along beside him.

Helen looked up at him with panic in her eyes, "I know I created this problem on my own, but I need you. You can't abandon me, not again!" She got up from the step and started to follow him around the shop, increasingly desperate, "Please, Ralph, I am so scared, can't you see that? What's happened to my life? I used to think I was in control of everything. Now it's all spinning around..." but loud sobs took over and she could no longer speak.

Ralph stopped and pulled Helen to him and hugged her tight, soothing her by gently rubbing her back, "Ssshh, it'll be fine. We'll sort it out. We'll find a way."

"I'm sorry, so sorry. I know this is my mess, but I have no one else I can turn to."

"It's OK, I can't imagine what you have been through

in the last few months. The thing is…I love Sam. We're at the beginning of things, but I know I love him. Do you understand?"

Helen pulled away from his hug and wiped her eyes, "I do, I understand. He's so nice and very, very handsome…but you've only just met him and if he is the right man for you then he'll wait, won't he? He'll understand I need you back, just for a while."

Ralph's chin fell to his chest and his throat tightened, "You have no idea what you are asking." Panic started to rise inside him, he couldn't breathe, the air was trapped in his lungs and his chest grew tighter and tighter. He stepped to the shop door and rested his head against the cool glass, hoping it would sooth him.

"I can't tell you how much it means to me that you would even think about doing this for me. But you need to do whatever you think is right, Ralph."

"Right? For who? You? Me? Sam?"

"You are a good person, Ralph."

"Please, let me think. I will need some time. Don't say anything to Sam, I can't talk to him about it yet. I need to get my head straight first."

Stanley sat and gently nudged his head against Ralph's knee, he didn't understand what was happening but he didn't like it. Not at all.

* * *

A few hours later, Stanley leapt out of the window display, pleased to see a friend approaching to break the tense silence in the shop.

Joe stuck his head around the door, "Hey, Ralph, what are you doing?"

"Nothing. Thinking. You?" Ralph said from behind his counter.

"Thinking too. Hard, isn't it?"

Ralph smiled weakly, "Yup, bloody hard."

"It's going to be a very long day. How are you Stan, my man?" Joe knelt down to fuss the little dog, who rolled on to his back to examine his friend from upside down.

"Stanley, stop being such a tart, leave Joe alone," Ralph called.

"Where's Helen, I thought I saw her doing your book display earlier?"

"She's gone for a walk. I'm glad you've come in, I wanted to say sorry for last night. It all got a bit out of hand."

Joe waved Ralph's apology away and sat on the floor, "It's fine, it wasn't a good evening for me, but I'm back on it now. I need to ask you a question, Ralph?"

"Sure, as long as it's not a hard one, my brain's a bit full at the moment."

"Is a handwritten letter better than an email?"

"It depends what it's for. If you're paying a gas bill, I wouldn't write them a letter."

"You weren't so funny when you first came here, I liked you then."

Ralph pulled a face, "So, tell me who you are writing to."

"Imogen," Joe said, rubbing Stanley's stomach.

"I see. I take it you've made a decision?"

"Yeah, I decided this morning. I'm staying here. So, the Rooftop Club will be staying together!"

Ralph nodded glumly, "For now. I'm sorry things didn't work out with Imogen."

Joe shrugged, "I guess we can't all hit the jackpot first

time, like you and Sam. There's so much to keep me in Rye...perhaps more now. Every time I thought about leaving, I came back to the things I couldn't give up. So, in the end it was obvious; Imogen wasn't enough to make me leave, so she's not the one."

Ralph got up and returned a book to its shelf, "Fair enough. So, you're thinking of sending Imogen a letter? Do you think that's the best way? When I ran away from Helen, I left her a few useless words on a biscuit packet, which was absolutely *not* the right thing to do. Karma has a way of making you pay for your mistakes – trust me, I'm learning that. You need to talk to her."

Joe shook his head, leaning back on his elbows, "I'm not sure I'd say the right thing. Anna was right last night, in a way, feelings are hard for me. I do have them, contrary to popular opinion, but I'm only just finding my way around them."

"You have to try. How about you write her a letter to work out what you want to say, then throw it away and call her? You'll have the words then."

Joe looked at him, "You think so?"

"Definitely, the new all-feeling Joe needs to do the right thing. One of us does."

"What do you mean?"

"Nothing."

"It's so goddamned hard though, isn't it? Doing the right thing."

Ralph laugh was hollow, "You have no idea."

Joe jumped to his feet, "Right, I'm gonna do it. Just one more question?"

"Yes?"

"Do you need any gnomes?"

161

CHAPTER 17

The small medium, cheese on
toast and a muriel.

The next week continued to be grey and miserable along the Sussex coast, mist and drizzle hugged the narrow streets of Rye keeping the town quiet. The craft shops, galleries, delicatessens and antique shops all remained largely empty.

Joe spent his time clearing out his storeroom, with a wave of energy having finally spoken with Imogen. He was so nervous that he couldn't really remember what he had said, but it can't have been too bad, as Imogen, in her usual straightforward way, told him she would probably be better off with someone who had more experience of relationships. Maybe someone whose party piece was better than jiggling his buttocks independently to *Staying Alive*. He could only accept this as a reasonable assessment of the situation and they had wished each other well.

Ralph had agreed with Helen that he needed a week to work things through in his head, so she gave him some space and went off to visit a friend in London. He attempted to cover his turmoil from Sam with a flurry of activity in the shop and developed a series of ideas to boost sales. He decided to launch the Beagle Book Club for children, featuring Stanley's Saturday Story held monthly in the bookshop. Ralph would select a book to read to the young club members each month and then there would be a competition for them to draw a picture about the story, which their parents needed to drop back into the shop before the next meeting. The entries would be displayed in the shop and the winner would receive a book token as a prize.

The most unpredictable sales initiative was Jane Scott's book signing for which she returned refreshed from her luxury spa break. Ralph had done quite a bit of publicity locally, but this had been swamped by Jane's publicist who seemed to have bombarded the whole of the south of England with the news. When Ralph closed the shop early on Wednesday there was already a queue forming outside. The evening followed a similar pattern to the football team's fair, with Jane Scott making a magnificent arrival in a hired limousine, exiting the vehicle only when a large crowd had gathered to cheer her. She gave a few well-rehearsed off-the-cuff remarks, read a chapter from her autobiography followed by a long meet and greet with each of her fans, who bought her book, had it signed and posed for several photographs with the famous actress.

Jane proved to be a consummate professional where her fans were concerned and gave each of them her full attention and they went away feeling they had touched a little piece of tinsel town. However, Sam couldn't be persuaded that Jane had been really generous to do the event, despite Ralph making more money in one evening than he had in the rest of the month put together. So, the day ended with tension for them both, but for entirely different reasons.

* * *

Also on Wednesday, Anna left The Cookery in the hands of Martin for the afternoon while she went shopping with Ruby. She was determined to remain on her best behaviour, which made her anxious, which in turn caused her to swear regularly, fall over things and try on clothes in all the wrong sizes. Eventually, Ruby couldn't resist it any longer and as Anna tried to walk in a pair of stilettoes she had put on the wrong feet she burst out laughing and couldn't stop. Anna looked at her with horror, then down at her feet squashed into the shoes and also started to laugh. Disgruntled staff members watched them stumble out of the shoe shop, having to hold each other up as they laughed their way to the station café.

After about twenty minutes, two cups of tea and a toasted teacake, Ruby was able to speak again without giggling, "I honestly cannot tell you when I have laughed so much."

"Well, I'm glad that crippling myself has been so amusing," Anna said with a fake grimace, before breaking back into a smile. "I don't know what I was thinking! I suppose I thought that now I am going to own two businesses I should dress more like a successful woman. Maybe a bit like you, linen and suits and silk and proper grown-up shoes."

"Anna, you have achieved everything so far by being yourself," Ruby said. "You've certainly done it without my help…"

"But…"

"No, Anna, I mean it. *You've* done this and you need to accept you are already a successful woman. So, kimonos and Daffy Duck t-shirts…"

"It's Donald Duck actually."

"Sorry, Donald Duck t-shirts are your signature style. Don't even think about changing into a boring old fuddy-duddy like me. I buy what I see on the model in a shop window or get the shop staff to put something together for me, it's got nothing to do with individual style or judgement. I haven't put an outfit together for myself since I was a child."

"Really?" Anna's eyes shone. "Get that tea down you then. We are about to find Ruby-style!"

Anna threw some money on the table and grabbed her coat and her mother and marched back to the High Street, "I know the perfect place – have you ever been to The Small Medium at Large?"

"I don't think so," Ruby said, hurrying along behind Anna. "Small, medium and large?"

"No, it's a boutique called The Small Medium *at* Large. Sue, who runs it, is a psychic. She's fabulous, she can work out exactly what a woman needs to wear AND she can have a rummage through your tealeaves while you're there, if you want."

Ruby blushed slightly and fiddled with her silk scarf, "Well, I'm not sure…"

"Come on, it'll be fun!"

Ruby couldn't argue with her daughter's enthusiasm

and she allowed herself to be led into an extraordinary shop right at the end of the High Street, with a purple exterior and bright pink interior.

"Anna! Babe with the best buns in town!" a rough voice bellowed from the back of the shop.

"Sue, it's an emergency. It's my mother – she's never bought her own clothes; she only buys what's displayed on shop dummies!"

"Shit a brick!" came back the deep throaty reply. "Right, clear the shop!" A large mound of paisley fabric shot out from behind a curtain and started flailing around, shooing a couple of young women out of the door, "Come back later, all hell's about to break loose!"

The mound of cloth flung the door shut and threw itself against it, pausing for long enough for Ruby to see that on top was a small head of bright white hair and an enormous pair of round glasses.

"Mum, this is Psychic Sue. Sue, this is Ruby, my mum."

Ruby held out her hand, "Very pleased to…"

"Hush, hush," Sue said, waving a tiny hand in the air. "How do you feel about loon pants?"

"Erm, well, I'm not sure I feel anything about them, I've never…"

"A yogini I met in Salamanca once told me loon pants are the ultimate apparel; they are loose fitting and allow your chakras to run entirely free. I have never worn anything else down thither since."

"Mum has a yogini, she's called Sharon."

"Indeed? Sharon? I see you and I shall very quickly be aligned, Ruby, mother of Anna," Sue said as she slowly approached Ruby, who had to fight hard not to back away into the safety of a rack of dungarees. "I can tell from the pinched tones of your aura that you are wearing entirely the wrong sized brassiere. We must begin there and work our way outwards!"

A little over two hours later, Ruby and Anna staggered out of the shop, clutching armfuls of paper bags. Anna waved at Sue, who was behind her silver glitter counter counting the large amount of cash Ruby had parted with for her new wardrobe of clothes. They stumbled back to The Cookery where Anna made them two mugs of tea.

"I feel like I've been run over by a steam roller," Ruby said.

"I know, she's a bit like that, isn't she?" Anna laughed. "I love your new clothes though; you are going to look amazing. You'll be fighting off the fellas now."

"Oh, no, I don't think so, these clothes are for me. The new me. I hope I'm brave enough to wear them."

"You're probably right, I mean, our success with men is hardly great, is it?" Anna said, suddenly looking serious. "Two marriages for you and none for me. Actually, if we are going to make a go of this mother and daughter thing, we need stuff in common, don't we? Like being manless. Is that a word? Manless?"

"I think most people would say single," Ruby said.

"Would they? Yes, I suppose they would. Anyway, it's something we have in common, being independent women. We don't need to go on dates and be charmed by some tosser in a Led Zepplin t-shirt."

Ruby looked at Anna and saw her genuine enthusiasm at finding something she could share with her mother. Then she thought of Joe and their plans for Friday night - he had said it wasn't a date, hadn't he? It was a drink between friends, to talk. However much she daydreamed about it being something more, he had made it very clear they were just friends. She smiled at Anna, "Two single, manless women about town, is that us?"

"Yes, that's us. Ruby Rose and Anna Rose...the Manless Roses! Hey, we could be a circus act – can you juggle? Never mind, you can learn. This is brilliant, the more we can find in common the better, right? And that's the other thing...erm...I've had a really great afternoon, but if this is going to work between us trust is going to be really important," Anna said, fiddling with her Donald Duck t-shirt. "Sorry to bring things down and I don't want to fight, I am trying to be less fighty, but if I am going to trust you again you need to be really honest with me. Like, if you start drinking or even thinking about it, please tell me. The more I know, the more I feel we can make this work. Do you understand?"

"Of course, I totally understand," Ruby smiled at Anna. "I am certainly not thinking about it, but I will do whatever you need me to do."

"Fine, so honesty is the best policy. Right?" Anna held her tea mug in the air.

"Right," Ruby raised her cup and they chinked the china together in agreement.

"To honesty and the Manless Roses!" Anna cried, startling an elderly couple at the next table who peered over their crosswords at them.

✻ ✻ ✻

On Thursday evening, Anna marched up the hill towards St Mary's church with a set of keys for The Copper Kettle.

"Keep up," she shouted behind her to Ralph.

"I'm going as fast as I can," he grumbled. "I don't know where you've got all this new energy from, and I don't know why I have to come with you."

"I need your help. There are weeks of work to do and I need your skills."

Ralph stopped, his heart sinking fast, "Weeks? Anna, look, I'm not sure I'm going to be able…"

Anna turned around to look at him, "Come on, I know you have a gammy leg, but you should be used to it by now." She took his arm and started to drag him up the hill, "I really, really need you. I haven't seen you all week, it's been bonkers, what with shopping with Mum, Jane Superstar Scott being in town, Joe nursing his first proper broken heart and me becoming the new Alana Sugar of Rye."

"Alana who?"

"You know, The Apprentice man. Face like a loofah. Alan Sugar, but I'm a lady, so Alana! Anyway, Fiona was beside herself when I told her I would buy the place and could do it in a few days, when Mum's money comes through and the legal stuff gets done."

"This is her chance for freedom," Ralph said.

"I know, there were tears and everything. Luckily, she hasn't got George with her at the moment, it's just her and that fat pink piglet in the house."

"Where's George gone?"

"He's gone to boarding school. You won't believe it, but Dew-drop Dobson had been saving money for years to send him to a posh school. Fiona told me, when the business started to fail he really needed the money he'd built up for George to help keep it afloat, so he spoke to Andy about it. But the swine told Dew-drop if he didn't give the money to George, he would move the whole family to Australia and he'd never see them again."

"You're kidding?"

"Nope, that's why he put The Copper Kettle on the market and a few days later old Dew-drop's heart stopped and he keeled over into the canal. Fiona didn't say as much, but it's obvious she blames Andy for causing it. I mean, it's not murder or anything, but the stress must have been too much for him."

"How much was it?"

"Nearly one hundred grand, he put it in trust through a solicitor so it can only be spent on school fees, that way Andy couldn't use it for anything else. Fiona says George is really enjoying it and she thinks he's better out of it all while she sorts things and escapes from Andy."

"It's good to hear things turn out well for people sometimes," Ralph said.

"What's that supposed to mean?" Anna held on to him until he came to halt. "What's up? I know something's wrong, just because I haven't been around doesn't mean you can't tell me stuff. You always tell me stuff. Why aren't you telling me stuff?"

"Please stop saying that word," he started up the hill again, keeping his head down.

"What word? Stuff?" Anna said, hurrying behind him. "What's got into you? Is it Helen stuff? Sorry. I mean she seems lovely and everything, but there is something going on with her. I don't know what, but she seems a bit, well, odd. Sometimes she looks at you in such a way that..."

"Stop!" he said. "We're here, can we get on with this, please?"

Anna put her hands on her hips, "No, not if that's

your attitude. I want you to help me because it's fun and we're best friends."

"Not you too," he scoffed. "I'm sorry, forget I said that. I'll help as much as I can, it'll take my mind of...you know...stuff."

"We're going to need to start a *stuff* swear box and you've just lost 50p," she said, triumphantly.

Ralph smiled, "If there's anything I need to tell you, I will, alright? I need to talk to Sam first."

"Fair enough-ski, but just so you know - I'm going to worry about you until then. And that worry is likely to manifest itself in feeding you copious amounts of food, so don't leave it too long or you will be enormous and Sam won't love you anymore and you won't be able to walk Stanley and he'll probably run away." Anna produced the keys for The Copper Kettle, "Is that clear?"

"As crystal. Let's get inside," Ralph said as he stepped back to look at the tearooms.

The building itself stood dark and alone on the corner next to the pretty church lychgate, opposite the dignified columns and arches of Rye's medieval marketplace and townhall. It was flat and wide, with a large white framed window running the width of the ground floor. The upstairs had two square bay windows, surrounded by typical Sussex terracotta tiles that covered the remaining façade.

"A lick of paint will bring it back to life," Ralph said, flicking a bit of peeling paint off the window ledge with the single crutch he had now taken to using. "Don't you think you need to emphasise its charm and age, not mess about trying to change it?"

"I know, I've been thinking about that...wait, let me unlock the door."

"Does Andy know you have the keys?" Ralph asked.

"That dirt-bag? No way. Fiona had to sneak out with them when he was at a dentist's appointment, she's grown so much in confidence since she knew I could buy the place," Anna said as she fiddled with the lock. "We have to be careful, though, she said Andy pops in with contractors sometimes. He still thinks he's going to turn it into some sort of high-class fencing operation for his stolen goods."

Ralph looked up and down the deserted street, "Do you think this is a good idea, then? If he sees us, it'll blow everything apart."

"Fiona says he's been in London today, so he won't be back until late. Ah, I'm in," she said as the key turned.

The door swung open and they were greeted by the smell of stale flour, grease and neglect. Ralph flicked a few switches and the tearoom lit-up with a gentle yellow glow, the fabric shades on the old wall lamps sending soft shadows across the ceiling and into the dusty corners.

"It's actually quite cosy," Anna said, walking between the tables. "I love the big wooden beams and the rough plaster on the walls, it looks properly old." She suddenly threw her arms out wide and began to twirl in the middle of the tables, "How exciting is this? The beginning of my empire, mine all mine."

"I hope this isn't going to go to your head."

"You know what I mean," Anna said, steadying herself against a wonky hostess trolley after one spin too many. "This is actually happening."

Ralph took a good look at his friend, her wild hair framing her happy round face, the new blonde streak at the front leaping straight up in the air, her crazy yellow swing coat swaying around her. He swallowed hard, every time he came to a conclusion about what he needed to do for Helen something or someone made him change his mind. This morning it was as simple as one of Sam's smiles over the breakfast table, now it was his best friend's joy. How could he leave her to take on this new venture alone after all she had done for him?

He forced a smile, "It's exciting and you deserve it. Tell me about your plans."

As he spoke, they heard the sound of a large car bouncing over the cobbles as it came up the hill towards them, "Quick, the lights!" Anna squealed.

Ralph limped back to the switches and plunged them into darkness. Anna threw herself under one of the tables and he flattened himself against the wall behind the door. The lights of the car swung past the front of the building and turned away into Market Street opposite. They held their breath, but it didn't slow down and soon disappeared.

"I don't think I'll become a spy," Anna's muffled voice moaned from under the table. "I'm not sure my bladder could stand it. If that car had stopped, there would have been another nasty stain on this carpet."

"Let's not hang around too long then." Ralph said, switching on a couple of the lights and drawing the fusty curtains across the window.

"OK, this is what I was thinking," Anna said, getting up from her hiding place. "The thing is that it's traditional, old fashioned in a really cute way, right? So, I should develop that idea, go back to the way it was - proper afternoon teas on nice china, cheese on toast, crumpets, Horlicks, Bovril, really nice blended teas in silver pots. Waitresses in uniforms with lace aprons and little caps. Make it a real treat to come here, a little bit of old England."

"It sounds perfect," Ralph said. "There isn't really anywhere like that in Rye. The tourists would flock to it and the locals will love somewhere classy to come and gossip."

Anna's eyes shone as she imagined the transformation, "And you see this space?" She pointed to the long empty wall running all the way to the back near the kitchen door. "Can you paint something on it for me? A sort of muriel."

"I don't think you really want a muriel. How about a mural?" he said with a smile.

"Alright, clever clogs."

Ralph started to examine the plaster on the wall, which was rough and stained a deep yellow, but looked quite sound, "What sort of thing? I mean, you'd be better to get a proper artist in."

"I don't want a proper artist, I want you...oh, that didn't come out right. Look, it has to be you, it'll make it really special. I don't mind what it is, maybe a big copper kettle, with lots of cakes, something like that. I want it to be big...but classy."

"Big, but classy? Right, well, maybe I can do a few sketches, but..."

"Brilliant! It'll be amazing, I know it will!" Anna flung her arms around him and whispered in his ear, "Remember, you can talk to me about anything."

Ralph hesitated, "I know..." and his phone pinged alerting him to an incoming text. "It's Sam, he says he needs me at Cinque before he kills Jane with a kipper."

"Really? How would you use a kipper for that?"

"No idea, but he sounds like he is going to find a way,

so I'd better go."

"Don't forget about the muriel for my wall," Anna shouted as he left the tearoom and headed back down the hill. "It will be a memorial muriel, something for the town to remember you by in years to come as one of Rye's most celebrated inhabitants!"

Ralph shook his head, not sure he would still be an inhabitant next week let alone in years to come.

CHAPTER 18

The joy of a fish finger sandwich, winter
coats and deadly pencils.

When Ralph arrived at Cinque, he found the restaurant and bar almost empty, with a few diners enjoying a quiet evening. He spotted Dawa behind the bar, "Hi, is there blood on the carpet yet?"

"Not at the moment, but it's early," Dawa said with a shrug. "They're in the kitchen."

"What are they doing?"

"No idea. Sam said something about distracting his mother by giving her something to think about other than throwing him under a bus to boost her career."

"I see," Ralph said, hesitating. "I suppose I should go in and help him."

"I suppose you should, would you like a fire extinguisher?"

"What for?"

Dawa smiled ruefully, "I believe they are very handy when dealing with fire breathing dragons."

Ralph chuckled and headed towards the kitchen swing doors, "I think I'll be alright; I can beat her off with my crutch if need be."

"I've got some garlic and a sharp wooden stake if that fails," Dawa called after him.

In the kitchen, Jane was perched on the edge of a stainless-steel counter filing her nails, "Ralph! This is so exciting; Sam is showing me how to make Scallops Agua-something. Apparently, it's Rye Scallop Week next week – isn't that fun for them? Who knew that scallops had their own week?"

"Yes, it's an annual thing, I think. The whole town joins in and they get through about fifteen thousand scallops, all from Rye Bay," Ralph said.

Sam appeared from the walk-in fridge looking exhausted and leant against one of the counters, "Ralph, thank goodness. Mum, I said you can't do that in here! We can't have nail filings everywhere."

"These are very expensive nails, darling, I'm sure they're not poisonous. They're fibreglass," Jane said, admiring them.

"Doesn't that make it worse?" Ralph said to Sam, who shrugged, clearly having lost all control of his mother.

Jane was looking over Ralph's shoulder. "Oh, hello!"

"Dawa was serving a customer and said I should come in," Helen said as she stood in the doorway. "I was getting a bit bored in London, so I thought I'd come back and see what you two were up to."

"How was your friend?" Ralph asked.

"She was fine, up to her neck in nappies and babygrows. It was fun...sort of."

"Great," Ralph said, without meaning it.

Jane poked Sam with her nail file, "Samuel, where are your manners? Aren't you going to introduce me?"

"Oh, haven't you met Helen yet?"

"Clearly not or I wouldn't ask," she said, turning her attention to Helen who shrank back slightly under her gaze. "Aren't men beasts? Their manners have developed so little over the millennia."

Sam sighed, "Mum, this is Helen. Helen this is my mother, Jane Scott."

Helen nodded, "Yes, I recognised her. It's really lovely to meet you, I'm a big fan."

"How kind," Jane said with a regal nod. "Do you work for Ralph?"

Helen giggled, "Not unless you count doing his ironing. I'm his wife."

Jane's jaw dropped and Ralph quickly added, "Helen's come down from Barnsley for a visit."

"Have you eaten yet?" Sam asked her.

"No, not yet, I was waiting to see what Ralph was doing," Helen said.

Jane hopped off the counter and walked slowly over to her, "Wait, I seem to be a little left behind here, your name is Helen?"

"Yes, that's right."

Jane shook her head, "And I thought for a moment you said you were Ralph's wife? But that can't be right."

Ralph moved protectively to stand with Helen, "She is – was – still is. We were...are married."

Jane Scott turned dramatically to Sam, "Oh darling, not again? You poor thing!" Then her eyes narrowed and she fixed her gaze on Ralph, "And as for you, I never..."

"Wait!" Sam said, taking a firm hold of his mother's

elbow. "They are separated. I know all about Helen, about *them*."

"Really? And you don't mind?"

"Why should I? There's nothing to be ashamed of here. I'm really pleased to get to know Helen," Sam said, guiding his mother towards the door.

"Wait, Sam, wait," Jane said, slipping out of Sam's tight grip. "So, let me get this straight. Sam, you are with Ralph. Ralph is with you and at the same time married to Helen. How very modern!" Her eyes seemed to glisten and she licked her lips as she took in the implications of the situation, before continuing in a much smoother tone, "Helen, darling girl, you must be exhausted, travelling all the way from London on your own."

"I came on the train, but it didn't take long," Helen said, fiddling with the buttons on her coat.

"You young women are so adventurous; I haven't been on a train in decades. Come on, let us girls go for a drink. I must find out all about you," Jane said as she started to lead Helen away. "Let's have something to eat together. Ralph, where do you recommend that's good around here?"

Ralph looked at her, "Jane, your son owns a restaurant."

"Yes, yes, but that's a bit too public, isn't it? Somewhere quiet, where we can all chat and get to know one another."

"There's The Mermaid Inn," Sam said, giving in to the juggernaut that was his mother.

"That sounds perfect. This town is so quaint, Helen, have you visited before?" Jane said as she pushed her through the swing doors.

Helen, looking stunned, allowed herself to be guided

away, "No, this is the first time."

As the women disappeared, Sam took Ralph's hand, "We need to watch my mother, did you see how she moved in on Helen like a crocodile sizing up its lunch?"

"Dawa warned me to be careful. I wish I'd brought the fire extinguisher," Ralph said, turning and hurrying out.

When they got back into the restaurant Dawa had a thunderous look on his face as he helped Jane into a long black fur coat, while she continued in full flow, "Dawa's such a dear, he can turn his hand to almost anything, you know. He used to beat people up for my husband, before he died, obviously..."

"I provided personal security," Dawa growled.

"That's what I said, now he's cleaning tables here for my son. Isn't that lovely, Helen? Our family is very loyal to its staff."

Just as Dawa's hand closed around the red handle of a fire extinguisher Sam stepped in and faced his mother, "Will you pack it in, Dawa is not staff. He was Dad's best friend and is family, as far as I'm concerned."

Jane Scott furrowed her brow as best she could through the cosmetic procedures that held it firmly in suspended animation, "But you pay him, don't you?"

"Yes, to run the restaurant..."

"Then he is staff, dear. Anyway, Helen doesn't want to hear all about our domestic arrangements, the poor girl needs a drink and something to eat. You look dead on your feet, darling. Sam, can your other staff manage the kitchen tonight, while we eat?"

"Yes, I suppose..."

"Excellent, you lead the way. Do we need a cab?"

Sam gritted his teeth, "No, it's round the corner, we

180

can walk."

Ralph held the door open for Jane and then Helen to step out into the street. Sam looked back at Dawa, "Sorry, I'll talk to her."

"Don't worry, I'm quite used to your mother. One day I'll kill her quietly with a pencil, it's easy. It leaves very little evidence."

Sam shrugged, "Fair enough. If you need help hiding the body, just give me a shout."

"Of course, Sam. Enjoy your evening...as best you can."

Outside, the little group stood under the light of a lamppost, their breath streaming in clouds into the air, "Are we all set?" Sam asked, trying to be cheery.

"Oh, no," Jane gasped. "I'm so sorry, I've left my handbag inside."

"I'll get it," Sam said.

"No, you go on with the others, this cold air has made me want a tinkle, I'll never make it in one piece. I'll catch you up in a few minutes," she tottered back up the steps to the restaurant.

"If Dawa is sharpening pencils, please don't speak to him," Sam called after her.

Jane paused in the doorway, "What was that, darling?"

"Nothing, Dawa will direct you to the pub, it's not far."

* * *

Sam, Ralph and Helen were comfortably settled in the rich surroundings of the six-hundred-year-old Giant's Fireplace Bar of The Mermaid Inn. The dark oak beams, deep red carpet and wooden furniture made the space feel warm as the February wind whistled outside. The fire in the huge fireplace was beginning to die and most of the other customers were preparing to leave.

Ralph pushed away his plate, "That feels better, you can't beat a fish finger sandwich on a winter's night."

"It's even better because my mother never arrived," Sam said with a grin.

"I hope she's alright," Helen said.

"Don't worry about her, she'd make it through a nuclear winter with her survival instincts. Are you sure you don't want a drink, Helen? Fizzy water is not very exciting."

Helen smiled, "I'm fine, thanks. This is such a lovely place, so old."

"There are all sorts of tales about smugglers meeting here," Ralph said. "Apparently one of the bedrooms upstairs has a rocking chair in it that rocks all on its own. The whole town is full of ghost stories. I can give you a tour tomorrow if you like, unless you were planning on heading back?"

"I'm not quite sure when I'll go back, we still have a few more things to sort out, don't we...if that's OK with you two? I don't want to impose and I know it's a bit awkward, but..."

"It's absolutely fine, it will give us a chance to talk," Ralph said, wincing slightly. "I mean about the divorce and...stuff."

Helen looked down at her hands, "Yes, I suppose it will."

Sam searched for something helpful to say, "I'm getting a coffee, anyone else?"

"Oh, yes, that would be lovely," Helen said. "Decaff if

they have any, please."

"It'll help warm you up, I can't believe you've still got your coat on," he chuckled. "Ralph?"

"Yes, please. Do you think you should call Jane?"

"Nope, it's possible Dawa has finished her off," Sam said.

In the silence of Sam's departure to the bar Ralph looked at Helen as she fiddled nervously with the rings on her fingers. He saw she had dark circles under her eyes and her face looked drawn and tense. He leant forward and laid a tentative hand on her knee, "Are you OK?"

Helen flinched slightly at his touch, then looked down at his hand, "Yes, fine. I think I've gone off baked cheese, with the...you know."

"I didn't mean your dinner, something else is wrong. Remember, we used to share everything."

Helen shook her head, "Not everything it seems. Your being gay never came up, for instance."

Ralph removed his hand and a rush of shame travelled down his spine, "No, of course."

"I didn't mean that," Helen said. "I'm sorry, that was unfair."

"I'd say it was perfectly fair, actually," Ralph said, his cheeks burning.

"It's just that spending those few days with Claire and her new baby in London, has got me even more spooked. She was exhausted and the baby never slept and there was so much to do and remember..."

Sam returned with a tray of coffees, "The mothership has texted, she got waylaid by some fans apparently. She'll meet us back at Cinque, so we get a bit more breathing space. What are you two talking about?"

Helen gave a faint smile and Ralph stirred his coffee as Sam looked from one to the other, "Oh, right. Shall I go back to the bar?"

"No, you don't have to," Helen said. "I'm sorry, I'm really tired. Sam, this must be awkward for you - your boyfriend's ex-wife turning up."

"Not at all, I'm glad you're here."

Ralph found Sam's hand under the table and gave it a squeeze, "Thank you."

"Nothing to thank me for. Helen, there's nothing to feel awkward about - unless you are planning to try and steal him away from me and then we may have to play tiddly winks for him."

Ralph swallowed hard and Helen laughed, "I've not played tiddly winks for years!"

"Good, I'll have an advantage then, because I wouldn't let him go without a fight. Anyway, you and I have so much to talk about - socks on the bathroom floor, for instance."

"Oh, no, I'd forgotten. Does he still do that?"

"Oh, yes. Not to mention an inability to put the lid back on any sort of jar."

"That drove me mad," Helen laughed.

"Now, look you two..."

"I assume he still won't eat tomato seeds, so you have to scrape them out when you make a salad?" Helen asked.

"It's like having a five-year-old in the house," Sam said, warming to his theme.

"It is not," Ralph protested. "They taste like snot."

Sam smiled at him, "You see, only a five-year-old would even know what snot tastes like."

The walk back was much livelier as Helen and Sam

bonded over Ralph's less desirable habits.

"It's not right to be mocking the lame," Ralph called , limping along behind them.

"We love you really," Sam said, holding the door of the restaurant open for Helen. "Madam."

"Why, thank you," Helen said as she moved inside.

"Tomato hater," Sam said to Ralph as he lumbered up the steps with his crutch.

"You are so going to pay for this," Ralph hissed.

"Is that a promise?" Sam replied with a wink and tweaked Ralph's bottom as he followed him inside.

"There you are," Jane Scott cried, putting her phone back in her bag and waving a cocktail glass at them from a table in the bar. "I'm so sorry I couldn't join you, sometimes the public are so demanding, but they do pay my wages - indirectly." She patted the empty space next to her on the curved leather seat, "Helen, come and sit with me, I want to know all about you."

"Actually...Oh, hi, Dawa," Ralph paused as Dawa walked out from behind the bar twirling a sharp pencil between his fingers.

"Just in time," he said in a low voice and disappeared into the kitchen.

Looking confused, Ralph continued, "Erm, yes, anyway...I'm going to take Helen home, it's getting late."

"No, that's no fun! Have a cocktail, they're lethal but entirely delicious."

"Helen's not drinking, Mother, let her go home," Sam said.

Jane's eyes narrowed, "Really?"

"No," Helen said. "Not at the moment."

Jane was staring intently at Helen, "That is such a pretty coat. That blue is just the right shade for your skin tone." She slid off the seat and made her way slowly towards her, "Is it cashmere?"

Helen hesitated as Jane closed in, "No, nothing so posh. Just plain old wool, I think."

"It's lovely, may I?" Jane Scott moved her cocktail glass into her other hand and reached out to feel the fabric along the front of the coat. As she ran her fingers over the buttons, she said, "The fit is remarkable...for off-the-peg."

"Mother," Sam warned.

"What, darling? It's just us girls talking about fashion, these men will never understand, not even the gay ones," she said.

Ralph needed to get away, the tension was beginning to make him feel unwell, "Shall we head off, Helen?"

"Good idea," Jane said. "This girl needs her sleep, look at her."

"It's the train journey, I suppose, I do feel a bit strange," Helen said.

"It must have been awful, especially in your condition," Jane said as she swirled the last of the cocktail in the glass and tipped it into her mouth.

"What...what do you mean?" Helen stammered.

"A pregnant woman travelling half-way across the country alone, I think you are tremendously brave!" Jane said, arching an eyebrow as best she could.

Sam turned to Ralph, "She's not..." then he looked at Helen. "You're not...are you?"

Helen slowly moved her hands to her stomach, smoothing the soft woollen folds of her coat over her stomach, "I'm sorry, Ralph should have told you."

Sam's voice was low, "Ralph knows?"

Helen looked at Ralph, "Of course. I know it's difficult

but…"

"How long?" Sam asked

Helen looked at him, tears in her eyes, "Five months. It's due in the middle of June…"

"Five months?" Sam said his mouth twisting tightly. "That's last September."

Helen shook her head as sobs overtook her, "I'm sorry, I don't feel well, I…" and she ran to the door and out into the street. Ralph watched her go, frozen to the spot, then looked at Sam with horror in his eyes. He reached out for him, "You don't understand, it's not…"

"Don't!" Sam yelled, pulling away and quickly walking through the bar and into his office, slamming the door behind him. Ralph didn't know what to do, he needed to go after Sam, but Helen was out in the cold, feeling unwell and alone.

Dawa stepped up to Ralph and laid a hand on his shoulder, "Make sure your wife's alright," he said.

Ralph nodded numbly, grateful for someone to tell him what to do, "I'll come back and talk to Sam," he said as he went out to find Helen. Dawa stood for a moment, then turned slowly to see Jane Scott sitting calmly back at her table delicately typing into her phone. The long, sharp pencil in his hands snapped.

CHAPTER 19

*The new Bonnie and Clyde, a barely
legal plan and Clint Eastwood.*

Early the next morning, Ralph stood in the doorway of The Bookery breathing in the chill air. Since breaking his leg he hadn't been able to go for any of his regular early runs to wake himself up and clear his head, but this morning he desperately needed to do both. He shivered and called for Stanley to come back from his trot along the High Street. The little dog dutifully returned, pausing only once to sniff an Indian take-away menu that was blowing down the road.

As he closed the door behind him, Ralph pulled the phone out of the pocket of his green shop apron and checked for messages, but there were none. He'd had little sleep having spent a large part of the night back at the hospital A&E Department, but this time with Helen. Eventually she was pronounced simply in need of more rest and less stress and they were sent home. He had called and texted Sam continuously until long into the early hours of the morning without any response. Finally, he had sent a text explaining the baby wasn't his, but he did have a big decision to make about his role in helping Helen see the next few months through safely. He had waited, but nothing came back and he had fallen asleep on the sofa. He only slept for a short while and then went straight to Sam's house, but it had been empty.

He limped across the shop and out into the hallway at the bottom of the stairs to the flat above and listened for signs of Helen being awake, but there was nothing. He returned to the counter, picked up his mug of coffee and poured a few more biscuits into the dog bowl at his feet. Stanley sniffed at them, preferring instead to come and sit by Ralph, his senses telling him all was not well.

"I'm fine, Stan," Ralph said as he fussed the dog's ears and looked into his big worried eyes. "We'll get through this...somehow. Looks like you might be moving to Yorkshire, how does that sound?"

Stanley didn't reply, but attacked an itch behind his ear with considerable enthusiasm. Ralph looked down at him and smiled, "If only my life was as straightforward as yours, Stan. You get an itch, you scratch it – problem solved, eh?" and he gently nudged the little dog with his foot, but his timing was bad as Stanley was off balance trying a particularly perilous manoeuvre to get to the irritating itch and tumbled over and down the step in the middle of the shop. "Stan!" Ralph jumped up, but Stanley was already back on his feet and barking as the door to the street burst open and Anna charged in.

"It's me," she bellowed. "I need you."

"Shit, Anna, you nearly gave me a heart attack!"

"Pardon your language! It's an emergency."

"I'm not in the mood for one of your emergencies today, I really don't need to fight with you or help you get a pancake off the ceiling or..."

"No, no, this is serious, last night was absolute chaos!"

"Tell me about it."

"Ralph, it's Fiona," Anna stood beside the counter, running her hands repeatedly through her hair and twisting curls around her fingers. "It's all kicked off, I had to hide her at Irene's last night."

"Hide Fiona? Why?"

Anna started to pace backwards and forwards, Stanley dancing out of the way of her swishing tie-died loon pants, "She came to the flat, banging on the door at midnight. Andy had found the paperwork the solicitor has prepared for us for the sale of The Copper Kettle. She thought she'd hidden it from him, but she didn't know he regularly sneaked through her things. He is such a shit-bag – language, I know, but he deserves it. Anyway, he found the documents and went mad, she managed to run when he was distracted with a phone call or something."

"Did he...? I mean, was she..."

"No, he didn't hit her. She says he hasn't ever been violent, it's all threats and emotional control, so far. But she said she'd never seen him so angry as last night, she was terrified."

Ralph stood and grabbed hold of Anna, "Please stop charging about, Stanley's going to have a fit if you don't, I've already kicked him down the step."

"What?" Anna looked down at Stanley, who was cowering under the counter.

"It was an accident. Why have you given Fiona to Irene?" Ralph asked.

"Well, my name is on the papers as the purchaser of the tearooms, so we thought he might come and look for her at mine. He knows she doesn't really have any friends and her family is all gone."

"I see, good idea. Did he come round?"

"No, I sat up all night with my pepper spray and a rolling pin, but nothing. He's more likely to turn up at The Cookery this morning, but at least there'll be customers there and Irene," Anna looked genuinely scared and Ralph put his arm around her.

"He won't try anything in public, besides, what can he do? The Copper Kettle is Fiona's, her father left it to her, not him."

"I know," Anna said, clutching him tightly. "But the thing is we wanted to get it all done and sorted, so Fiona could quietly disappear when she had the money. It would be too late for him to stop it then and he wouldn't be able to find her."

Ralph looked up as he heard voices outside the shop and saw the familiar bird-like shape of Irene stalking towards the door, ushering Fiona in front of her.

Irene opened the door and pushed Fiona inside, "Mission accomplished," she said closing the door and leaning heavily against it, peering out into the street. "No sign of the target, we're clear."

"She thinks she's Clint Eastwood," Ralph whispered to Anna, making her smile. "Hi Fiona, how are you doing?"

"I'm fine, thanks. I can't believe I've caused all this fuss and inconvenienced you all like this," she said, looking very small in the middle of the large shop.

Anna pulled away from Ralph and wiped her eyes,

"You have done nothing wrong, it's your tit of a husband who's the problem. Sorry for the 'tit', but it's justified."

"Do you want me to see if Joe's in the shop and got any weapons? Knives, flame throwers?" Irene asked without taking her eyes off the street.

"Irene, we are not at war," Anna said, seeing Fiona's alarmed face. "I appreciate you putting Fiona in your spare room, but we are not planning for a siege. Why don't you go and get things ready in The Cookery? We'll have to get stuff out of the freezer, I won't have time to bake today. Oh, and can you give Martin a ring and see if he's free to come in and spend the day with us, please?"

"Back-up? Good thinking," Irene pulled the door open and winced.

"Are you OK? Is it your kidneys? It must be the stress."

"No, my kidneys have never felt better. It's my fingers, they're stiff as I had hold of the breadknife under my pillow all night. I'll be fine, leave it all to me...I'm on it," she said as she sidled out of the door, looking up and down the street before setting off in a crouched run.

"Well, I'm glad someone is enjoying this," Anna said, closing the door. "Please don't worry about Irene, Fiona, she seems mad...well, she *is* mad...but she's harmless and she can drop a big bloke as fifty paces with a look."

"She was so kind last night and has said I can stay as long as I like, but I can't hide for ever. I'll be fine, I'll go back to the house this morning and get the papers...."

"Is that a good idea?" Ralph asked.

"Surely the solicitor can issue more contracts," Anna said.

"Yes, but we also need Dad's death certificate and probate stuff to go with them – I'd put them all together.

I was going to bring everything for you to sign today. Without it all we won't be able to complete the sale and getting duplicates could take ages."

"Damn," Anna said, starting to pace again. "We're stuffed. I mean, I've got the money all ready to transfer, but we need to sign the paperwork really, don't we?"

Fiona stood and watched Anna march back and forth in front of her, "Yes, we can't do anything without the papers. I know how to get in if he's not there, I don't have a key you see, I just ran last night and didn't take anything with me..."

"Bastard," Anna snorted as she did an about turn at the travel books.

"There's a window in the study at the side of the house, it's got a dodgy latch. It's easy to pop the window open with a bit of force, I can get in that way and find the papers."

"No, it's too much of a risk," Ralph said, stepping aside as Anna paced past him to the biographies. "If he finds you, he could flip. You can't go back."

"I agree," Anna said on her way to the romance section. "It has to be us; we'll go in and get them."

"What?" Ralph gasped. "We can't break into his house."

Anna stopped next to the long Catherine Cookson shelf, "It's not just his house, it's Fiona's too. She can give us permission to go in, so we are barely breaking the law...or hardly at all. Are we?" She looked at Fiona.

"No, I shouldn't think so, but what if he finds you? I can't let you take that risk," Fiona said, tears shining in her eyes. "This is all such a mess; I should have left him years ago."

"Now, you can stop that right now," Anna said,

fiercely. "This is a minor setback - we can do this! Right, Ralph?"

"Actually..." Ralph started to say.

Anna turned to him, "Don't dip out on me now, you're my partner in crime."

Ralph put his hands up, "Listen, Bonnie...or Clyde, whichever you are, calm down. Haven't you forgotten something?" He pointed down to his damaged leg, "I'm in no state to be climbing through windows and shinning up drainpipes. I'd be more of a hindrance than a help."

"Poop, I forgot about that. You and your delicate bone structure," Anna said.

They all jumped and Anna screamed as the door burst open again, "Oh, what a beautiful mornin'," Joe sang loudly, his hands tucked into the belt of his snug jeans.

"What the hell?" Anna cried. "You moron!"

Joe looked crestfallen, "I've had better reactions to my singing."

"Sorry, you made us jump, that's all," Ralph said.

"This is not the morning to come creeping up on people," Anna huffed.

Joe shut the door, "Singing Oklahoma is hardly creeping about, to be fair. What's up? Anything I can help with?"

Three pairs of eyes all looked at him, Anna slowly took a step towards him, "You are perfect."

Joe frowned, "It has been said, but why have you all gone weird on me?"

"We have a situation and we need you to break into Fiona's house," she said, holding up both hands. "Before you say anything, here's the thing; Fiona's husband has found out she's selling The Copper Kettle from under him and she had to escape last night. The papers we need to complete the sale quickly are still in the house, so, we need to get in through a dodgy window, find them and get out again. You and me, together. So?"

Joe looked from Anna to Fiona, then to Ralph who nodded at him.

Joe shrugged, "OK."

"Just like that? You'll do it?" Ralph said.

"Listen, I've known Anna a long time and I've never heard her be so clear and succinct..."

"Thanks," she said.

"...It's normally jabbering nonsense."

"Don't spoil it..."

"I know Fiona's situation...sorry, Fiona," Joe said to her and she nodded. "So, let's do this thing. Get in, get some papers, get out and Fiona is free, right?"

"Pretty much," Ralph said.

"I am so grateful," Fiona said, stepping forward. "This feels like my only chance to get a clean break. If I can't sell the café I'm stuck. I have nothing of my own and if I try and divorce Andy, he'll fight me every step of the way."

Joe smiled at her, "Hey, it's not a problem. When shall we go in?"

"Well, tonight would be the best time," Fiona said. "He plays snooker on Friday from about six o'clock until at least eleven. He never misses it because he does a lot of business at the sports club."

"Perfect," Anna said, her eyes sparkling. Despite her fears, the excitement of getting one over on Andy was exhilarating.

"I saw him stuff the envelope with all the documents in a drawer in his desk, so you could try there first,"

Fiona said.

"Great, then you'll need some of your things, Fiona, won't you? We can nip upstairs and pack a bag for you."

"Actually, I already have a bag packed. I'd started to put things together I might need, a few clothes, my passport, that sort of thing. It's in George's room, under his bed, Andy never goes in there. I should have put the papers in there too, it was so stupid."

"It doesn't matter, we'll get it all," Joe said. "How are you at driving, Ralph, can you manage it with your foot? We'll need a getaway driver in case we need to make a quick exit."

"Oooh, that's a good idea," Anna said.

Ralph turned away from them, "Actually, this is not the best time for me."

Joe sensed Ralph's distress, "What's going on?"

"It's a long story," he said. "But I really need to be here."

"Come on," Joe said. "We're having a day of drama, whatever is happening can't be as bad as Fiona's situation."

Ralph looked at Joe, the emotions he'd been holding back threatening to overwhelm him. He took a deep breath, "I need to talk to Sam, but he's disappeared."

Anna moved quickly to his side, "Why? What's happened? Is it his mother? I said..."

"No, it's not Jane. It's Helen, she's pregnant."

There was silence as they took in the news. Finally, Joe spoke, "Is it yours?"

Ralph sat on the stool behind the counter, "No."

"Then I don't see the problem. I mean it's a bit...unusual, but not your problem."

Ralph shook his head but looked defeated.

"Oh, sweetheart, I know what this is. It's guilt," Anna said, putting her arms around him. "You think she's on her own because of you running off, don't you? And you probably think she wouldn't be pregnant with someone else's baby if you had been a proper husband?" Ralph nodded and she went on, "Did you talk to Sam about it?"

Ralph shook his head miserably, "I wanted to get my head straight first, she's in such a state about it and has no one else to turn to. If I needed to go back with Helen and look after her, I had to be sure and...oh, I don't know, I've messed it all up anyway. Sam found out she was pregnant before I could tell him it wasn't mine and now I can't find him. I need to talk to Helen, but she's not awake yet. I can't lose him."

"You won't have to, Sam's a good guy. He won't let you down."

Joe pulled out his phone, "He'll need time to process it, that's all. You know what he's like, if he feels threatened he retreats and hides. I'll see if I can find him."

"Thanks. So, you see, I can't really come and help you burglar Fiona's house, I need to be here."

"We'll be fine," Joe said, holding the phone to his ear. "He's not answering my call either. Knowing him he's turned it off or thrown it down the toilet. I'll keep trying. Don't worry, Ralph or you Fiona, you've got The Rye Rooftop Club on the case, we were born for this sort of thing! Right, Anna?"

"Not half!" she said, offering Joe a high-five just as he turned away and made for the door. "Joe! Joe, high five!"

"Yep," he called over his shoulder as he typed a text to Sam. "Five's good for me, see you then," and he was gone.

Anna grinned at Fiona, "We're a great team, it'll be

fine."

"I hope so," Fiona said. "Look, I can't sit around while you all do so much for me. I'm going to go and speak to the solicitor, he was a friend of Dad's, I'll see if there is another way to do this. I'll let you know if he comes up with anything, then I'll go back to Irene's."

Anna's hands shot in the air, "Irene! I'd better check on her, she's probably set up a barricade or pots of burning chilli oil over the door by now. Ralph, you need to see Helen and talk to her. I know you've been friends for a long time and shared a lot, but she needs to understand everything you've got here and what you'll be giving up if you go back with her." She began to choke with emotion, "I know you'll make the right decision... but...please don't go," and she turned and ran out of the shop.

When Ralph got upstairs the flat was still quiet and Helen's door firmly closed. He stood outside for a moment, then knocked gently. There was no response, so he knocked again more loudly. Still nothing.

"This is ridiculous," he said and turned the door handle. The bed was empty. It had been neatly made and Helen's suitcase sat on the end of it, open with everything folded inside. He checked the rest of the flat, but there was no sign of her, she must have left while he was downstairs.

Ralph spent the rest of the day with his heart leaping every time he saw anyone in a baseball cap pass the shop, hoping it was Sam. By closing time he had seen and heard nothing from either him or Helen. Where the hell were they?

CHAPTER 20

*The getaway driver, dumplings
and forward rolls.*

Irene put a cup of milky tea on the table and flopped into the chair beside it. She stretched out her hand and wiggled the fingers to ease the stiffness still present from her night on guard with the breadknife. Andy had not appeared during the day and the café door was now locked, so Martin had returned to his hostel to finish knitting the particularly tricky collar of a waistcoat he was making for one of Irene's grandchildren. The customers had all gone home before darkness and drizzle had set in, and Irene was planning to enjoy ten minutes with her feet up before heading home to make dinner for her and Fiona. She was looking forward to having some adult company in the house for a change and she had decided to revisit her dumpling recipe, which had proved popular in the 1980's. As Irene mused the delights of suet, Anna appeared from her flat above

The Cookery.

"Good lord, I thought it was the Ninjas come for me," Irene said, taking in Anna's outfit.

Anna looked at her reflection in the coffee machine; black school plimsolls, black culottes with a stripe of silver sequins running down the seam of each leg, a black and grey poncho, all topped off with a black beany hat with a red pom-pom at its crown.

"Too much?" she asked.

"For a clown's funeral, no. For breaking and entering, perhaps a bit. I think if anyone caught sight of you, they'd probably remember enough details to give a full description."

"These are the only things I had in black, except the dress I wore to Dew-drop's funeral and that didn't seem appropriate. I'll be fine, it's dark and Andy's not going to be there anyway," Anna said, tucking some free-wheeling copper curls back inside the hat.

A few minutes later Joe arrived, dressed more conventionally in jeans, black boots and a black leather jacket and scarf, "Hey, we look like twins," he said as Anna let him in.

"If Arnold Schwarzenegger and Jimmy Kranky were related," Irene sniffed. "I told Anna I would go with you; I've had to break into people's houses so many times that it's second nature now."

"Really?"

"I wasn't taking things. My Celine went through a phase of stealing, so I had to go back late at night and put it all back. Piece of cake, if you know what you're doing."

Joe shook his head, "Irene, you should write a book, your life is incredible."

Irene got up to rinse her cup, "I couldn't, if I told the truth half my lot would be in prison and the other half would be in the funny farm. Right, I'll leave you to it. Hopefully, if you're not in Wormwood Scrubs, I'll see you later when you bring the documents round for Fiona. Happy hunting."

Once Irene had departed to tackle her dumplings, Anna made them each a coffee to pass the time until Andy would have left for his snooker match. She slopped the coffee over the side of the cups as she brought them to the table, "I'm a bit nervous. I was gung-ho earlier – it was exciting to be fighting back for Fiona, but now it's dark outside it doesn't seem quite so exciting."

"We'll be fine," Joe reassured her. "We're collecting some of Fiona's stuff from her house, that's all – only not via the front door."

"If you put it like that it doesn't sound so bad. Did you get someone to be the getaway driver?"

"Yep, I asked a friend. They'll be here anytime now."

"Fab. Do you want anything to eat before we go?" Anna said, nervously playing with her pom-pom.

"Do you really need the hat?" Joe asked.

"It covers my hair, which is pretty obvious, isn't it?"

"No more than a bright red pom-pom bouncing around."

Before they could continue their discussion, there was a tap on the door and Joe got up to open it, "Hey," he said. "Thanks so much for doing this."

"It's no problem, I'm glad I could help. I've never driven a getaway car before!"

"Mum?" Anna stood in shock as Ruby came into the café.

She looked chic in a short pink puffer jacket, with fur lined hood, pink jeans with paisley turn-ups and a white t-shirt showing Snoopy laying on his doghouse watching sequin-covered clouds float by.

"Hello, darling, how does the outfit look?" Ruby said. "Joe, Anna helped me find the new me, with the help of Psychic Sue. According to her, my aura is pink – which you can only tell when your underwear is appropriate, so I'm told. What do you think?"

"It's cute, I love it," he said with a grin.

She blushed, "Really? You have to try new things, I suppose. Like breaking into a house. It's so exciting, isn't it?"

"You're our driver?" Anna said.

"Yes, didn't Joe tell you?"

"No, he didn't," Anna said, glaring at Joe. "Why on earth are you dressed in pink? We're breaking into someone's house not going for a pyjama party."

"I think she looks great," Joe said.

"Well, it is a great outfit, I helped chose it...but not for burglary!"

Ruby stepped forward and put her handbag firmly on the table, "Well, I understood you were doing the actual burglary and I was merely the driver. I love this outfit we chose together and I am having a drink with a... friend, after we've finished, so I thought it would be a good time to wear it."

"But...but..." Anna couldn't find the words, so slumped in her chair and drank her coffee with an exaggerated frown on her face.

"I am a perfectly competent driver. I have a brand-new car, which can be very nippy and I know the roads around Rye like the back of my hand. Now, Joe, I don't think it's a problem, but I've forgotten to bring some other shoes," she pointed down to her feet, which were inside a pair of elegant peep-toed shoes with surprisingly high wedge heels. "They're new too, but it's been so long since I've worn heels, you see. I had meant to put something flatter in the car, but I got a bit behind - I'm not really very competent in these at the moment. Do you think they'll be OK?"

Joe laughed, "They'll be fine, we're not planning on running around anywhere and you'll be in the car the whole time. You look amazing, by the way – pink aura and all!"

Ruby blushed, tucking her hair behind her ear, "Thank you. Now, I'll nip to the loo and then shall we go?"

"No time like the present," Joe said, watching her walk away.

Anna leant across the table and whispered, "Joe, my mother is not a getaway driver."

"We don't know that until she's had a go," Joe grinned.

"I can't believe you've got her involved."

"Jeez, Anna, listen to yourself! Your mother is doing everything she can to try and prove herself to you. Unless you give her a chance, she will never be able to even start to make amends for whatever it is you blame her for."

"You have no idea the person she was..."

"Exactly! I asked her because I'm interested in finding out what sort of person she is now, you should too - the rest is all history."

"Right, are we ready for a big adventure then team?" Ruby asked as she returned.

"Always," Joe said.

Anna smiled a little too brightly, "Fine, let's go."

* * *

Twenty minutes later they pulled up in a quiet street on the outskirts of Rye, Ruby switched off the engine and they sat in silence except for the sound of hot metal quietly ticking as the car began to cool.

"A VW Beetle? As a get-away car?" Anna moaned from the back seat.

"Have you never seen a Herbie, the VW, film?" Ruby said. "Herbie Rides Again? He was a VW racing Beetle, he...."

"This is not a film, Mum..."

Joe coughed.

Anna looked at him, then turned back to Ruby, "Never mind, stay here and be ready to get us away whenever we appear." Anna started to scramble forward to get out of the two-door car.

Ruby turned to Joe, "Well, there's no car in the drive, so the coast is clear. Wouldn't we be better to go round the back? All these houses have back gates that open on to the lane behind. It would be a lot less conspicuous."

Anna looked at her, "How do you know that?"

"I grew up round here. The cricket ground is just round that corner, me and your father spent many happy hours behind the pavilion when we were first dating."

Joe chuckled, "That's my sort of date."

"Eeew, gross," Anna said.

"Anna, you are not twelve, for goodness' sake," Ruby said, laughing with Joe.

"Come on then, let's head to the back," Joe said.

Ruby took them down the road and turned left onto a narrow lane that led behind the row of large semi-detached houses. They counted along and stopped outside what they calculated to be Fiona's back garden gate. They got out, closed the car doors quietly and stood for a few moments getting used to the dark.

"Right," Anna whispered. "You stay here, Mum. We shouldn't be long."

"But don't you want me to act as look out in case he comes back early? That's what they do in the films - someone stays outside and signals if anyone comes home."

Anna and Joe looked at Ruby in surprise, "Good thinking," Joe said. "You're good at this."

"With all that pink you'll have to stand in a flower bed," Anna said as she started to open the back gate.

"You said it suited me," Ruby said.

"It does, just not for...oh, never mind, come on."

It took a few good shoves to get the gate open over the weeds that had grown up behind it and, once they were through, they started to tip-toe across the lawn. Ruby found it rough going, so took off her new shoes and put one in each jacket pocket. They then continued to creep forwards, keeping to the shadows at the side of the garden.

As they got to the house, Joe pointed out a path to their right, "The dodgy window must be round there. Ruby, you go to the front and let us know if Andy comes back. If he does, signal then race back to the car and we'll follow. OK?"

"Yes, but what's the signal?" Ruby said.

"What do you mean?" Anna asked.

"Well, it's usually a bird noise, like an owl or a pigeon."

"Not your bloody films again?"

"She's right, Anna, we need to know what to listen out for," Joe said. "How about an owl?"

Ruby pulled a face, "Oh, I can't do an owl. I'm not good at birds generally, actually."

Anna hopped from foot to foot, "Then why did you suggest it?"

"I didn't suggest it, I said that's what they usually have in films. I can do a cat."

"A cat would be perfect," Joe said, putting his arm round her and guiding her towards the front of the house. "We'll listen out for a cat."

"Good luck," Ruby whispered as she disappeared into the darkness in front of them.

"A bloody cat!" Anna hissed.

"Shut up, she's trying her best. Now come on, we need to see if we can get through this window."

They moved slowly around the house and stopped at a large sash window that sat at Joe's waist height and rose high above his head. It had a peeling wooden frame, which he felt his way along with his fingers. It gave slightly as he applied pressure and rattled it gently, the noise making them both hold their breath, but they could sense no movement from inside the silent house. He then pushed the frame inwards, managing to get a finger underneath it and with a sharp movement pulled upwards. The window groaned reluctantly and rattled its way up, opening a half meter gap at the bottom.

"Easy," he said. "After you, crazy lady," he gestured inside and then joined his hands into a cup shape and bent down. Anna put her foot into his hands and as she started to hop up, he lifted her quickly over the sill and through the window. She landed on her head, doing a floppy forward roll across the room and finishing in a heap next to a coffee table made from a bored looking elephant holding a thick sheet of glass on its back.

"Sorry," Joe said as he joined her inside. "Were you a gymnast?"

"Do I look like a gymnast?"

"Fair point. I know a joke about gymnasts...."

"This is not the time, Joe. I'm not sure when the right time is for one of your jokes, but this definitely is not it," Anna said, getting to her feet and looking around the room. It was square with a large bay window at the front and an old-fashioned oak desk in the middle. She ran her hand across it, "Stolen, I bet." There was a leather Chesterfield sofa under the window, a sideboard similar to the old desk and a few bookshelves that held a one or two books.

"Come on," Anna said, creeping to the door. "We need to get Fiona's bag from George's bedroom."

"Right, you do that and I'll look for the papers."

Anna turned, "No, come with me. I don't like the dark."

"Now she tells me," Joe said as he joined her at the door. "Let's put the torches on from our phones, but keep them pointed at the floor."

Anna pulled her phone out of her pocket and switched on the torch function, which lit the dark brown carpet in the hallway, "Upstairs and first door on the left, Fiona said."

Joe lit his phone up as well and began to follow Anna who was moving painfully slowly, pausing after each step, "He's coming back tonight not Christmas," Joe said in her ear. "Get a move on."

They made their way up the stairs, their hearts beating faster with every creak from under the well-worn carpet. They located George's room by football hero Cristiano Ronaldo being pinned to the door. Inside, Joe knelt next to the bed while Anna shone the torch on him, "Got it," he said, fumbling deep underneath. Anna squealed as her phone started to vibrate, and the opening bars of The Nolans' 1980 chart-topper *I'm in the Mood for Dancing* started to play loudly in the silence.

Anna panicked and dropped the phone, "Shit, shit, shit. Sorry, language." When it hit the floor the torch went out and Joe scrambled to find it, The Nolans getting into their full harmonious stride by now.

Anna started to stamp wildly about with her plimsolls, trying to stop the noise and Joe hit out at her flailing legs, "Quit that, you're going to break my hand. I've got it."

He handed it back to her and she quickly cancelled the incoming call, "It was Irene, shall I call her back?"

Joe looked at her incredulously, "No! Of course not."

"No, no, of course not."

"I can't believe you didn't turn it off, jeez. Silence it and put it in your pocket, we'll go back down without the lights," he picked up Fiona's suitcase, went out on to the landing and down the stairs quickly and quietly. Anna crept along behind him, her heart hammering in her chest, thinking that maybe a life of crime was not necessarily a potential career side-line for her after all.

At the front of the house, Ruby was doing her best to keep warm and look inconspicuous up close to the privet hedge, quietly singing to herself a selection of Wham! hits. She was just getting into her stride with

Club Tropicana when car headlights lit up the road. She scooted back to the path beside the house and tucked herself around the corner of the building, hoping the car would simply pass by, however, it began to slow.

"No, no, no," she hissed, getting ready to slip off her shoes again, which she had put back on to keep her feet warm. "Keep going, please, please."

But the headlights slowed almost to a stop and started to turn into the drive, confirming it was Andy returning home sooner than expected. Instinctively, Ruby spun around on the spot, forgetting her lack of experience with her current wedge-heeled footwear and toppled over onto the gravel path with a thud.

CHAPTER 21

The schools for burglars, a trampoline and Olga Korbut.

I nside the dark study Anna removed her head from a cupboard in the sideboard, "Did you hear something?"

Joe paused with his hand deep in a desk drawer, "Probably next door's dog or something. Keep looking." He went back to work searching for the papers, but Anna stayed alert as the oddest sound blew in through the open window, "Moo-ee-aa."

"What the hell was that?"

"It was nothing..."

"Sshh, listen."

"Mee-ooo."

"It's going past the window," Anna whispered and tip-toed towards it. Looking out she saw her mother on all fours, crawling along the path to the back of the house making the strange high-pitched sound, "What are you doing?"

Ruby jumped, then twisted around on the ground to look up at Anna, "Meow."

"Mother, you can speak, I'm right here."

"Oh, yes, sorry. He's back! Andy's just pulled into the drive."

As Ruby uttered these fateful words, Joe and Anna heard the distinctive sound of a key turning in the lock of the front door, "Shit," Anna said and dropped to the floor in the study.

"Sofa!" Joe hissed as he tucked himself into the footwell of the old oak desk. Anna got the message and crawled quickly across the room to the Chesterfield sofa and jammed herself behind it, dragging Fiona's suitcase in after her just in time as the room burst into light and Andy entered, throwing his car keys onto the desk.

Neither Joe nor Anna could see him, but they could hear him stomping about the room muttering to himself, "Damn, cheap rubbish. I'm gonna stick it right up the arse of...where is it? God damn it!"

Andy was standing in front of his desk, his pudgy knees centimetres from Joe's face as he curled his six-foot frame into the smallest ball he could manage. Andy was wildly pulling open drawers and slamming them back again, with a new and inventive curse for each one. Just as he pulled the desk chair up behind him to sit down the doorbell rang and he swore again as he set off back to the hallway. Joe let out his breath, relieved Andy's knees had narrowly saved themselves the shock of knocking up against a large Canadian hardware shop owner crouched under the desk.

They listened to Andy open the front door, "What?" he snapped.

Joe started to unfold himself, "Oh, hello," said a breathless voice that sounded an awful lot like Ruby. "Are you the householder?"

"What a bloody stupid question? Do I look like a burglar?"

"No, no, not at all. Good point," Ruby went on as Joe backed his rear end out of the desk. "I represent the ladies of the, erm, cricket club. I'm collecting money for, erm, new stumps. Nice new, big ones..."

"Oh, fuck off!" Andy shouted and the door slammed shut. His footsteps beat a path back to the study and Joe tried to get back under the desk with little success, having no idea how he had fitted the first-time around. Luckily, Andy avoided the desk and went instead to the sideboard next to the sofa. Anna closed her eyes, her pom-pom tightly gripped between her teeth to prevent any untoward sounds escaping, as he banged more doors and drawers. Eventually, he cried out with triumph, "Got you, you bastard!" Then, around the end of the sofa she saw a small pink hand with fat little fingers appear with a phone charger plug in its grip.

"Where are you? Damn it!" The chubby fingers felt their way along the skirting board, backwards and forwards trying to locate the socket that sat on the wall next to Anna's left plimsoll. After several painful seconds he found the empty socket, plugged in the charger and the hand disappeared. A moment later the small sofa shuddered as Andy dropped his not inconsiderable bulk onto it with a long sigh, causing it to slide along the floor and pin Anna against the wall. For a moment everything went silent and none of the three occupants of the room moved...then the silence was broken.

"Mee-oo-ow!" floated in from outside the window,

followed by the rapid crunch of gravel under foot.

"What the...?" Andy wheezed as he launched himself up off the sofa, giving Anna an opportunity to shove it away from her and start breathing again. She listened to Andy lean out of the window, "If I catch you, you mangy sod, I'm going to string you up from the nearest tree!" and the sash window was slammed back into place. Then there was quiet as he stood by the window, realising it shouldn't have been open in the first place.

"Idiot, Fiona. No idea about security!" he muttered viciously to himself, before returning and dumping himself back down, skidding the sofa backwards and trapping Anna again in a vice-like grip.

"Ah, Ken, it's Andy," he said into his phone. "Yes, I'm back home, got my phone on the charger now. Cheap Chinese shit, honestly, I wouldn't wipe my arse with it...I know, right?...Anyway, what were you saying before, when it died and cut you off? Something about your kid nearly getting nicked?"

Andy listened for a moment, taking in what was being said to him at the other end of the line. Anna's ribs began to creak, so tightly was she now packed against the wall. Then above her head she noticed a hand coming over the back of the sofa towards her, it didn't quite reach her but started to wipe something from one of its fingers on to the grubby leather. Once the item, which Anna presumed was the contents of one of Andy's nostrils, had been duly transferred the hand went away again.

"But what was he doing on his own? He knows the rules, never go into anyone's house on your own, you always need two. One to look out for the old bastards and one to nick what we need. Did he get anything?

There were supposed to be medals and pucker silver tankards in that one...What, nothing? Stupid sod. Well, he'll have to go out again, we've got a proper old stately home waiting, massive it is. They've got all sorts in there and the owners are away at their place in France from tomorrow for four weeks. Apart from cleaners on a Wednesday, it'll be empty. Even he can't mess that one up...I know, in our day breaking and entering had some skill, right? Now, they're just thugs with a crowbar - we should start a school, some sort of tech for burglars," Andy let out a wheezy laugh. "Probably get a bloody grant for it too...I know. Right, I've got stuff to do, a crap being the first of 'em. I'll speak to you tomorrow, right? OK, OK." Andy finished his call and tossed the phone down onto the sofa, then heaved himself upright again and they heard him move into the hallway and up the stairs.

Joe quickly freed himself from the desk as Anna pushed back against the sofa, crawling around the end of it on her belly, pushing the suitcase in front of her. He looked up over the desktop, "Alright?"

"My internal organs have been so squashed they'll be no good for a donor if I get knocked down by a bus."

"What?"

"Never mind, we've got to get out of here," she whispered.

"Not without those papers, there's one drawer I never got to look in, hang on."

"Quick, please," Anna pleaded as she edged her way towards the window and started to try and open it without making any noise. "I think the window's stuck!"

"Hang on...bank statements, pizza menu, school fees

invoice...ah! Got it, The Copper Kettle papers, all handily in an envelope. Let me check - yep, probate, death certificate, the lot," Joe held up a large brown envelope and waved it at Anna.

"Brilliant, now we need to go," she mouthed at him. "But I can't open the window."

Joe hurried round the desk, "Here, let me try." He reached across Anna and started to push and pull the window frame, but it was stuck firm, "Shit, you're right."

"What are we going to do?" Anna asked as they heard a toilet flush somewhere above them. They looked at each other, eyes wide, "I am not going behind that sofa again, there's snot everywhere!"

"Front door," Joe said, picking up the suitcase and sprinting for the hallway. As he got there, Anna close behind him, they heard an upstairs door open followed by footsteps on the landing.

"Back, back," Joe hissed, retreating into the study, shutting the door and shoving the ugly elephant coffee table across it. "Get ready to jump, we'll have to go straight over next door's fence or he'll see us run down the garden."

Anna looked out of the window at the high wooden fence that faced her, "I'll never get over that," she said.

"Who's there?" Andy's voice came from the stairs.

"You're going to have to channel Olga Korbut again and make like an Olympic gymnast. Ready?" Joe said quickly, as he gave the window frame an almighty thump and ripped it noisily upwards.

"Oy!" Andy yelled as he found the study door shut and blocked.

Anna scrambled out of the window and charged into

the bushes beside the path and started to climb the fence, aided by an attractive but inexpensive decorative trellis. She heard Joe throw out the suitcase with a thud behind her, the next second she felt a pair of hands grab her buttocks and shove her up and over the fence at great speed. Having heaved her over, Joe took the case in one hand and used the other to climb the trellis himself, hoping the flimsy structure would hold his weight. He could hear Andy cursing and shouting as he pushed the door open, moving the small but surprisingly hefty elephant aside. As Joe's head came above the top of fence, he was startled to see Anna's face rising up before him with a look of frozen horror on it before she fell back down again. A moment later up she came again, her hands waving wildly in the air. He looked down over the fence to see that he had thrown her over and straight onto a large trampoline that was now propelling Anna up and down at speed.

"Jesus Christ," he shouted and launched himself over the fence, just as Andy's head appeared through the window.

"I see you!" he yelled as Joe's black boots disappeared from view. "You won't get away with this. You have no idea whose house you've been in. You will regret this..."

By this time Joe had dragged Anna off the trampoline and they were charging down next door's garden, lit beautifully by a security light in full view of a startled elderly couple sitting on their sofa finishing a crossword. They reached the gate and ran out into the lane, where the bright red VW Beetle was revved and ready to go. The headlights burst into life and they flew to the car, Anna clambering in the back before Joe popped the front seat back in place and got in next to Ruby, "Go, go, go," he panted.

Ruby did not need telling twice and both Anna and Joe were thrown back against their seats as she took off at speed, burning a great deal of rubber as she went. They struggled into their seatbelts as Ruby whooped loudly, "This is so exciting! I remember driving through France with your father, Anna, in a little 2CV. It had rust holes in the floor so you could see the road underneath you, oh, it was thrilling! I was driving in bare feet then too."

Joe looked down and saw that Ruby was indeed driving without shoes as she floored the accelerator, "I think we're OK now, Ruby, perhaps we don't need quite this much speed."

"Let's make sure we're clear," she said, adrenaline pushing her on. "Hold tight," she yelled as they came to the end of the lane and took a tight left bend at speed coming face to face with a Fiat Panda and a startled looking driver with a neat tweed cap and twitching moustaches. They screamed to a halt with a few centimetres between the bonnets, but before they could catch their breath Ruby had slammed into reverse and they were charging back up the lane again. "Just like the old days," she beamed at Joe and Anna, who both sat upright with a hint of green around the edges of their pale faces.

They passed the end of Fiona's garden again at full throttle, only this time they were travelling backwards, and soon reached the other end of the lane. Ruby came to a brief halt, turned them around and set off on the main road in a more sedate manner with a grin from ear to ear.

CHAPTER 22

*The rooftop air, indecent Italian trousers
and goosebumps.*

Helen twisted her wedding ring around her finger as she stared at a faded print of lovers walking hand in hand along the shores of Lake Como. The tiny Italian restaurant was warm and they didn't seem to mind she had been sitting in the window picking around the edges of her vegetarian lasagne for the last two hours. She couldn't face moving again, having spent a long day walking aimlessly among the myriad of Rye's cafes and gift shops. She had bought some pretty handmade baby clothes in a shop, cryptically called Ethel Loves Me, where a nice lady – presumably Ethel - told her in colourful detail of the near-death experience she had been through with her first pregnancy. She was desperate to get back to her small room in Ralph's flat and lay down, but that meant facing him and her future and she couldn't do it – not yet.

She looked at the dull gold band on her finger - when had it stopped being bright and shiny? She had noticed Ralph no longer wore his ring, but that wasn't the only change in him. As she had chatted with him and Sam in The Mermaid Inn the night before, Ralph was more animated, more alive than she ever remembered seeing him. There was a spark between him and Sam that she and Ralph had never had. They seemed so comfortable with each other that she had felt a pang of jealousy, as she watched them laugh and casually touch each other's arm or hand. Ralph had started a new life for himself here and although she still loved him as her best friend, and desperately needed him, it was clear it was time to let him go.

A young waiter in trousers too tight for both decency and comfort asked if she needed anything else. She stared at him blankly, "Like what?"

He looked surprised, "Erm, well, another drink perhaps or a dessert?"

Helen ran her hand across her braids, "Oh, yes, of course. Sorry, I was miles away. Could I see the dessert menu, please?"

This baby made her hungry, usually for fat and sugar, something she had trained herself to avoid for most of her life, but these days what baby demanded, baby got. Despite her slim figure she had been fortunate to conceal her condition from everyone, until now. Luckily, her appalling bank uniform was designed to make any kind of body shape into a square and, for once, she had been grateful for it. However, with only four months to go the baby bump was too obvious to hide any longer and her constant fatigue needed more explanation than it being a cold or headache. When she got home she needed to make proper plans for the birth, for time off work, for her future...their future. She had to face up to the fact that very soon she would be a mother and her child would look to her for everything. She couldn't ignore it any longer.

Through the window Helen saw the warm glow of a café opposite, where a woman sat reading a book and sipping a frothy coffee, next to her a little girl was reading her own book, her thumb in her mouth. Both seemed content and oblivious to the world turning around them. She looked down at her wedding ring and smiled. Then she pulled it over her knuckle and laid it on the white tablecloth. It was no longer a perfect circle; one side had been flattened over time. The ring that had once meant so much, now looked flimsy and battered.

As the waiter returned with a laminated menu, she dropped the ring into her bag and looked up at him, "I'm sorry, I have to go. Could I have the bill, please?"

She watched as his tightly packed trousers trudged away and smiled because she knew what she had to do.

✻ ✻ ✻

The pebble skimmed the surface of the sea for no more than a second before plunging below a white-capped wave, "Oh, for goodness' sake," Ruby sighed. "I used to be so good at this."

"I'll take your word for it," Joe chuckled as he searched for his own flat stone.

"It's so long since I've tried. Actually, it's been a long time since I've even been to the beach," Ruby turned to look at Joe's smart, shore-side house behind them, silhouetted against the night sky. "You are so lucky to live here."

"I know. It was Auntie B's place, she let me live here when she wanted to move to the apartment over the store and be in the town centre. Now she's not here, it's all mine," he threw a stone low and fast across the dark water.

"Oh, you've got it! Look, it's gone miles," Ruby shouted, pointing after it. She studied his handsome face, lit tenderly by the moon, "Thanks for being so good about not going to a bar or anywhere like that tonight. After crawling around that garden, I really wasn't in a state to be seen in public."

"No problem, this is fun. Right?" he asked.

She smiled, "It certainly is. I used to come down to Camber Sands when I first passed my driving test. The road going past your house is so long and straight. It doesn't really go anywhere, so it was quiet. Alan, he was my husband...my first husband. That makes me sound so old, doesn't it?"

Joe looked at her, the wind blowing her hair back away from her face, her eyes bright and the cares gone that usually seemed to hold her, "Not at all, it's kind of glamorous," he said.

"Really? You Canadians are simple creatures, aren't you?" and she skipped sideways as she avoided Joe's hand that shot out to give her a shove. "Honestly, if you think having two husbands is the height of glamour, there can't be a lot of excitement in Canada."

"Listen, we have snow up to our nipples in the winter and sun that blisters the pavement all summer, we need to find pleasure where we can."

Ruby giggled and looked back at the row of houses running along the beach, "I don't think these houses had been built when we used to come here. This road became our racetrack and I'm sure we wouldn't have got away with it if people had lived here."

"You used to race?" he looked at her with shock. "Mind you, I don't know why I'm surprised, after your Formula 1 performance earlier."

She smiled as long forgotten memories moved back into view, "We used my Auntie Beryl's powder blue Triumph Toledo and let rip up and down here, doing handbrake turns at each end. I loved it. Oh, my goodness, they were good days - barbecues on the beach, skinny dipping in the sea...it was freezing. It was so different then, I mean, *I* was so different, so innocent."

"Not so innocent, if you were swimming naked with your boyfriend on a public beach," Joe teased.

Ruby put her hands on her hips, "Do you disapprove, Joe? I'm surprised, a man with your reputation."

He laughed, "So, you are aware of my reputation, are you?"

"Most definitely. Although, I have to say, it all seems highly exaggerated."

He put his finger to his lips, "Sshh, don't tell anyone I'm really quite dull."

"Oh, you are not dull, far from it, but you are more sensitive than anyone gives you credit for. You are a charming, kind man, as well as being a good listener," she met the gaze of his crystal blue eyes, then looked away. "Sorry."

"No need to apologise, not many people know the real Joe, I guess," he threw another stone high and long above the waves. "But what about you? Who knew you are a skinny dipping, speed freak?"

"*Was* a skinny dipping, speed freak. That was a different person," Ruby said.

"A different time, maybe, but the same person. She's still there," he said, reaching out and moving a strand of blonde hair from her face. "I saw her tonight."

"No, Joe, too much time has passed. I'm an old woman now."

Joe stepped back, "Why do you do that? Why do you put yourself down, just like Anna does? You are not an old woman, I don't see anyone here matching that description. I see a beautiful woman. A glamorous woman. A cat impersonator - a *bad* cat impersonator. A getaway driver extraordinaire and a woman who is certainly still capable of skinny dipping...come on!" He backed away from her, stumbling down the shingle bank towards the edge of the sea.

Ruby watched as he struggled out of his leather jacket and threw his scarf aside. Next, he pulled his shirt over his head, revealing beautifully broad shoulders, a strong chest with one pierced nipple and flat stomach. She gasped and threw her hand over her mouth, "Joe!" she called after him.

Joe couldn't hear her as he got closer to the waves, but she saw him pause and hop about as he pulled off his boots and then his socks. He whooped as he stood barefoot on the cold, wet sand. Then he unbuckled his belt and with one fluid motion pulled his jeans down and stepped free of them, revealing a lack of any underwear. Ruby froze at the breath-taking view of Joe standing before her and tears stung her eyes. She had never seen anything so beautiful in her entire life.

"Come on then," Joe shouted across the wind and the waves. "Time to prove the real Ruby is still here!" He took a step into the water, "Shiiiit, that's freezing!"

Ruby blinked, her heart pounding. Joe held his hand out towards her, a handsome smile on his face, his body strong and enticing. Slowly she made her way towards him, every part of her longing to touch him, to enjoy this beautiful man. As she came to him she saw his eyes shining as he looked at her and she laid a hand on his chest, which was soft and warm despite a covering of goosebumps from the cold. The touch sent a shiver through her and she leant into him and placed a soft kiss on his cheek.

"You are magnificent," Ruby whispered. "But I can't, I'm so sorry. I made a promise," she turned and quickly crossed the beach without looking back. With shaking hands she found her keys and somehow managed to open the car and drive away, despite tears blurring her view.

* * *

Anna and Ralph turned as they heard the doors to Auntie B's flat open onto the roof terrace.

"Here comes the other Raffles," Ralph said, leaning back against the railing, the rooftops shining with frost behind him

"Eh?" Joe grunted wandering over to the make-shift bar.

"Raffles, the famous cat burglar," Ralph explained.

"Don't mention cats," Anna said from her seat at the little iron table. "I didn't tell you about Mum's fool proof warning system, did I?"

Joe popped the cap off a bottle of beer and took a long drink, "Did you get the paperwork to Fiona?"

Anna nodded, "Yes, it's all signed so she can take it to

the solicitor first thing in the morning. He knew Dewdrop Dobson, so has agreed to come in at the weekend."

"Good," Joe said as he sat heavily beside Anna with a sigh.

Ralph pushed himself off the railing and joined them. There was silence as they sipped their drinks and contemplated their very different days, staring into the small flame of Auntie B's candle.

"Sorry to interrupt," Sam said as he stepped out of Ralph's flat, with no cap on his head his sandy hair hung across his face.

"You're back!" Anna said, jumping up. "Where have you been? Has something happened, you look awful? Is it the restaurant? Is it Dawa? Oh no, that's all we need, he was a nice man with such lovely teeth..."

Sam looked at her, "What on earth are you talking about?"

Anna put her hands on top of her head, "Sorry, it's been such a strange evening. I got a bit...you know... bonkers. Sorry."

Ralph stood up, "You disappeared."

Sam raked his fingers through his hair, "I'm so sorry, when I found out Helen was pregnant with your baby, I freaked out. I'm really sorry - it's not about me, I know that. You have a lot to sort out, so whatever you decide is fine with me."

"No, no, you don't understand. If you'd stopped and listened...didn't you read my text?" Ralph said, moving to him.

"I gave my phone to my mum; I couldn't talk to anyone. I think she turned it off or put it somewhere."

"Sam, you can't keep doing this to me! Listen, the baby's not mine! It's someone else's. Helen slept with a guy, just once, before I left."

"What?"

"Is this a bad time?" said another voice from behind them.

They turned to see Helen standing on the edge of the terrace, "No, not at all," Ralph said, hopping over to her, his bad leg dangling in the air. "Where have *you* been as well? I've been going mad. Why does everyone disappear on me?"

She smiled thinly, "You may want to think about that question, with your particular history," she said and punched him sharply in the bicep. "I needed a bit of time, it all got too much."

"I think we have all had a lot going on and what we need at this point is a good joke," Joe said, raising his arms in the air like a circus master.

"No good looking at you then," Anna said.

"I shall ignore that. What do you call a baby potato?"

Anna groaned, "I don't know."

"A small fry!" There was a brief silence, "OK, as you are all a bit distracted, this might be a good time to add that I went skinny dipping with Anna's mum. I thought you should know." Joe got up quickly and returned to the bar.

"What the hell...?" Anna shouted.

"Nothing happened! She ran off. I think I freaked her out when I stripped off, but I thought I ought to mention it in case she said anything."

Sam wiped a tear from his cheek and looked at Ralph, "I can't believe it's over; I should have talked to you..."

"Yes, you damn well should." Ralph took a breath, "Look, we still need to talk, it's not that simple..."

Helen took hold of Ralph's arm, "Please, I need to say

something."

Before she could finish they all jumped as a heavy banging from below cut through the quiet of the night. The sound continued in a vicious rhythm; thump, thump, thump as someone hammered on one of the doors downstairs. Then they heard distant shouts, floating over the roof from the High Street.

"Who is it?" Anna whispered.

"Sshh," Joe said. "Listen."

They all stood still until the intermittent words floating up to them became clearer, "...OPEN...BASTARDS...I KNOW...FIONA...NOT...AWAY."

Anna gasped, "Piss, oops - language, but it's Andy!"

CHAPTER 23

*The Delta Rooftop Force, a deal
is done and Jolene.*

The distant shouts continued to ring around the roof terrace, "Who's Andy?" Helen asked.

"Fiona's husband," Anna said.

"We broke into his house tonight," Joe added.

"What?" Sam said.

Ralph shook his head, "You see what you've missed? It's a long story."

"I think he's at your door, Anna," Joe said. "He must be outside The Cookery. Stay here, I'll go down."

"Not on your own you won't," Anna said, downing the remainder of her glass of wine in one gulp.

Ralph picked up his crutch, "We'll all go, he'll feel more intimidated then."

"Well, you're not leaving me out," Helen said as she followed Joe into Anna's flat.

Joe laughed, "That's what I like to hear, fighting spirit.

Come on then, Delta Rooftop Force, let's go into battle!"

Ralph turned back to Sam, "Are you with us?"

Sam looked at him, "I'll always be with you...if you want me."

"Sam..." Ralph said.

"I'm sorry I vanished, I should have stayed and talked. It's a knee jerk reaction..."

The banging seemed to be getting louder from below, "Can we talk about this after we deal with the maniac trying to take Anna's door of its hinges?" Ralph asked.

Sam nodded, "I have no idea what's happening, but from now on - where you go, I go."

"You may regret saying that," Ralph said as he made his way into Anna's flat.

By the time he and Sam had caught up, the others were all standing in Anna's hallway watching the front door visibly shake and bounce with each assault from the outside.

"If he's damaged my hand painted *There is No Place like Home* sign, I'll kill him," Anna muttered as she opened the door. "What is the matter with you? You could have damaged this door. There is a perfectly good doorbell here that plays an excellent electronic version of Dolly Parton's *Jolene*," she said, pointing to a plastic bell push at the side of the door. "What do you want?"

Andy took a moment to take in the group behind her, but soon found his voice, "Where is she? Eh? I know she's hiding and I bet you know where she is. Stupid cow, if she thinks she can break into my house..."

"Easy now, tiger..." Joe said, moving beside Anna and forcing Andy to step back.

"I'll handle this," Anna said. "Right, let's get this straight. You are Fiona's husband, correct?"

"Yes, of course."

"There's no, *of course,* about it," Anna snapped. "Fiona is an attractive woman and you are the last person I expected her to be married to. You were batting way above your weight there, Sunny Jim. And there is quite a lot of weight to bat, let's be honest."

"What the..." Andy roared, but was cut off by Anna's raised finger in front of his face.

"She's amazing," Helen whispered as she watched Anna in full flow.

"Fiona has left you, which is about the best thing she has done for years, I would imagine. She has also decided to sell her café."

"That is..."

"Oh, shut up and listen. It is *her* café, not yours, hers. And as of tomorrow, it will be mine. The papers are all signed and will be with the solicitor first thing in the morning and there is nothing you can do about it. Fiona is hidden well away from anywhere you can find her and, even if you did, there's a fire breathing dragon guarding her so you won't stand a chance."

"What?" Sam whispered to Ralph.

"She means Irene...another long story," Ralph said.

Anna continued her lecture, "So, the best thing you can do is toddle off back to your tacky elephant coffee table and whatever mouldy cave you crawled out of and..."

Andy's chubby finger pointed straight at Anna, "It was you!"

Anna hesitated, "What do you mean?"

"You broke into my house! It was you climbing over the fence. How else would you know about the elephant?"

"Well...look, that's none of your business really. I've never met an elephant...I don't even know where you live..."

"I bet it was him," Andy said, gaining confidence by the minute and pointing at Ralph. "The pretty boy, I saw him with you at the do after the old man's funeral. I thought he was a poofter, I never thought he'd have the guts to do anything like this..."

Anna stiffened, "Now you really are getting on my tit ends..."

Joe nudged Anna to one side as he stepped into the doorway, his towering frame casting a shadow across Andy's small round one, "OK my friend, you want to know the truth? It was me, I came and got Fiona's papers and some of her belongings. You want to know something else? You are going to do absolutely nothing about it."

Despite his height disadvantage, Andy stood his ground against Joe, "And why is that?" he sneered. "All I have to do is call the police, get them to fingerprint my place and that'll be you two locked in a cell before the end of the night," he pulled his phone out of his jacket pocket.

"Poop," Anna said. "I never thought about fingerprints."

"Ha," Andy laughed, triumphantly. "Not so clever now are you, cookery girl? You think you can steal my shop from under me, do you? Well, no one gets one over on me. I've been doing stuff like this for way too long to be beaten by a bunch of pansies and...and..." he waved his hand at Anna, trying to find the right word to describe her.

"Hobbits?" Joe suggested, helpfully.

"Exactly," Andy snorted.

"Oy," Anna said.

"Sorry, but I thought the little guy needed a bit of help, he is so out of his depth," Joe replied, enjoying himself, leaning casually against the door frame.

Andy raised his phone, "I won't need any help from you, when I get the police here and have you arrested."

"Ah, but you won't be doing that, will you?" Joe said.

Andy paused and a greasy smile dimpled his bulbous cheeks, "Well, I don't have to, provided those sale documents for the café are in my hands within the next half an hour."

"Nope."

"Your fingerprints are all over my house."

Anna started to twist the edge of her poncho in her hands, "But we were asked to go to the house by Fiona. It's her house too, she has a right to her things. The police would never arrest us for that."

"Maybe not for that, but the expensive antiques that also went missing tonight and the mysterious disappearance of a Rolex watch from my desk drawer are certainly worth them investigating, don't you think?"

"What antiques? What watch?" Anna said, panic rising in her voice.

Joe had not moved from his position in the doorway, "Don't worry, Anna, nothing else is missing, except a couple of his brain cells. He is not going to do anything but sit back and let the sale of The Copper Kettle go through tomorrow. Oh, and he's going to leave Fiona well alone without contesting any element of the divorce settlement."

Andy started to laugh a nasty, wheezy chuckle from the back of his throat, "We're not in the wild west now, cowboy," he laughed. "You can't intimidate me - I have the law on my side."

Joe pushed himself off the door frame and took a step towards Andy, who jumped back with a yelp, "That must be a first for you! And I reckon I can intimidate you all I like, because I really don't think the police are going to be interested in us when they hear this," he reached into his back pocket and pulled out his phone.

Andy stared at him, "What are you talking about?"

Joe tapped the phone then held it out in front of him, adjusting the volume so everyone could hear. There were a few thumps and bumps as if the phone was being picked up or moved as it was recording, then as clear as if he had spoken in front of them came Andy's voice;

"Ah, Ken, it's Andy. Yes, I'm back home, got my phone on the charger now. Cheap Chinese shit, honestly, I wouldn't wipe my arse with it...I know, right?...Anyway, what were you saying before, when it died and cut you off? Something about your kid nearly getting nicked?..."

The colour in the real Andy's face started to drain away as the recording played on, revealing the conversation he'd had earlier in the evening while Joe and Anna were hiding in his study, outlining details of the correct way to burgle a house and the new target of the stately home to be broken into by his associates.

"That proves n-nothing...nothing," Andy stammered, looking as if he didn't believe that at all.

"Oh, I think it would be of great interest to the police, especially if we add to that a statement by your wife detailing all your dirty little dealings over the years and the location of all your knocked-off goods," Joe said.

Andy stared at him, his mouth silently opening and closing like demented goldfish.

Joe patted Andy on the shoulder, "Good, I'll take it we have a deal then. So, you can crawl back to your house. The sale of The Copper Kettle will go through tomorrow, as planned. Fiona will divorce you and if I hear of you making it difficult for her in any way, this little broadcast will be winging its way to the Sussex Constabulary. Have I made myself clear?"

Andy stood for a moment and looked at all five faces in front of him, then his shoulders sagged and he nodded.

"Good, a pleasure doing business with you," Joe said, before leaning down and putting his face within a few centimetres of Andy's. "Oh, by the way, if you step out of line or I ever hear you speak about your wife like you have tonight, I will find you and I will tear you into very small, fatty little pieces. Now, on your way."

Andy seemed to rock back on his heels and it looked like he might fall over or be sick or both, but he managed to pull himself together sufficiently to stand his ground. As he stared at the group his eyes suddenly dropped to the ground, where Stanley had appeared from between Ralph and Sam's legs. Having followed the sound of his friends to see what was going on, he had taken one look at Andy in a standoff against the Rooftop Club and made a swift character judgement. He bared his teeth, growled from the back of his throat and began to stalk slowly towards him.

Andy stepped away, trying to move as quickly as he could without turning his back on the dog or wanting to be seen to be running. He began to speed up, keeping a watch over his shoulder as Stanley continued his menacing approach.

"Stanley!" Ralph called. "Come here!"

The little dog hesitated, making sure his small round prey was not going to return, and then trotted back to Ralph's side.

"Bloody hell," Anna said. "Remind me never to get on the wrong side of a Beagle or a Canadian. I didn't know you'd recorded that."

"We all have our little secrets," Joe said with a wink.

"That was amazing," Helen said. "Just like in the movies."

Joe squared his shoulders and turned to them, "Sometimes things need to be said and done. There is right and there is wrong - and he was in the wrong."

Helen swallowed hard and looked at Ralph, "He's right, Ralph. Please can we talk. I really need to tell you..."

"There's Dawa," Anna said, pointing across the street.

Sam pushed past her and Joe, "Dawa!" he called as he saw him running towards them.

CHAPTER 24

The bacon sandwiches, spontaneous combustion and a spider's web.

The sound and smell of hot, sizzling bacon spread through The Cookery, calming frayed nerves. Sam and Ralph sat hand in hand at a table near the counter, while Helen hugged a warm cup of herbal tea opposite them and yawned.

"Have you heard from Joe?" Ralph called into the kitchen.

Anna turned from the stove with a plate full of fried bacon and started to fill freshly cut rolls with generous piles of rashers, "Yes, he texted to say Fiona is fine, no sign of Andy at Irene's place. She hasn't even had any vile texts from him tonight, which is a good sign. I still can't believe Joe thought to record Andy's crooked conversation, it never even crossed my mind – although, knowing me, I'd have started serenading him with The Nolans from behind his sofa."

Once everyone had a plate of food and teacups were topped up, Anna settled down at the table with them, "Right, Dawa, spill. What's Jane tinseltown-tits Scott done now?"

Just as Dawa opened his mouth there was a knock on the café door and he groaned, plunging his head into his hands, "Now what?"

Ralph limped over to the door, "Hang on, it's Martin."

"Good evening, one and all," Martin said as he stepped inside. "Just checking all is well. Eleven o'clock on a Friday night seems a little late for carousing in the café."

"Come in, come in," Anna called. "It's been a proper night of drama, but there are bacon sandwiches if you want one?"

Martin hesitated, "I wouldn't want to intrude."

"You're not intruding at all, the more the merrier," Dawa said, scrubbing his hands through his beard. "About twenty minutes ago, I came over with urgent news and Anna has refused to let me speak about it until everyone has tea and sandwiches, so if you've ever fancied seeing a man spontaneously combust, this could be your lucky night."

Anna waved a Romney, Hythe and Dymchurch Steam Railway tea towel at him, as she bustled around the kitchen preparing another sandwich for Martin, "Shush, Dawa, we've been through enough for one night without being engulfed by another emergency on an empty stomach."

Helen clicked her fingers at Ralph to get his attention, "I'm vegetarian, remember, I don't eat bacon."

"Oh, of course, sorry. Anna...." he said.

"No, no, it's alright, don't make a fuss, you eat mine though," Helen whispered, pushing the plate towards him.

"What?" Anna said, passing a sandwich to Martin, who had settled in next to Sam.

Ralph held up Helen's plate, "Helen's a vegetarian."

"Sorry, I forgot. Let me get you something else."

"I'm fine really," Helen said.

"Look..." Dawa started.

"Nonsense, you need feeding, as does the baby. Would you like an omelette?" Anna asked.

Dawa tried again, "Please..."

"Christ! Dawa, do Sikh's eat bacon? I've given you pig and now I've said Christ to a Sikh. I'm going to go to hell, not that I'm a Catholic..."

"Anna!" Dawa wailed, making everyone jump. "I'm sorry, I didn't mean to shout but this is very important. Anna, please don't worry, I and many other Sikh's eat pork. I am Sikh by birth, but I no longer practice any aspect of the religion except some of the customs of dress, such as my turban. So, can you please sit down and allow me to speak?"

Anna wiped her face with the tea towel and sat down, "Yes, go ahead. Soz."

Looking embarrassed, Helen took her plate back, "I'll have some of the bun. It's fine."

"Dawa," Sam said. "Please tell us what's going on."

Dawa took a breath and straightened his tie, "Very well. Since your mother spotted Helen was pregnant, it has been clear to me that she was up to something, I just couldn't work out what. Earlier this evening she was in the bar of Cinque and I heard her talking on her phone to someone in London. From what I could ascertain it was a journalist. I do not know who, but they are on their way down to Rye even as I speak."

"That doesn't sound promising," Martin said.

"Too bloody right," Sam said, rubbing his hands together anxiously. "What did she say to them?"

"I heard Jane talking about a story, she said it would be an exclusive for this journalist, featuring...I'm sorry, Sam, but featuring her son and his gay lover's pregnant wife."

"Oh crap," Sam whispered.

"No!" Anna said, her bacon sandwich hanging limply in mid-air on the way to her mouth. "She wouldn't, would she?"

"Oh yes, she would," Sam nodded.

"She would sell a story about her own son to the papers? But why would she do that?"

Dawa swallowed a mouthful of tea, "So her profile would go up. She'd probably follow it with exclusive interviews of the dotting mother, supporting her bereft son, being strong and brave."

"Exactly, all publicity is good publicity in her world," Sam said, his face pale as he thought of the wave of attention coming his way .

"The woman is a disgrace," Martin said.

"She is also a cock-womble – sorry, I know there are children almost present," Anna added, pointing to Helen's stomach. "Where is she now?"

"She's still at Cinque for the time being. I was watching her in case the journalist arrives," Dawa said. "I called your phone, Sam, but it rang in her handbag. I had to make up something about needing to talk to you about the dodgy fridge." He got to his feet, "I told her I would only be gone a few minutes, so I think I should get back and keep an eye on her. Sam, you need to decide how you want to handle this. I have a number of options

I could suggest, but they are perhaps a last resort. You know what I mean."

"The pencil?" Sam said.

"Come to the restaurant as soon as you can, I will try and keep her occupied until then. Thank you for your hospitality, Anna," Dawa said with a small bow and left the café.

"Doesn't he have lovely manners?" Anna sighed.

"Anna, focus, please," Ralph said, then looked over at Helen, who was watching the drama unfold in front of her with wide eyes, "Welcome to The Rye Rooftop Club! It's not always like this, I promise," he said with a grimace.

Helen sat forward, "I'm so sorry, this is all my fault. Sam, you must understand this baby is not Ralph's."

"He knows," Ralph said. "But we haven't talked about what happens next..."

"Next?" Sam said, running his hands through his hair. "What do you mean next? The problem isn't yours. Sorry, Helen."

"It's fine, Sam," Helen looked down at her hand and saw the faint indentation where her wedding ring had been. "But you are wrong about one thing...it's not a *problem* at all. It's my *baby*. I've been thinking of it as trouble, but now I know this little person is my future – she is not my problem."

Ralph looked at his wife and best friend of so many years and her pretty, drawn face, "You shouldn't have to do this alone. I won't let you down when you need me, I don't know how, but..."

Helen reached out to him, "No, Ralph, you don't understand..." she felt all the eyes around the table on her and took a deep breath. "Look, I know you have enough to deal with at the moment with Sam's mother and I am so sorry for causing all this trouble. I also know it was wrong to ask you to come back with me, I had no idea how much you had here. Your amazing new life and new friends. Something you deserve – this is your place and your time. Meeting you all has inspired me more than you can imagine. It's time for me to stop being so scared and find out who I can be without you, Ralph. I don't have long until I will be responsible for a small human, so I have to try. Once I am my own person, perhaps I will find my Rooftop Club - my tribe, like you have."

Anna reached over and took her hand, "I think you are going to be fine," she said, then paused. "She? Did you say your baby was a she?"

"Yes, it's a girl."

Anna gasped, "Will you call her Anna?"

"Erm...I'll think about it."

Anna blushed, "Sorry, I don't know why I said that. I got a bit carried away. I'm quite tired."

"But you are going to need help," Ralph said.

Helen looked at him and then punched him hard in the shoulder, "Too right I am. You have to come and visit and baby sit and change nappies and paint her bedroom - both of you. What you and Sam have together is wonderful and seeing you fight for each other has made me want to fight for my child in the same way. I am also going to drag my family further into my life, warts and all. They don't get off that lightly, just disapproving from the side-lines. And I'm going to have a clear-out of people who call themselves my friend, but offer me nothing."

Ralph moved around the table and embraced her,

"Thank you. I still love you, you know."

"I know, me too. But, Ralph, you did such an important thing for me. The shock of you leaving has finally woken me up, made me see I needed to begin my own life too. You chose to be you, Ralph, and now it's time for me to be the real me...and you know what? I really want to be a mother."

Anna dabbed her eyes with her tea towel, "Isn't it brilliant how things all work out in the end? Like Little House on The Prairie, even when the poor little girl went blind or the donkey died..."

Sam sighed and ignored Anna, "You will be amazing, Helen, and we will always be there for you when you need us, but when Anna says everything has worked out, that is not strictly true. Remember my mother?"

Helen looked back at Sam, "But there's no story now; it's not Ralph's child."

Sam gave a hollow laugh, "You really don't know my mother, she won't worry about letting the truth get in her way. She'll still tell the story to the journalist with all the gory bits coloured in. Then you'll have to admit to the world you had an affair and that'll be a whole new story, loads more coverage for my mother. I'd have to leave the restaurant - it would be a nightmare for me to be there with everyone gawping at us. Ralph may have to give up The Bookery, because people will judge him, regardless of the truth."

"What have I done?" Helen gasped.

Ralph blinked, "It wouldn't be that bad, surely."

"Ralph," Sam said, leaning across the table. "I've been through this before, when my love life was splashed across the papers...twice. They are relentless. Now there's social media and the celebrity magazines too, they'll want the story to run and run for weeks. In the middle of it all like a giant spider will be my mother, crawling her way back to the top of the casting director's lists for juicy roles. She will be forgotten no more and will leave us all behind dangling in her web."

"But surely you can talk some sense into her if she knew the damage it would cause," Anna said with a mouth full of bacon sandwich.

Sam sat back in his chair and locked his fingers behind his head, "Fat chance, at times like this she doesn't see anyone else, only herself and her name up in lights again. It'll only be later she will look back and see what she's done."

"There has to be something we can do," Ralph said.

Sam shook his head, "If there is we don't have much time, the journalist could be here any minute."

They all began talking at once; Anna suggesting various ways to poison the journalist, Helen wanting to take the blame for the confusion and let the unwanted attention fall on her, Ralph believing Jane could still be persuaded not to ruin her son's life for her own gain, Sam wondering whether it was ethical to get Dawa to take the journalist outside and beat him into silence – or better still, do the same to his mother. As they all spoke over each other, Martin, who had sat quietly for some time, rose to his feet and headed to the door, "Martin?" Anna called. "Where are you going?"

Martin stood in the doorway, pulled his tartan hat tightly over his ears and looked back at them, his eyes unusually cold under their bushy grey eyebrows, "Leave her to me," he said and closed the door behind him.

CHAPTER 25

The secret assassin, the wasp and Tom Thumb.

I n The Cookery there was a brief moment of confused silence, broken by them all leaping to their feet, grabbing their coats and making for the door.

"Do you think Martin's a secret assassin?" Anna asked as she pushed them all out and locked up behind her.

"Not unless he does them in with his knitting needles," Ralph said, trying to keep up with Sam who was ahead of them.

Sam caught up with Martin, "What are you going to do?"

Martin kept his focus ahead as he strode over the cobbles, "As a former schoolteacher I have dealt with far more devious individuals than your mother. After some of those little psychopaths, Jane Scott will be a walk in the park."

"Fine, but try not to let any bruises show. Go for the

body," Sam said, only half joking.

Cinque came into view, its name illuminated in red paint above the door and most of the internal lights extinguished as it was late and closed to customers. The glass and steel door opened and Dawa stepped out, his tie pulled askew and the top button of his shirt undone, "She's still here. The journalist has called her to say he is about an hour away. What's the plan?" he asked Sam.

Martin marched past him into the restaurant and all eyes followed his disappearing back.

"No idea," Sam said. "Martin's in charge," then he quickly led the way inside.

They found Martin in the bar standing in front of Jane who looked a little startled, perched precariously on top of a bar stool. They could not hear what Martin was saying as he was speaking barely above a whisper, but when he heard them all piling in behind him he looked at them and frowned. He then turned back to Jane and took her gently but firmly by the elbow, forcing her to slide off the high stool. He did not release his grip, despite her protestations, and marched her to the other end of the bar where the door stood open to the small cupboard that doubled as Sam's office. He manoeuvred her inside, stepped in after her and slammed the door shut behind them.

"What's he up to?" Dawa asked.

"Not a clue, but did you see his face?" Ralph said. "It was like he was going into battle over the top of the trenches."

"Sshh," Anna said, tip-toeing to the door. They all followed, trying to listen to the conversation inside. They could hear muffled shouts, mainly from Jane, then an ominous quiet.

"Was that a thump?" Sam said.

"It sounded like a thump," Anna whispered, putting her ear to the door. "What does a thump mean? Was it a 'he's killed her' sort of thump?"

"Anna!" Ralph said. "Martin is not going to kill Sam's mother."

"It's gone really quiet," Anna hissed. "No, wait, he's saying something. I think he called her a wasp! He said, *Come, come you wasp. You are too angry*. What does that mean?"

"It's Shakespeare," Dawa said. "Taming of The Shrew, I think."

Anna looked at him with wide eyes, "You have so many hidden depths, Dawa. It's amazing. Oh, and remind me to talk to you about your dentist later...hang on," she stuck her ear back against the door. "It's just mumbling now; I can't make out what they're saying."

They stood in an awkward semi-circle for what felt like a long time, but eventually the door slowly opened and they stepped back. First to exit the office was Martin, with a pleasant smile on his face.

"So sorry to keep you all waiting," he stepped aside and Jane appeared behind him, looking pale. "Your mother and I have reached an understanding, haven't we, Jane?" He spoke as if to a small child who needed gentle encouragement to behave well.

Jane nodded, but said nothing as Martin continued, "We have contacted the journalist in question by text message and he will find local accommodation tonight, before meeting with her in the morning."

Sam looked alarmed, "She's still going to talk to him?"

"Indeed, Sam, and she has quite a tale to tell. Don't you, Jane?"

Jane nodded again, "I'd like to go home now please, Sam, I am very tired and would like to go to bed."

Sam looked at Martin, who smiled his agreement, "Erm...OK."

"Do you want me to come with you?" Ralph asked.

Sam nodded, "Absolutely."

"We'll need to pick Stanley up on the way back, then," he added. "He's been on his own all night and his bladder is probably the size of a hammock by now. Will you be alright, Helen?" Ralph said.

"Yes, of course, I can walk back with Anna. I've still got your spare key."

Anna smiled, "Yes, that's fine. We can have a good old girlie chat and talk about names for the baby. I was wondering about Anastasia!"

❖ ❖ ❖

"Let me get this straight," Irene said the next morning, leaning heavily on The Cookery's counter. "You pulled off the heist in Fiona's house, fought off her abusive, criminal husband and then foiled some evil plot by Sam's mother to ruin his life? All in one night?"

"Well, you make it sound like I did it alone, but that was more or less it," Anna said, as she popped a batch of pies into the oven.

"It's like Mission Impossible! Mind you, I can't always follow the plot of them films. That little man, what's his name? Tom Thumb?"

"Tom Cruise."

"Yes, him, he's very good at climbing things. I like those bits. But why did you have to jump up and down on a trampoline?"

"I didn't. It was on the other side of the fence when Joe threw me over. It was lucky it was there or I might have broken something."

"You're lucky you didn't break the fence with those hips," Irene sniffed. "So, how did Martin get that Jane Scott to play ball, then?"

"No idea, he won't say. He's coming in to cover for me this morning, so you can use your interrogation techniques on him to find out."

Irene stiffened, "I don't know what you mean?"

"Talk of the devil," Anna said as Martin arrived for work, in a new purple knitted tank top. "That's snazzy!"

Martin looked down proudly at his new jumper, "I made it last night when I couldn't sleep. They ordered the wrong colour wool for me at the shop, but I rather liked it so I made something for myself."

"Well, it's different, I'll give you that," Irene said as Rosie arrived for her Saturday shift. "Oh, here's the flower fairy. Come on you, there are cushions need checking for crumbs."

"Thanks for helping out this morning," Anna said to Martin, as Irene and Rosie began to bicker and set up for the day. "I need to head to the shops and get some supplies in."

"Well, I am glad to be of service."

"While I've got you here, I have some news," Anna said. "It looks like the purchase of The Copper Kettle is going to go through, so I need to get organised as quickly as possible. How would you like to be my full time cook?"

Martin looked stunned, "Me? In your new café?"

"Yes, I really need someone I can trust. I'll base myself here and teach you everything. It'll be mostly heating pies, making scones, cakes and sandwiches for afternoon teas, that sort of thing. You are so good at that; I'd be happy to leave you there alone."

"I would be absolutely delighted, old thing, but I'm not entirely sure I'm your man," he turned away from Anna, putting his hands deep into his pockets.

"Oh, but you are, I really want you to do it. The thing is though, there isn't much money to get it up and running, so I wondered if you would accept part of your wages as living in the flat above The Copper Kettle? If you lived there rent free, I could then pay you a bit on top. In time when things get established, we can thrash out a proper deal. I'm sorry to ask, but I thought it might help us both."

Martin cleared his throat, emotion getting the better of him, "It sounds like a perfect arrangement, but I would like a little time to think about it, if I may?"

Anna was surprised, but said "Oh, yes, of course. Please do."

Martin smiled shyly at her, "I am very flattered to be asked, but I have to be sure I won't let you down. I would not forgive myself if that happened."

"I can't imagine you ever letting me down," Anna said.

"You forget that a short while ago I was on the streets after living on little but brandy for years. Although I may appear to be doing well, it is often something of a struggle, especially at times when my wife is being particularly frenzied about something inconsequential relating to my past or the divorce. I do not wish to appear ungrateful, but a few days to settle my mind and ensure this is the correct path to take would help me enormously."

Anna gave him a hug, "You take all the time you need."

"There is no time for cuddling in the kitchen," Irene called from the front of the café. "There are people out there in sandals waiting for us to open. Why they want to wear open-toed shoes on a Saturday in February is beyond me. Sunday maybe, but not Saturdays."

* * *

In Sam's house on the other side of town, two pieces of wholemeal toast popped out of the toaster and fell back into the metal slots. The room was quiet, except for the occasional sipping of coffee.

Ralph looked at Sam and cocked his head fiercely towards Jane, who sat beside them. Sam shook his head and stirred some soggy cornflakes in a bowl in front of him. Ralph pulled a face and mouthed "*Ask her!*". Sam shook his head again and mouthed back "*You ask her!*". Stanley sat in the corner of the room watching them both, like a spectator at a tennis match, then he stuck his head down near the floor and scratched furiously at his ear, concerned his hearing was failing.

"I believe the toast is ready," Jane said and got up to bring it to the table.

"Not for me, thanks," Ralph said. "I'll need to take Stanley home in a minute and open The Bookery."

'Don't go!' Sam mouthed urgently.

"What is the matter with you two this morning?" Jane asked, returning with the toast on a plate. "I thought you had patched things up, now Ralph's impending fatherhood isn't an issue."

Sam looked at her in astonishment, "You know about

that?"

"Of course," she said. "Martin put me fully in the picture last night."

"Mum, look, Martin was trying to help me...us, but if he hit you then that is not acceptable," Sam said.

"Hit me?" Jane laughed. "What on earth made you think he hit me?"

Sam threw his spoon into his cornflakes, "Because you are sitting at my kitchen table with a bloody great big black eye, that's why!"

Jane touched her right eye tentatively, the circle of blue bruising edged with green and yellow, "Oh, this? Martin didn't do this." She then picked up a piece of toast and begin to delicately spread butter over it.

"But how did you get it, Jane?" Ralph asked in exasperation. "You didn't have it before you went into the cupboard..."

"Office..." Sam corrected.

"Sorry, office."

Jane sighed and laid down her knife, "I know you are both keen to know what Martin and I discussed last night, but I'm sorry I can't tell you. We spoke in absolute confidence. He was very helpful and I can see more clearly now - despite this eye."

"But..." Sam started to say.

"No, Samuel, no buts. You have to trust me," and she returned her attention to the toast.

Sam dropped his head onto the table in despair at the thought of doing the impossible.

"You have your hair in your cornflakes," Ralph told him.

Sam didn't move, "I know."

"I think I'll go to work," Ralph said, standing and collecting Stanley's lead.

"That's it, go on, leave me," Sam said from the depths of his cereal bowl.

"You'll get a bad neck if you stay like that, Samuel," Jane said, then turned to Ralph. "I may pop in later, there's a new book I thought I might try."

"Yes, fine, see you later then."

The last thing he saw as he left the kitchen was Sam's hand waving at him slowly, his hair still soaking up the milk from his bowl.

CHAPTER 26

*The great survivor, a good man
and sharp pencils.*

Stanley enjoyed his usual meet and greet on the way into town, saying hello to passing locals who had got to know him during their many walks around the jumbled streets of Rye. Ralph let Stanley lead the way slowly back to the High Street, his head still spinning from the revelations of the last few days. He walked in a daze, not even noticing his aching leg, until he found himself outside The Bookery.

He stood under the old iron lamppost and stared at the shop – just as he had on his first night in Rye. The reading lamps in the window were still shining their bright colours onto the display of books for Mother's Day, and the motto he had hand-painted across the bottom of the window stood out clearly, *'Let your adventure begin...'*. However mad things got around him, calm was restored when he came back here, where it all started –

but not today. Everything he had gained by coming to Rye was now in the hands of Jane Scott - and he had absolutely no reason to trust her with that responsibility.

Ralph's phone started to ring. He pulled it out and saw Sam's name on the screen, "Hi, what's up?"

"She's gone!" Sam said on the other end of the line.

"Who?"

"My mother! I went upstairs for a couple of minutes and then I heard the front door shut and she was gone."

"What's she up to now?"

"Hang on, I've got a text...."

Ralph looked at the gifts in his window for Mother's Day, and he thought of the book of *Fifty Cruises To Do Before You Die,* that was wrapped and ready to post to his own mother in Derbyshire. He thought about how lucky he was that his relationship with her was so uncomplicated.

Sam's voice was urgent when he came back on the line, "Are you still there? Ralph?"

"Yes, still here."

"It was Dawa, he says Mum's at Cinque waiting for the journalist. What do we do?"

"Bloody hell," Ralph shouted. "We get there as quickly as we can," and he turned around, dragging Stanley behind him, who had fancied a little lie down in his shop window bed and was not at all keen on another walk. "I'm on my way."

"Me too, see you there."

The phone went dead as Ralph started to hobble to the restaurant as fast as his plastic boot would allow. He was pretty sure they wouldn't be wrapping any gifts or signing a card for Jane this year - or any year to come - if she went ahead with her plan to betray Sam and Helen.

A few minutes later Sam came running full pelt towards him from the other direction as they met outside Cinque. The door flew open and Dawa beckoned them both inside.

"Quick, the journalist just got here," he said, his voice low. "I've put them on a table at the far side of the restaurant. I have also sharpened several pencils to a very fine point, so if you need me to take her out, just say."

"The perfect Mother's Day gift," Sam growled.

"If you get into the cupboard, she shouldn't see you . Don't shut the door completely and you'll be able to hear them."

Sam scowled, "It is my *office*, how many..."

"This is not the time," Ralph whispered pushing Sam across the bar.

They managed to get into the cupboard without being spotted by Jane or her guest, who sat with his back to them, displaying a head of shiny black hair and a quite extraordinary amount of dandruff. Sam pulled the door too behind them, but left it open enough to see and hear what was going on. Dawa went back to the bar and finished preparing the coffees that had been requested for the meeting.

Jane was wearing dark glasses, a plunging neckline of impressive proportions and was listening to the nasal whine of the journalist's voice, "Thank you so much for reaching out to me, Jane. It has been quite a while since we've heard from you, we'd begun to wonder if you had faded gracefully into retirement."

She stiffened, but maintained her broad smile, "Oh, Bernard..."

"Bobby," the journalist corrected her.

"Really? Like the socks?"

"I don't think so."

"Never mind. Darling, Bobby, it has been a difficult time for me, but out of the darkness perhaps there can be some light. If what I have been through can help just one other person, then I can begin to heal."

"What the hell is she talking about?" Ralph whispered in Sam's ear, as they clung to the inside of the door.

Sam grimaced, "Your guess is as good as mine, but if she mentions your name or Helen's I'm going to set the fire alarm off!"

The conversation at the table paused as Dawa delivered two coffees. He deftly served them, never taking his eyes off Jane who didn't look at him, choosing instead to rifle through her handbag for a prop in the shape of a small handkerchief.

"Thank you, that will be all," she said and Dawa's knuckles turned white as he gripped the tray and forced himself to walk away without decapitating her with it.

"I don't understand," Bobby said, scratching his head and releasing a flurry of snowy flakes onto the shoulders of his cheap, shiny suit. "I thought when you called yesterday, we were talking about your son, his lover and a wife with a baby?"

Sam stretched out his hand to feel for the fire alarm point on the wall of the cupboard.

"Wherever did you get that idea from, Bobby? You are such a busy man, perhaps you were thinking of someone else?" Jane said.

"Not at all, you told me..."

"The point is this, I am prepared to tell you the full story of my fight for survival against..." she hesitated, waited the perfect time to build tension, then slowly reached up and took off her dark glasses revealing the livid black eye. The performance had the desired effect and Bobby gasped, so she went on, "...my fight for survival against my abusive lover!"

Ralph gripped Sam tightly behind the door, "Well, I never saw that coming."

"Me neither, I may not have to set the sprinklers off after all," Sam said, finding Ralph's hand in the darkness and holding it tight.

"Jane, this is terrible! Who did this to you?" Bobby asked, pushing his phone, which was recording the conversation, closer to her.

"The name is not important. I, like many women, am a survivor. It is the story of that survival that should be told. Even a woman like me, an icon with all the talents at her disposa, can fall prey to pain and injustice by simply loving the wrong man."

Sam pulled the door shut, cutting off both the sound and light from the restaurant, "What are you doing?" Ralph hissed.

"I've heard enough. You can read all about it in the papers next week. I've seen her give performances like that all my life, I know how it goes."

"Martin is a genius if that was his idea."

"He certainly is and we owe him, big time, but the main thing is it's over," he reached out to Ralph and pulled him close.

"I can't believe it," Ralph sighed, relaxing against Sam. "I'm not sure I'm cut out for all this chaos. I mean, I came down here for a quiet life."

Sam laughed lifting Ralph's chin up until they were nose to nose, "No you didn't, you came here for a *different* and more authentic life and I for one am bloody glad you did." They kissed and Sam slipped his hands down into the back pockets of Ralph's jeans, pulling him closer.

"Now then," Ralph chuckled. "Don't start something you can't finish in this cupboard..."

"It's an office," Sam breathed into his ear.

"Whatever, but we are not alone."

"Yes, we are."

"Nope," Ralph said, rattling Stanley's lead and making the little dog look up and bark.

"Sshh," they both laughed.

"Perhaps you're right. One day soon it will just be the three of us, living a simple life, no dramas, no revelations, no mayhem," Sam said, laying his head on Ralph's shoulder.

"Do you think we'd get bored?"

"Never. I'll cook, you'll paint, Stanley will do whatever Stanley does. I can't imagine ever getting bored with that."

"No, maybe not – I take it you have no plans to do your vanishing act again any time soon."

"I know, I haven't got that flight or fight response sorted yet, I'm so sorry," Sam said, hanging his head.

"No, you haven't. I would much rather you stayed and fought. There is nothing we can't face if we do it together."

"You reckon?"

"Absolutely, there can't be much left for Rye to throw at us, can there? I mean, it's a tiny place, but there is one hell of a lot going on here."

Sam screwed up his face and nodded, "OK, I promise not to run next time something spooks me...or if I do, to go round the block and come back again."

Ralph grinned, "Perfect. You are a very nice man, whatever anyone says about you."

"Who said something about me?"

"Nobody, but I'll fight them for you if they do."

"Would you? You once offered to fight Dawa for me, until he picked you up by the trousers, but it was a lovely thing you were trying to do."

"Please stop reminding me of that."

Sam paused and cupped his hands around Ralph's face, "Let me think...erm...no." Then he kissed him.

There was a gentle knock on the door and Stanley barked, scrambling to reach the handle and let the visitor in. Sam stepped back from Ralph and straightened his shirt, then flicked Ralph's hair back into place, before opening the door. His mother stood outside, with her hands on her hips,

"Well, thank goodness that's all over," she said.

"I don't know what you mean," Sam said with a guilty look at Ralph.

"My interview with that slimy man! However, we artists must do what must be done to survive on *this goodly frame, this earth,*" Jane turned and made her way back to the bar, where she put down her handbag and started looking through it.

"Is that Shakespeare again?" Ralph whispered to Sam.

Jane turned to him, "You recognised it? Shakespeare was my first love; I had forgotten how much it meant to me until Martin reminded me. He saw my performance in *The Taming of the Shrew* you know - when I was a girl, of course. He has been a fan ever since." She then took a hand mirror from her bag and with a tissue started to wipe at the bruising around her eye. As she rubbed, the colour started to smudge and then transfer to the tissue.

"Is that make-up?" Sam gasped. "It's not real?"

"Of course it's not real, darling. What did you think happened? I bashed myself on a door handle last night?" she laughed. "That nasty Bobby person took some photos for his little rag and next week the world will wake up to Jane Scott, The Great Survivor! Martin is such a clever man, despite his extraordinary taste in knitwear. Remind me to buy him a new hat as well, that tartan thing has to go. Anyway, my publicist will get me a few friendly interviews, breakfast telly, lunch time stuff and maybe something deeper with the Times magazine, then we sit back and wait for the phone to ring with some lovely parts that should at least bag me a BAFTA nomination - not before time."

The made-up bruise was now gone and she re-applied her normal make-up, "My darling boys, you look shocked. Let me tell you, *It is not in the stars to hold our destiny, but in ourselves.* In other words, if I don't make my own luck, no one else will."

Sam leant on the bar, "Mum, you amaze me - you frighten the life out of me, but you also amaze me."

Jane looked at him, her face softening, "Do I Sam? What a lovely thing to say. In fact, I think that is the first really nice thing you have ever said to me."

"Now, don't start getting emotional."

"There's no chance of that, darling, not with the price of this mascara." She put her make-up away and closed her bag, then moved to him and carefully brushed his hair away from his face, "I know one should never judge a man by his friends, I mean look at Jesus and that nasty Judas chap, but it is clear by the people you have sur-rounded yourself with that you are a good boy...sorry, a good *man*. Sam, I am very proud of you and your father would be too."

"Thanks, Mum," Sam said and gave his mother a proper hug, something he had not done since he was a boy.

Dawa stood behind the bar and he caught Ralph's eye, "Looks like I won't be buying any new pencils for a while," he said. "Shame."

CHAPTER 27

*The moment to let go, a photograph
and a rat up a drainpipe.*

t Cinque, Sam had long sittings for lunch and dinner, so it wasn't until he got home late that night that he found Jane had gone. Her room was empty and the expensive luggage missing, but she had left him a note saying she had dashed back to London to handle the next stage of her rebirth as a tragic heroine.

Sam sat on the end of her bed and for a moment he missed her, but then he thought about the real women, trapped in painful relationships, like Fiona, who his mother was about to run roughshod over for her own gain. He knew his mother was an extraordinary woman, but she was not a good one. To say that about the person who is supposed to be his greatest protector was painful. However, she was the one person he should be able to look up to and be proud of, but he found he could not.

A shadow fell across him and he looked up at Ralph, who stood in the doorway looking sleepy, "Sorry, did I wake you?"

"No, I was just dozing, waiting for you," Ralph said. "Are you OK?"

"Not really, I couldn't wait for her to go, but..." he stopped and put his head in his hands.

Ralph moved to the bed, pulling Sam into his arms, "But, what? Tell me."

Sam's voice was ragged as he started to cry, "I miss her...but I don't think I ever want to see her again."

Ralph held Sam tightly, rocking him gently in his arms until the sobs began to subside. Then he gently lifted him to his feet, led him to their bedroom and put him to bed. Eventually they both fell into a deep sleep entwined in each other, with Stanley creeping up and settling on the end of the bed, completing their own family that would protect and care for each other without question or the expectation of anything in return.

✳ ✳ ✳

The next few days were tense for everyone in the Rooftop Club, as they waited for the results of their weekend activities to play out.

They scoured the press and social media for any word of Jane, but there was nothing. A mini tornado in Wales seemed to take up most of the attention, until Jane's story broke on Wednesday. This was the same day Fiona received a letter from Andy's solicitor telling her that as their house was registered in Andy's name alone, he would be keeping it in lieu of her having the tearooms.

As Ralph was closing up The Bookery, Anna brought Fiona and the letter to him, "Can you believe what the little tit-bag has done now?" she said as she stomped around the shop. "I'm not even going to apologise for the language because he deserves it. After what Joe said to him, I mean, is he stupid?"

Ralph finished reading the letter, "Well, I think we can assume he is not the brightest bulb on the Christmas tree." He went to the basement stairs at the back of the shop and called down, "Helen, Martin, can you come up? We need a council of war."

The shop door burst open and Joe came in at speed, his head down over his phone "She's all over the place now, like a bad bout of herpes" he said, then looked up from his phone. "Oh, sorry. Hi all, just trying to keep up with Jane Scott's coverage across the internet, it's crazy. Everyone seems to be talking about it, all the press are covering it. She certainly knows how to get attention; I'll give her that."

"Poor Sam," Helen said as she and Martin emerged from the basement, where they had been unpacking a new delivery of children's books ready for Stanley's first Beagle Book Club meeting. "I hope he's OK."

"He's staying put in the kitchen at the restaurant," Ralph said. "Dawa is acting as doorman, keeping the media away, so he's alright. Irene has offered to go over with her rolling pin if things get out of hand, so he'll be quite safe. He doesn't want to read or see anything about his mother, so don't anyone say anything, please."

"Certainly not, old thing," Martin said. "The less he knows about it the better. I'm rather sorry I even suggested it to her."

Ralph shook his head, "No, please don't be, you saved

us from a far worse situation. We need to ride it out."

"Martin," Fiona said. "Jane Scott may be taking advantage of other people's misfortunes, but what she is also doing is highlighting the debate about women who are trapped like I was. That has to be a positive outcome and if it helps even one woman to free herself, then you have done a very good thing."

"Thank you, I take your point and I'm grateful," Martin said.

Anna stamped her foot, "That's all very well, but what about this letter? We can't let him get away with it."

"What letter?" Joe asked.

"My husband says he is going to keep the house for himself," Fiona said, taking the letter from Anna and beginning to fold it away. "I knew Andy would need to feel he'd won some sort of victory. I expect he thinks I'll give in and let him have it, but I'll be damned if I will!"

"Here bleedin' here," Anna said. "Let's dob him in to the police like we said we would."

Fiona twisted the letter in her hands, "I really don't want to unless I absolutely have to. I've worked so hard not to let any of this impact on George, having me testify in court against his father would break his heart."

"I get it, but we had a deal with your husband," Joe said. "He has broken it and can't get away with that. If he does, then goodness knows what he thinks he can get away with. We really need him to disappear with his tail between his legs."

"We do indeed, but how?" Martin said.

"I did have one idea, but you will probably think it's ridiculous" Fiona said, moving to the middle of the shop and looking around at them all. "I was passing the offices of the Rye Observer yesterday. They display a range of photographs that have been taken locally but didn't make it into the paper. There was a photograph there of Andy with Jane Scott, he insisted on having one taken at the football team's fair. I took one on my phone too. Do you remember, Ralph?"

"Yes, it's etched on my memory."

"Well, for reasons we can all understand, Jane Scott has refused to name the person who gave her a black eye - her imaginary boyfriend," Fiona began to pace up and down as she thought through her idea. "Now, suppose he was not imaginary anymore. Suppose a photograph begins to be circulated across the internet of her with an unnamed man. It doesn't need to say he is the actual man in question, but social media is well known for people putting two and two together and reaching five, isn't it?"

"Brilliant!" Joe said. "So, we start to circulate the photo of Jane and Andy, just asking the question whether this could be the man who gave her the black eye and - boom, it'll go viral!"

Fiona smiled at them all, "Yes, then Andy will be in the sort of spotlight he doesn't want and will have to disappear like a...a..."

"Pink rat back up a drainpipe," Anna said, clapping her hands.

"All we need to do is to let him know that the photo was leaked as a warning to him of what else we have up our sleeve," Joe said.

"He'll be terrified of the attention," Fiona said. "He will have to lay low - I'm sure none of his dodgy friends will want to give him any stolen goods to sell while he has so much attention on him, will they? His income will suddenly stop and he'll be stuck. He'll need to sell our house and unless he agrees to split the proceeds fairly with me, I can delay and hold things up, so he gets nothing."

Anna put her hands on her hips, "Now this is girl power in action! I'm loving the new Fiona."

"I know," Fiona said, grinning shyly. "Me too. But how will we do it?"

"I'm on it," Joe said. "Ping me the photo from your phone and I'll get it out there. Then when it's had the desired effect, I can text Andy and let him know where it came from."

"No, let me," Fiona said. "I'll send you the photo, but when it's time to let him know who was behind it - I will tell him. I think it's about time he actually saw me fight back."

"Good for you," Joe said as everyone applauded and Anna threw her kimono covered arms around Fiona.

Anna stood back and looked at them all, "We make quite a team, don't we? The Rye Rooftop Club just got a whole lot bigger and better and ballsier! I love it!"

"Well, I'm afraid I am a temporary member," Helen said, moving slowly to the door to Ralph's flat. "I have a scan booked for tomorrow, so I have to go home. It's time to get ready for the arrival of my daughter."

"Another fabulous team," Anna said, rushing towards Helen. "I'm feeling very huggy today, so it's your turn, lady," and she engulfed Helen in a big green kimono hug.

"I am not sure whether this is the right moment, but as we seem to be resolving a number of matters, I suspect it is," Martin said. "If the offer is still open, Anna, may I accept the position of cook you kindly offered me?"

"You bloody well can," Anna shouted. "Sorry, language, but it deserves it and you get the next bloody squeeze," and she charged across the shop and embraced a shocked looking Martin.

When he was released, he smoothed his ruffled eyebrows and wiped his eye, "I think I may be allergic to your perfume," he mumbled.

"I'm not wearing any," Anna said.

"Ah, yes, I see," Martin said. "Then it must be that I am extremely grateful for finding a new family that has given me the strength and the support to kick the booze and start again. I would like to thank you all."

"I'll drink to that," Joe said, raising an imaginary glass in the air. "Oh, sorry, that's in bad taste considering your, you know..." and he looked mortified as everyone else started to giggle.

"Joe, I think that may be the funniest joke you have told so far," Martin said as he began to laugh loudly, slapping his knees with joy.

"Come on everyone, let's parade Helen to her car and give her a proper send off," Anna cried as she pushed Helen out of the shop and up the stairs to Ralph's flat, to help her pack for her journey into motherhood.

CHAPTER 28

*The Sistine Chapel, spirit animals
and broken promises.*

With the sale complete on The Copper Kettle, Anna launched into the transformation of her new tearooms with her usual fierce energy. She set her heart on opening over the Mother's Day weekend, which was less than two weeks away, so she was constantly running up and down the hill as the tired old tearooms got new carpets, furniture, lighting and an updated kitchen. Martin joined her in The Cookery during the day to learn everything he needed to know about the new menu for The Copper Kettle.

Every evening, as the night took over from day, the Rooftop Club would gather there and follow Anna's frantic instructions to paint the walls and ceilings, clean surfaces, polish furniture and bring new life to Dew-drop Dobson's old business.

On Friday evening there was a knock on the tearoom's door and Fiona poked her head inside, "Hello, everyone."

"Fiona!" Anna said. "Come in, come in. How are you?"

"I'm fine, thank you."

"Wait, what is this vision I see before me?" Anna said, her arms thrown wide.

Fiona looked embarrassed, "Do I look alright? I haven't worn dungarees since I was about twelve, but I absolutely love them. The lady in the shop said something about them allowing my chakras to breath freely."

"Psychic Sue! I knew she'd sort you out. I'm surprised she didn't get you to buy the brightly coloured ones, she usually does."

"Oh, she tried," Fiona laughed. "But I put my foot down and stuck with the blue denim. Despite the colour she thinks my aura is, I'm not ready for anything too drastic yet."

"The butterfly is amazing," Ana said, coming closer to examine the pattern on the bib of the dungarees made from multi-coloured diamante beads.

"Hmm, well, I was persuaded the butterfly was my spirit animal," Fiona said, looking down at it. "I'm not sure I believe all that mumbo jumbo, but Sue said she felt I was emerging from a dark place into the light, like a butterfly from its cocoon. I mean how did she know that? I've never been in that shop before."

Anna nodded seriously, "She knows, she's psychic."

"Butterflies saved me once too," Joe said from the top of a ladder behind Anna. "I used to do an act in a club in Bangkok, and my big finish was standing on a tower of beer bottles with just a paper cut-out of a Red Admiral over my..."

"Don't get distracted from your work, please," Anna

said, rattling his ladder. "There is a time and a place for tales of your sordid past and this is not it. We have a deadline to hit!"

Fiona giggled and looked around. She saw the yellowing walls covered with light cream paint, a rich blue carpet on the floor and new glass wall lights in a traditional carriage style, "This place looks amazing, so fresh and bright. You are all working so hard."

Joe had returned to painting the old oak ceiling beams, "We have a pretty good task master and an incentive – bacon sandwiches at midnight and cocoa before we go to bed, all provided by the boss."

"Only if you work hard enough," Anna said, slapping his bottom through the tight shorts he was wearing. "Ow, that hurt, you could crack walnuts with those buttocks. Don't look Fiona, you'll be scarred for life."

Fiona laughed, "I won't, don't worry."

Joe looked disappointed, "You won't look or you won't be scarred for life?"

"Both," Fiona giggled, blushing slightly. "What are you doing, Ralph?"

Ralph and Stanley were sitting on the floor under the long wall on the far side of the room with a long ruler and a pencil, "Believe it or not, I am trying to draw an enormous copper kettle and a pile of cakes. It looked easy when I drew it on a sketch pad, now it has to be about ten times bigger it's getting complicated. Stanley's good at maths so he's doing the scaling up."

"You'll be fine," Anna said, waving her hand at him. "You never heard da Vinci complain when he painted the Sistine Chapel."

She turned as she heard footsteps coming down the narrow stairs from the flat above, "Michelangelo, dear thing, not da Vinci," Martin said as he appeared carrying a large cardboard box.

"Thank you, Martin," Ralph said.

"Alright, alright, but he was painting in the cold, upside down, about a mile in the sky above medieval Rome in a funny little hat, which you are not. You are sitting on the floor with a cup of tea in the middle of Rye, so knuckle down," Anna turned her attention to Martin. "Is that the last box?"

Martin placed it on top of a pile of others near the door, "It is. There's just the furniture now."

Fiona looked at the boxes, "Is that all?" she asked.

"Yes, I'm afraid so," Anna said. "Your father didn't seem to have many personal possessions; he was…quite minimalist."

Fiona nodded sadly, "Yes, he wasn't really bothered about comfort. Thank you for packing them, Martin."

"It was a pleasure," Martin said. "Ruby helped, of course, she's upstairs finishing cleaning the bedroom. That large box has all of his drawings in it, which are exquisite, I must say."

"Thank you, he did love his birds. Would you like any for the tearooms, Anna? No, no, why would you?"

"Actually, I'd love to have some," Anna said. "I know Dobson and I didn't really get on, but he did give me my first chance as a baker and it was here, too. So, it would be nice to have some continuity. There's a wall by the loos that needs something, I think if we put four or five of his smaller drawings on there, it would be great."

Fiona smiled, "I'd love that. It would almost be like he was still here, in a way."

"Perfect, shall we have a look then?" Martin said, opening the box.

They sorted through the many delicate pen and ink drawings of local birds and selected pictures in matching frames, which Martin set about mounting on the wall.

"How's George, by the way? Does he know about your divorce?" Anna asked as she helped Fiona seal the boxes of her father's possessions.

Fiona nodded, "Yes, but he doesn't seem too fazed by it at the moment. He loves his new school and really enjoys being a boarder. He seems to like the routine, and he's even lost a little weight."

"Well, that's good. Are you going to leave him there?"

Fiona nodded, "For the time being, we can't afford for him to board forever, even with Dad's money, but while he's happy I think it's the best thing for him. Anyway, I don't actually have anywhere to put him even if he did come home." She banged the top of a box with her hand, "Oh, that's what I came to tell you! Sorry, I forgot with the butterflies and everything. Andy has agreed to split the sale of the house fifty-fifty."

Martin stopped hammering in a nail, "Has he? That's excellent news, so your little ruse worked?"

Fiona chuckled, "It worked perfectly. The photo went viral within minutes. Andy was mortified, he kept going online and denying he was Jane Scott's evil attacker. The more he said, the worse it got. He had some terrible abuse, so he took down all his social media accounts, then people started coming to the door and he got banned from the snooker club. If it wasn't Andy, I'd have felt sorry for him."

"That's my girl," Anna said.

Ralph turned to them, "And the added bonus was that Jane Scott was equally mortified by being associated with someone like Andy. She couldn't believe anyone would think she would choose him...sorry, no offence, Fiona."

"Oh, none taken, I really don't know what I was thinking," Fiona said, fiddling with her hair, which was no longer in its tight plait, but hanging in loose curls across her shoulders. "Anyway, the even better news is that we accepted an asking price offer on the house today!"

Anna cheered, "That's amazing, freedom at last!"

"I know and I've sent him the divorce papers too." Fiona paused and looked at Anna, "Actually, may I ask you something?"

"Of course," Anna said.

Fiona hesitated then took her arm and led her away from the others and into the kitchen, "I was wondering what you were going to do with Dad's flat upstairs? You see, I have no idea what to do next really, but I certainly need to get my own place. I hope you don't mind me asking, but would I be able to rent the flat from you for a while, just until I decide what to do?"

Anna bit her lip, "Oh dear, I would happily let you live there, but the thing is I've promised it to Martin as part of his deal to be the cook here. He needs to get out of his homeless hostel, you see, so it seemed like the perfect solution."

"It is, that's such a good idea. I'll leave the furniture for him. Please don't worry about me, it was just a thought. There's bound to be somewhere else local that's empty, I will start looking."

Anna frowned, "Hang on, hang on, I think I may have a solution for you. Leave it with me for a few days, if you can bear staying with Irene for a bit longer."

"Oh yes, that's fine. Mind you, if I eat any more dumplings I think I'm going to need to buy bigger clothes," Fiona hesitated again and looked at her nails.

"Was there something else?" Anna asked.

"I hate to keep asking you for things, you have done so much already."

"Oh, forget that, I'm having the time of my life being a tycoon and owning a chain of cafés," Anna said, waving her arms around the kitchen. "Come on, spill."

"Well, I was wondering if you were going to be hiring any waitresses? I don't really have any experience to offer and I..."

"Yes and yes," Anna said, taking hold of Fiona's hands. "Yes, I am hiring waitresses and, yes, you are my first choice. Welcome to the business."

"Really? Are you sure?"

"No, I said it for a laugh! Of course I'm sure."

"Thank you so much. I need to start putting those boxes in my car and get back to Irene's, she's getting very frustrated with a new jigsaw of Blue Peter presenters through the ages and I promised to help. I'll call in and see you tomorrow to sort things out."

"I'll give you a hand," Anna said and she squeezed past Joe who was coming into the kitchen.

"All the beams have got their first coat, so I'll let them dry for a while," he said.

"Brilliant, ta," Anna called back to him.

He went to the sink to rinse the varnish off the brushes and turned as he heard someone come in behind him. It was Ruby, with a bucket of dirty water.

"Hi."

"Oh, hi," she said, looking flustered. "Sorry, I...I wanted to empty this bucket, it's got dirty water in it."

He held his hand out, "Here pass it over, I'll do it."

"Thanks," she said and held it out to him, aware of their fingers brushing together as he took hold of the handle.

"Where have you been?" Joe said with his back to her.

"Nowhere, what do you mean?"

He turned and leant against the sink, "Ruby, since our date on the beach after burgling Fiona's house I have barely seen you. You won't return my calls and when we're here at the same time, you make sure we're never alone."

"We've been busy, that's all," Ruby responded, her stomach doing somersaults. "You have the shop, I have...well, it's been difficult."

"I'm sorry if I embarrassed you on the beach, that was the last thing I wanted to do," Joe said. "Although, I think I probably embarrassed myself more than you."

"No, Joe, you didn't embarrass yourself – I did. It was me who ran away and left you there all...all..."

"Naked?" he grinned.

Ruby couldn't help but smile, "Yes."

"Look, I'm going to embarrass myself again, but I made you something...to apologise."

"You do not have anything to apologise for, you really shouldn't have gone to any trouble."

"You haven't seen it yet," he said and lifted a cardboard box from inside a kitchen cupboard. He placed it on the counter and reached in and brought out a large brown cake. It had a steep slope running from one side to the other, down which a small amount of watery icing seemed to be sliding. He placed it carefully on the countertop, "I know baking is your thing, so I thought I'd have a go. It's my first ever cake."

"Really? You made that?"

"Yup, with my own bare hands and a little help from YouTube," he crossed his arms and stood back proudly. "Now, I will be the first to admit it doesn't look exactly like the picture, but I think it has a certain...flare."

Ruby put her hand to her mouth to stifle a laugh, "It does...it does have flare. I can see that." She came across the room to take a closer look, "It was very sweet of you."

"Cakes are your thing, Ruby, and I wanted to understand it. I know that's crazy..."

"No, it's such a lovely thought. May I try some?"

Joe looked shocked, "Seriously? You want to eat it?"

"Of course, it looks...delicious."

"OK, as long as you have insurance," he said, pulling a knife out of a drawer and cutting her a small slice.

Ruby picked it up and gingerly took a bite, "Well, I can truly say it is... absolutely...awful!"

"That bad?"

She put the rest of the piece back on the counter, "Yes, I'm afraid so, but I honestly appreciate the gesture."

She looked at his face as he showed his disappointment and reached out, laying her hand on his chest, just as she had done on the beach. The feeling of his warmth and strength was exactly as she had remembered it night after night since then. In her dreams, instead of walking away she had leaned forward and kissed him. Without thinking, that's what she did now.

Joe was taken by surprise, but quickly responded to the soft touch of Ruby's lips. He slipped his arms around her waist and whispered, "I'm going to need to bake more often."

"Well, some practice would be good," she said and

tried to step back, but he held her tight against him.

"Please let me say this. I've been thinking about it for ages, I even wrote it down to try and make sense of it when I couldn't get it straight in my head. So here goes." He took a deep breath and started to speak slowly and carefully, as if determined to get it right, "When I first started dating Imogen it felt like a huge achievement. I had an actual relationship! Who knew I could do that? But that was the best thing about it, it was never really going to go beyond that. When I met you, it felt completely different. It was so...natural. It took me ages to work out why, but it felt like happiness. That probably sounds real sappy, but I am more relaxed with you than any woman I'd ever met. I am myself. We fit, Ruby, and I had hoped if you felt like giving us a go, I might even find my best self. Then I went and ruined it by being my old self and stripping naked and frightening you off..."

"Oh Joe, it wasn't you I was frightened of..."

"Stop it!" Anna gasped from the doorway. "What are you doing?"

Ruby pushed herself away from Joe, "Anna, I'm sorry..."

Joe frowned, "Ruby, stop being sorry. I'm not. I loved kissing you."

"You kissed?" Anna stormed at her mother. "I knew I couldn't trust you. I told you honesty was the most important thing to me and now you are carrying on behind my back, with *him* of all people. You made a promise!"

"Woah, woah," Joe said, looking from mother to daughter. "What promise?"

"Please don't, Anna," Ruby said.

"We both swore off men. She promised we'd be manless together! We don't need men LIKE YOU!" Anna yelled.

Ralph's head appeared around the kitchen door, "Sorry to interrupt, but you do know they can hear you across the channel in France, don't you?"

"I should go, I've ruined everything," Ruby said, pushing past Ralph, picking up her coat and running out of the front door.

Joe turned on Anna, "Why did you make her promise that? Why shouldn't she have a bit of happiness, just because you can't ever do anything on your own?"

"Yes, I can. It's blokes like you who are the problem. Always messing women about. Skipping from one to another. Never being honest or committed or...or... real!"

"Blokes like me? I'm not good enough, is that it? I'm not honest or real? So, I'm not capable of actually loving someone, nor is Ruby, until *you* say so. Jeez, I don't know why I keep trying to fit in here!"

"Me neither!"

"Anna, that's enough," Ralph snapped. "Joe of course you fit in, you don't need to keep trying. You're the heart of us...of our family."

"No, Ralph," Joe said, looking up at the ceiling. "I'm not. My grandmother was and I'm just a poor extension of her, that's the only reason I'm still here. I keep trying to be accepted as me, but...well, that's not enough. Maybe I'll leave, go back to Canada."

"Please don't..." Ralph said, but Joe had already left the kitchen and they heard the front door slam behind him.

Anna looked at Ralph, pain written across her face, "I didn't mean it, I was shocked. I...Is he really going to leave?"

Ralph looked her straight in the eye, "You haven't given him much reason to stay, have you?"

CHAPTER 29

*The fragility of love, Captain Pugwash
and eye-patches.*

As the next morning dawned, Sam turned over in bed to find neither Ralph nor Stanley in their usual places beside him. It had been a busy night at Cinque, so he was hoping for a peaceful lie-in above the bookshop, but by the clattering and banging from the kitchen he doubted there was much chance of that happening. He threw back the covers, padded through the dark flat and swore as his bare feet kicked something hard and sharp.

Ralph's voice came from the kitchen, where he was crouching on the floor, "You're up."

"It would appear so," Sam said, rubbing his foot as he looked at half the contents of Ralph's kitchen cupboards spread over the landing. "What the hell are you doing? Are we having a jumble sale?"

"I need to make a pirate's eye-patch - or several, if I

can."

"Of all the answers I expected, that was not one of them."

"I'm sure I've seen some black plastic tubs in here somewhere."

Sam leant on the kitchen door frame, "Look, I admire your commitment to keeping sexy-time creative, but I'm not sure dressing up as pirates is really going to be my thing."

Ralph batted Stanley away, who was trying his best to gain access to the cupboard for a good explore, "Clear off, Stan. Can you take him out for a walk, please? Then you need to help me make a dozen pirate eye-patches, then you need to go and talk to Joe..."

"Hang on, hang on, what's the rush?" Sam said, still thinking of the warm bed he had just left.

"It's the first day of our Beagle Book Club for the kids, remember? They come, I read them a story and then they have to go away and draw a picture and win a book voucher. It's a pirate story, Captain Pugwash, because the bloke who wrote it lived in Rye. I wanted them all to have an eye-patch, but I only remembered it this morning. I've been so busy helping Anna with her new place, then with the bust up between her and Joe last night I forgot all about them."

"Right, that makes more sense. So, I'm on dog duty then we make pirate patches, then I talk to Joe. Why am I taking to Joe, shouldn't it be Anna?"

"She tried last night. She chased all over town and down to his house at Camber Sands trying to find him, but we don't know where he is...or he wouldn't answer the door to her. You're his mate and you weren't involved, so he might talk to you."

"Got you," Sam said, heading back to the bedroom.

Ralph called after him, "As soon as I find the black plastic, I'm heading straight down to The Bookery, so meet me there."

Sam appeared in the kitchen doorway again, "Erm, just one thing."

Ralph sighed, "What?"

"You may need to think about..." he pointed down at Ralph. "Before you go into the shop."

"What? Oh, yes, fair point," Ralph said, looking at himself and realising in his panic he had forgotten to get dressed.

"And one more thought, make an extra eye-patch – you never know, I might change my mind about playing pirates later," Sam winked, only just moving quickly enough to avoid a spaghetti spoon that flew past his head, over the banister and clattered its way down the stairs.

Half an hour later, they were both sitting on the floor of The Bookery, fully clothed, but surrounded by pieces of black plastic, sheets of coloured paper, lengths of elastic, scissors and glue.

"This is fun," Sam said as he threaded a piece of elastic through an eye-patch. "It's our first proper date for ages. I've missed this, just you and me."

"Stanley, come here, I need to try this pirate hat on you," Ralph said. "I know, but you can't say our relationship is ever boring"

"After recent weeks, that is a huge understatement."

Ralph tied a piece of string around Stanley's head that held a small paper pirate's hat with skull and crossbones painted on it, "There you are Stan, that looks great."

Stanley shook his head, but the hat seemed to be

stuck between his ears, so he decided to give it a go for a while and trotted off to investigate a spider that was visiting the travel section.

"Of the times I allowed myself to think about what it might be like to live as gay man and have a relationship, I'm not sure I ever imagined it like this," Ralph said, watching Sam start to thread elastic through another eye-patch.

Sam smiled at him, "No? Is the reality better or worse?"

"Oh, better, a million times better...and weirder."

"You know this isn't normal, don't you? Everything that's happened to you since you came to Rye? Things will settle down, I promise."

Ralph leant against Sam and rested his head on his shoulder, "I hope not, it all makes the drama of running away from my entire life and coming out seem insignificant. I don't feel like an alien or out of place amongst the madness here. Does that sound wrong?"

"It makes perfect sense. Perhaps everything that happens in Rye is the new normal?" Sam laughed. "It's the rest of the world that's strange and alien, not us."

"Perhaps, but whatever it is, I feel the most comfortable and confident I have ever been."

Sam put his arm around Ralph's shoulder, "Really? And you are happy, aren't you?"

"Very, thanks to you," Ralph kissed Sam's stubbly cheek. "Are you? Now your mum is out of the picture?"

"Absolutely. You and Stanley are the only family I need...oh, Martin."

"Martin? You think of him as family?"

"No, well, yes, but he's here...look," Sam pointed to the street, where Martin stood outside smiling at them.

"Sorry to interrupt," Martin said as he opened the door. "I didn't want to knock, you both looked so comfortable together in that moment, it was a joy to behold. It quite took me back to a time in my youth, with my brother before...Sorry, you don't want me chattering on and spoiling things."

Ralph smiled at Sam, "Don't worry, Martin, we were just having a few moments to ourselves amongst the craziness. Come in, how are things going?"

Martin stepped into the shop, undoing the large leather buttons on his chunky blue cardigan, "Very well, thank you. I honestly can't remember when I was so busy. I am knitting a vast array of garments long into the night for people. Then I'm working with Anna to prepare myself for the opening of The Copper Kettle - today I am attempting to perfect her new recipe for cheddar cheese and Bovril cake. She tells me it's quite the thing in South Africa, but I am not convinced Rye is ready for the Transvaal. However, I am not complaining, this is the most productive I have been since my days of stealing from the rich to give to the poor." He bent down to greet Stanley who had got bored tormenting the spider and had come to say hello.

Sam finished tying up another eye-patch, "When were you stealing from the rich?" he asked.

"Oh, more distant memories - back in the mists of time long forgotten, old thing," Martin said, avoiding eye contact by fussing Stanley.

Anna crashed through the shop doorway, "Have you seen it? The sign?" she said.

"What sign?" Ralph asked.

"Next door in the window of Let's Screw. It says *Manager Wanted!*" Anna said. "He's really going."

"Sam is going to talk to Joe this morning, he'll sort it out."

"Is Joe going somewhere?" Martin said.

Sam started to collect up the finished eye-patches, "There was a bit of a ding-dong last night, Anna found Joe kissing Ruby and *someone* went into orbit."

"Well, wouldn't you?" Anna said. "A: she's my mother. B: she betrayed my trust. C: she has now caused the break-up of the Rooftop Club, of our family, because Joe is going back to Canada."

Martin looked at Anna sternly, "Did she really cause the trouble, Anna? Or was she perhaps expressing a perfectly acceptable moment of tenderness with someone she may care for?"

Anna stared at him, her eyes wide, "Martin, you weren't there…"

"Not on this occasion, but I have seen it happen before - a moment of simple affection between two people tearing a family apart." He suddenly turned and walked to the door, looking a little older and frailer than when he had arrived. As he opened it, he stopped and looked back at Sam, Ralph and then Anna, "Love is so incredibly delicate it can be easily lost. Is it not our job as friends and family to do everything we can to keep it alive and help it grow?" He turned and shut the door quietly behind him.

There was silence in the shop, then Sam said, "What was that all about?"

"I think there is a story to be told about Martin and his family, something from his past," Ralph said.

Anna shuffled her feet, "I suppose you think this was all my fault?"

"Yes," Sam and Ralph said together.

She nodded, "You're right, it was."

"Really?" Ralph said.

"I haven't slept all night. Why do I do this? Go mad and say such awful things to people I care about. I'm such a terrible person!" Anna wrapped her arms around herself.

"You're not a terrible person, Anna," Ralph said. "But you have to deal with your issues with your mother."

"I know, I know. That's what I spent the night thinking about and I know why I went so mad. I was jealous."

Sam frowned, "You still have feelings for Joe?"

"No, oh lordy, no," she wiped a tear from her cheek with a corner of yellow kimono. "Joe and I only had a brief thing - *very* brief - and I got over that a long time ago. No, I realised I was jealous he was going to take her away from me, just when I'd found her again." She took a deep breath and buried her head in her hands.

Ralph and Sam both moved to her and wrapped her in a double-sided hug, "That's crazy. Can't you see you are the most important thing in her life?" Ralph said. "Look at all the effort she's gone to, stopping drinking and re-inventing herself so she can be your mum again."

"But I lost my dad when I was so little and she withdrew into the booze and met awful Derek and married him. I never had her to myself, just me and my mum. I thought that perhaps now I had everything – two businesses, the best friends in the world and my mum. I wanted her for myself," she sobbed.

"You can still have all those things, Anna," Sam said. "But in the same way you have a full life and a whole load of people to love, surely Ruby can have that too? It doesn't mean she'll love you any less."

"I suppose," Anna sniffed, buried deep between them.

"I've spoiled everything, haven't I?"

Ralph and Sam stood back, leaving her huddled inside her bright yellow kimono that had designs of green frogs jumping from lily pad to lily pad, "There is nothing you can't fix. Speak to your mum," Ralph said. "Tell her exactly what you told us. Sam will find Joe and get him to see sense."

"You think he won't go?"

"He can't go - the Rooftop Club needs him."

Anna wiped her eyes, "You're right, we can do this. You can do this, can't you, Sam?"

Sam smiled, "I'll try. I've got to find him first, but he can't hide from us forever – I'll apply for the job of manager of Let's Screw if I have to."

"You are amazing," Anna said, sniffing back the tears and looking brighter. "What would I do without either of you? Actually, don't answer that, I'm not sure the answer would be pleasant. Right, I'm off to open The Cookery and try and speak to Mum...why is Stanley wearing a pirate hat?"

"Never mind, you go and save the Rooftop Club and let me worry about the pirates."

CHAPTER 30

The Rye Bermuda Triangle, Seaman
Stanley and the need to go.

The children's event was due to start at ten, but Ralph had to open the doors early to accommodate the large crowd that was beginning to block the pavement and spill into the road. Sam returned just in time to help organise everyone, "Joe won't answer my calls, his doorbell or me nearly kicking the door of the shop down," he whispered to Ralph.

"Anna says she can't find her mother either. Rye is a tiny town, how come people can hide so easily here?"

Sam looked embarrassed, "Are you talking about me too? I've hidden from you twice in the short time I've known you."

"Actually, I wasn't, but as you've had practice you of all people should be able to work out where they go. But before we solve the mystery of the Rye Bermuda Triangle - what am I going to do with this lot?" Ralph said, looking panic stricken as more and more people flooded into the shop.

"Make more eye-patches?"

"Not funny! I thought we might get about ten or fifteen kids, there have to be at least thirty here."

Sam took Ralph by the hand and pulled him out of the shop onto the street, "Listen, this is what you wanted - a shop full of people. You are going to make a killing today. Deep breath, straighten your eye-patch and get back in there. I'll get as many grown-ups as I can next door to Anna's for some breakfast, then you can swash-your-buckle or whatever you need to do for the kids. We're a team, remember, we can do it."

Ralph looked at Sam, "We can. Together. We've faced worse, right?"

"If we can handle my mother, we can handle a few kids who like pirate ships."

"True, if we can deal with her, we can cope with a whole bloody Armada. Let's do this!"

They turned and went back into The Bookery. Sam worked his way through the crowd encouraging parents to pop next door to wake themselves up with coffee and fried breakfasts. He set his jaw and ignored the occasional whisper that followed him around the shop, "Isn't that..?", "His mother's Jane Scott. Don't you remember all that stuff in the papers?" After a while he got used to it and laughed his way through, realising only a small number of people actually read the papers and even fewer remembered what was in them, so he was able to smile and clear the shop of the majority of the adults without incident.

This left Ralph with a large group of children and a few grandparents who remembered Captain Pugwash from the telly and fancied a trip down memory lane. Quite a few of the Rye Rovers were present, including Elliot, out of his Pocahontas costume this time. Ralph got all the children to sit in the lower half of the shop on cushions he had borrowed from the chairs in The Cookery. A couple of the grandparents gamely tried to get down on to a cushion, although most were too worried about how they would get up again. So, they perched on the edge of the window display and smiled at Ralph, waiting for the show to begin.

Ralph was not a natural performer and although he'd practised reading the book out loud a few times, he was completely unprepared to face such a large and enthusiastic audience. He hopped up to sit on the counter and turned to face the sea of little faces below him, many of whom were squinting at him with only one eye as the other was covered by a black plastic eye-patch. Ralph froze, he didn't know what to say and his mouth was suddenly like the inside of a dirty old drawer. Luckily, as always, Stanley came to the rescue and his little paper pirate's hat could be seen bobbing along amongst the children, who squealed with delight as he went about his business of meeting and greeting every one of them.

"As you can see," Ralph said, quieting the crowd. "My first mate, Seaman Stanley, is the leader of the Beagle Book Club and he is very pleased to see so many of you here today."

From there, Ralph found his voice and his reading of the first Captain Pugwash book was greeted with hushed silence, giggles and gasps in all the right places. When he closed the book, he received a huge cheer and Stanley joined in with a volley of over excited barks, until he tumbled off the narrow step he had settled on and into the crowd of children. They all leapt to their feet to check he was all right and play with their pirate king.

"Hello, Elliot," Ralph said to the blue-spectacled goalkeeper. "Did you enjoy that?"

Elliot and his freckles looked up at Ralph seriously, "It was really good. You do good voices."

"Thank you, Elliot. Would you like me to tighten the elastic on your eye-patch? It's fallen down round your neck."

Elliot looked down at it, "No thank you. I like it there, it's like a necklace." The small boy paused and studied his feet for a moment, "Is that alright?" he said in a quiet voice.

Ralph knelt down, so he was directly in the boy's eyeline, "That, Elliot, is perfectly alright. In fact, I think it looks way better there than stuck over your eye, so you can't see where you are going."

Elliot smiled, "Good, I didn't know whether it clashed with my t-shirt."

Ralph couldn't decide whether to laugh or cry that the boy's greatest concern was a possible fashion faux pas rather than a fear of being different, "I think black goes with everything," he managed to say. "It looks great."

"Thank you," Elliot said, before skipping happily off to his grandad, who was trying to juggle a pile of Captain Pugwash books with others on roses, white wine and Mary Quant.

"Is he OK?" Sam asked, coming up behind Ralph.

"I think Elliot is more than OK. In fact, I'm pretty sure he will be running the world one day...or if he's not, he should be."

"Good, so come and serve this enormous queue of people who want to buy books from you," Sam turned Ralph around so he could see the crowd gathered at the counter. "Time to make some money, Mr Bookseller."

❊ ❊ ❊

That evening, Ralph, Sam and Anna gathered on the roof terrace for an emergency meeting.

"I think that's genius," Anna said, leaning against the rickety bar while Sam poured her a glass of wine.

"I feel bad lying to him, but it was the only way," Sam said. "I wouldn't lean too hard on that post, Anna, this bar looks more and more dodgy every day. Joe knows my number, so he ignored me every time I called. But, one of the kitchen staff calling him on their phone meant they got straight through. They've got an interview tomorrow at eleven for the position of manager of Let's Screw. He'll be mad when he sees me at the door instead, but at least he won't be able to ignore me."

"Let's hope he sees sense. Until he can find a manager to run the shop he can't really go anywhere, can he?" Ralph said, resting against the railing on the edge of the terrace. "Did you see that? The roof of the bar seemed to move. I swear those old trellis panels are rotten, let alone those posts holding the roof up. It's not going to last to the summer."

"It's been here years," Anna said, giving the bar a shake. "It'll outlast me, I tell you...Crap!" As she spoke, the thin wooden panels creaked and slid sideways. She managed to hold them upright, but the shift in balance caused the flimsy thatched roof to lunge away from its supports. "Sam, quick!" she yelled.

Sam turned just as the first pole fell away and the roof flapped down towards Anna's head. He leapt across to hold it up, but not before Anna got a decent thwack across the shoulders. He pulled the roof off her and held it up, steadying the other support as he did so, "Ralph, come on, we need you."

Ralph managed to hold on to the other flimsy support pole that kept the remainder of the roof in the air. They all stood for a moment, breathing heavily, waiting to see what trick the bar had up its sleeve next, but everything seemed to have settled and it stayed as it was.

"Now what?" Anna said, still holding the front section together.

Sam assessed the damage, releasing the roof carefully and letting it hang, "I can go to the restaurant and get some screws and stuff to put it back together. I've got a few tools there. Will you guys be OK for a few minutes?" He started to back away across the terrace.

"We'll be fine, but don't be long," Ralph said. "Won't we Anna."

"It'll be a nice rest actually," Anna said. "Standing still for a while."

Sam turned and disappeared through the wooden double doors into Ralph's flat.

"I hope he won't be ages, I think I might need a wee," Anna said.

"Why didn't you say that before Sam left?"

"I didn't know then."

"He's only been gone ten seconds. I'll admit women's bladders are a mystery to me, but honestly, Anna..."

"Alright, don't start...it's the stress."

"Think of something else. Let's talk about the people in the houses down there, under the roofs we can see.

How's the woman with the elephant who's got big back doors?"

Anna snorted, "Her *house* has got big back doors, not her imaginary elephant...ooh, don't make me laugh. I need to go really badly... I'm not sure I can hold it."

"For goodness' sake..."

"Help!!" Anna shouted.

"What are you doing?"

"HELP!! SOMEONE!" Anna yelled at the top of her voice. "I'm going to have to let go and run...PLEASE, someone HELP!"

As Anna was preparing to let the bar out of her grasp, they heard the rattling of the doors at the far end of the terrace that led into Auntie B's old flat, "Holy cow, it's a ghost!" Anna hissed. "Auntie B's heard me and she's..."

"Ghosts do not open doors!" Ralph said. "Joe! Is that you?"

Joe stepped onto the terrace and stood looking at them, his hands deep in the pockets of his jacket, "What's going on?" he said.

"Where have you been?" Anna asked.

"The bar's collapsing. Sam's gone to Cinque to get some tools," as Ralph spoke the loose end of the roof gave an ominous creak and shifted further towards the ground.

"Wait," Joe said. "I have stuff in the shop downstairs," and he shot back into Auntie B's flat.

"Is that where he's been the whole time? Upstairs in Auntie B's flat?" Anna said.

"He must have been, none of us thought to look there," Ralph said with a smile. "Talk about hiding in plain sight."

"I'm so glad he's still here," Anna said, emotion choking her voice. "Perhaps this bar collapsed deliberately to bring us all together on the rooftop."

Ralph shrugged, "I doubt it...hey, I thought you needed the toilet."

"Oh, yes, I forgot all about it when I saw Joe. Now you've mentioned it again I need to go!"

"Well, you'll have to wait, he won't be long."

A few minutes later Joe returned with two long fence posts over his shoulder and a heavy tool bag in his hand, "Still in one piece?"

"Virginitas intacto!" Anna said, brightly. "And the bar hasn't fallen down either."

Joe set the fence posts down without a smile, "Well, I can see one of those statements is true."

Anna gave a hollow laugh, "Cheeky bugger. Come on, Mr Fixit, let's see you do your thing."

Joe quickly got to work without uttering a word, fixing a base and fence post to the terrace floor, which allowed the loose corner of the roof to be pushed back securely into place. He then replaced the other support with the remaining new sturdier post.

"I'm so glad I get to talk to you," Anna said as he worked. "I was so out of order, with you and Mum, it was the shock. You both have a right to do whatever you want; you don't need permission from me. You'd be a great catch for anyone, even Mum. That sounded bad, but she would be lucky to have you...get you...be with you - you know what I mean. You can't leave us because I messed up again. You don't belong in Canada; you belong here with us. You hold us together – look at you, literally putting us back together now."

Joe stood up, without so much as a glance at Anna, "Right, you can let go, that should hold."

Anna stepped back, "Brilliant. You are not just a pretty face, are you?"

Joe started to pack his tools away, "No, I think that's probably all I am," he said dully.

"No, Joe, no," Anna said. "I am truly, truly sorry."

"You say that every time," he said.

"What can I do to convince you?" Anna cried, tears welling in her eyes.

Joe stood up, his tool bag in his hand, "Nothing."

Ralph stepped between them, "Joe, please, none of us want you to go. We always fight, it's part of being a family, isn't it? That's what we do, but we never stop loving each other."

"I guess," Joe said, hefting the heavy bag into his other hand. "I'm not really angry with you. I don't know what to do - I really liked Ruby and now she won't speak to me. I opened myself like I've never done before...it felt...I felt...anyway, I've booked a flight to go back and see my family for a while."

"When?" Ralph asked.

"A week on Sunday."

"Mother's Day?"

"Yeah, I guess so. I'm not sure when I'll be back. I'm not sure what I'll find in Canada, but it's where I was born and my brother and sister are there. Not that I know them now really. Anyway, tomorrow I hope to find someone to manage the shop..."

"Ah," Ralph said, looking at his shoes. "About that. The interview at eleven is actually with Sam. You wouldn't answer his calls and we couldn't find you, so he got one of the restaurant staff to call you. He was going to come and talk to you in the morning."

Joe nodded, his eyes showing no emotion, "I see. Well,

I have two other interviews, so I guess I'll be luckier with them…unless they're fake too?"

Ralph shook his head, "No, nothing to do with us."

"I think I need a break, that's all. I'll probably come back, but I'm not sure yet. I'm trying to find a tenant for the flat, so you'll have a new member of the Rooftop Club to fill the gap."

Anna sobbed quietly, "I don't want anyone else. I want you."

"How's Ruby?" Joe asked.

Anna shook her head, unable to speak, so Ralph answered for her, "We don't really know, Anna can't find her."

Joe looked worried, "You mean she's not at home? You don't think she's started drinking again?"

"I don't know," Anna said. "I hope not. I've tried the few friends she mentioned, even Sharon, that Yoga woman she goes to. No one has seen her."

"I'm sure she'll be fine," Ralph said. "She's probably visiting a relative or something."

"We haven't got any," Anna said. "Only old Auntie Beryl, but I don't know if she's even alive."

Joe started towards Auntie B's flat, "Text me when you find her, I want to know she's safe. Tell her…tell her, I'll miss her. She's very special." He didn't turn back, but went through the doors and locked them behind him.

"He's really going, isn't he?" Anna said.

"It looks like it…unless."

"Unless what?" Anna said, hope leaping into her eyes.

"There's only one person who has a chance of persuading him to stay."

"Who?"

"Your mother."

CHAPTER 31

*The new tenant, a sunset and a member
of the aristocracy.*

A week later Joe, Ralph and Martin stood on the roof terrace and watched the last pieces of daylight burn away over the rooftops.

"When I'm confused, I come to watch the sunset and think," Joe said, without enthusiasm. "It doesn't help though; it leaves me in the dark."

Ralph smiled, "I'm going to miss your jokes."

"Liar."

"I can't believe you are actually going tomorrow. I really thought we could persuade you to stay."

"Sorry, my friend. It's time to go," Joe said, finishing the last of his beer, enjoying the heavy malt taste of the local Harvey's bitter.

Ralph turned and started towards Auntie B's flat, "Maybe."

"No *maybe*, Ralph…"

"OK. Come on you two, we have work to do," Ralph called over his shoulder.

"Ah yes, judging time," Martin said as he and Joe followed Ralph. "The great artist Matisse once said *Every child is an artist, the problem is how to remain an artist once we grow up.*"

"It's so good to still have some quotes floating around up here," Joe said, putting his arm around Martin. "Auntie B was the queen of them, I miss her."

Martin stopped in the doorway to the flat and looked at Joe. "I notice you call her Auntie B now, not Grandma?"

"Sure, Grandma wasn't who she was to me. I mean, it doesn't change how much I loved her, but she is and will always be Auntie B."

"I understand," Martin said, laying a hand on Joe's arm and giving a gentle squeeze. "Come, let us see the joys we have to judge," he turned to take in the artwork of the Beagle Book Club Ralph had spread across the floor of Auntie B's living room.

Joe scratched his beard, "How many are there?"

"Twenty-seven," Ralph said from the floor, where he was sitting amongst pictures of pirates, canons firing and various interpretations of Captain Pugwash on the deck of the Black Pig. "It's amazing, parents have been bringing them in all week and almost every single person has bought something while they were there. It's been my best week for sales since Christmas. It's saved my bacon; I can tell you."

Martin settled down into a small cream armchair, "The book club was an inspired idea. Encouraging children to enjoy stories and to create art is an end in itself, but then to use it for commercial success is to be applauded, old thing, it truly is. As a child I painted in secret, as too many of my scribbles found their way on to the fire."

"That's a bit harsh," Joe said.

"My father was a harsh man. In many ways it spurred me on, as I was told I shouldn't waste his time with anymore pictures until they could match the ones on the walls of his study."

"Good, were they?"

"I liked the Gainsborough's and the Rossetti, but I was never keen on the ones by Constable. Anything that looks good on a tea tray is hard to tolerate, don't you think?" Martin blinked as Ralph and Joe looked at him open mouthed.

"There you are," Anna said, swooping in through the doors from the roof terrace dressed for bed in a fluffy pink dressing gown. "What's going on? Hi Joe," she added, sheepishly.

"Hi," Joe said as he examined some of the pictures. "Any news of your mum?"

"No, nothing. I am really starting to worry, not a single sighting for a whole week."

Joe sighed, "She'll be fine. I think she needs a bit of space from you…and me."

"Maybe," Anna said. "Sorry I'm late, I needed to soak in the bath for a while, I was shattered."

"It's OK, we haven't started yet," Ralph said. "So, is The Copper Kettle ready?"

Anna flopped into the armchair next to Martin, "Who knows, but ready or not we open tomorrow at ten sharp," she scrabbled to sit upright and then produced a squashed paper bag from the pocket of her dressing gown. "Oh, twat-buckets! Sorry, language, but I sat on them. These are for you lot, just something to say thank you for all your help this week. I can't believe it's Mother's Day tomorrow and we are actually going to open," she held out the bag and Joe looked inside cautiously.

"What were they before you sat on them?"

"They were delicious chocolate truffles, thank you for asking," Anna said, shaking the packet at Ralph. "Martin made them actually."

Ralph reached into the bag, "Oh, in that case..."

"To one of Anna's recipes," Martin said.

"Ah," Ralph paused holding a chocolate to his lips. "What's in them?"

Martin smiled, "The very best Belgian chocolate and red wine."

"Really, is that all?" Ralph asked, suspiciously. "The last ones Anna made had popping candy in them."

Anna winced, "I may have overdone the popping candy in that trial batch."

"It's really good," Ralph said, reaching out for another, but Anna slapped his hand away.

"No more if you haven't persuaded Joe to stay," she said, stuffing them back into her fluffy pink pocket.

Joe frowned, all week he had heard every reason why he shouldn't leave Rye, why returning to Canada would be a huge mistake, how much everyone here loved him. But he had finally made a decision about his future and, right or wrong, he was going to do it.

"Dear things, shall we begin the job in hand? We do have rather a lot to achieve this evening," Martin said, calmly. "There are still a couple of rooms for us to clear."

"Oh, yes, Auntie B's things," Anna said. "Has it been really awful?"

Joe closed the door to the terrace and sat beside Ralph on the carpet, "Actually, it's not been as bad as I thought it would be. She had everything in such good order, almost as if she knew. The place needs to be lived in again and it's not fair to delay any more. I should have done it weeks ago."

"But until you find a tenant there's no rush, is there?" Ralph said.

Anna looked at Ralph, "Didn't he tell you?"

"Tell me what?"

"I'm sure I did," Joe said. "I have a new tenant...you have a new member of the Rooftop Club."

Ralph's heart sank, things really were changing and a stranger would be replacing Joe and Auntie B, "What are they like?"

Anna giggled, "Don't worry, they'll fit in pretty easily."

Joe smiled at Ralph, "It was Anna's idea actually and it sorts out quite a few issues."

"Who is it?"

"Martin, of course," Joe said. "Martin is the latest permanent member of The Rye Rooftop Club!"

"I do hope that is not a problem, old thing?"

Anna twirled her dressing gown cord, "Isn't it brilliant? At first Martin was going to live above The Copper Kettle, but then Fiona asked if she could move in as she couldn't go back to her house, obvs. So, I thought if she paid me rent, I could afford to give Martin a proper wage and he could afford to have his own place here and be a real part of the club. It all made sense."

"I'm only sorry I didn't think of it, Martin," Joe said.

"Don't worry, Joe, everything seems to have worked out well and the timing is perfect. I will be honoured to be the custodian of your grandmother's flat and to be a true part of The Rye Rooftop Club. I only hope I'm not too dull for you all."

Ralph laughed, "There is no way we could ever describe you as dull – I mean, with everything you've been through, plus you confessed to being some sort of criminal Robin Hood in the past – stealing from the rich to give to the poor. Now we find out you lived somewhere as a child that had priceless masterpieces on the wall – I wouldn't be surprised if you told us you were a Russian spy, as well!"

"Not a spy for the Russians, no," Martin said with a wink.

Anna shot forwards in her chair, "What? You were a spy?"

"I think that was a joke," Ralph said. "It was a joke, wasn't it?"

"Quite probably," Martin said. "Now, shall we get back to these competition entries, we need to pick a winner?"

Ralph nodded, "Good idea. Oh, by the way, I sent Helen a Mother's Day card. I know she hasn't actually given birth yet, but I signed it from all of us."

"Talking of post..." Joe said as he scrambled to his feet and left the room.

"That is a lovely thought," Martin said to Ralph. "I trust she is well?"

"Yes, she's doing OK. Since she got back she's put our house on the market and plans to move in with an old friend, who's also recently split up with her partner, so they are going to share baby duties."

Joe came back into the room, "Sorry about that, the new postman has been leaving all Auntie B's post with me in the shop. Something came for you, Martin, I completely forgot." He handed him a couple of envelopes.

"Thank you. I hope you don't mind, but I took the liberty of telling my soon-to-be former wife of my new place, so that her solicitor can find me."

Joe crouched down on the floor again, "It made me laugh, both envelopes were addressed to Lord Martin. I suppose that's your wife being funny, is it?"

Martin glanced quickly at the envelopes and tucked them behind him in the armchair, "It would be quite a discovery if she was found to have a sense of humour."

"Then why *Lord* Martin?"

Martin hesitated, considering how much honesty was required as he officially joined the Rooftop Club. In the end he shrugged and pulled the envelopes out from behind him, "It is my official title."

They all stared at him.

"Wait, you're a lord?" Joe asked. "Like a proper lord?"

"I can imagine it's hard to believe, but, yes."

"How come you never told us?" Ralph said.

"There didn't seem any need, old thing. What would have been the benefit of telling you? It's not something in which I take any pride. I have certainly done nothing to deserve it, apart from surviving longer than my father...and my older brother," Martin shuffled the envelopes in his hands.

Anna pulled out the flattened bag of chocolates and popped one in her mouth, "So, is Martin your surname or your first name?"

"It is my family name, but people have always simply referred to me as Martin since school days. My full name is Phillip Colborn Edward Martin, Earl of Groombridge. Listen, this is all history, literally. To you and everyone else I am Martin, and I trust we can continue as before.

It's all nonsense and makes no difference in the real world."

"But what about the other stuff?" Ralph asked. "You told Sam and I that you used to steal from the rich, is that true?"

Martin sighed and sat back, his long thin hands brushing the fabric on the chair arms, "There are things in my past of which I am proud and many more of which I am not. If it is alright with you all, I will tell you my story in time, but not now. Perhaps it will be of sufficient interest to lure Joe back to these shores one day?"

"Sorry," Anna said. "Can I ask you one question, though?"

"Of course," Martin said.

"Were you really a spy?"

Martin chuckled, "No, I was never a spy."

Anna flopped back against her chair, "Thank goodness. I'll sleep better knowing that and I'm going to need all the rest I can get before tomorrow."

"Then we must resolve another puzzle, dear thing. Who has won the first Beagle Book Club art competition?"

Ralph held up a thick piece of cardboard with the face of Captain Pugwash on it, "This is my favourite," he said. The face was created entirely out of dried pasta, his hair and moustache were spaghetti, painstakingly painted black, the nose was a large piece of macaroni turned pink and the eyebrows were whole-wheat fusilli.

"I would agree, it is a triumph," Martin said, giving the picture a thumbs up.

"It works for me," Joe agreed. "Who did it?"

Ralph read from the back of the painting, "A girl called Laura Panter, aged eight and three quarters. I don't know her."

"I do," Anna said. "She's lovely, her mum drives the mobile library. She has fabulous hair – Laura, not her mother. It goes in all sorts of directions, on a good day I'm sure she can pick up Sky telly with it."

"Poor girl," Ralph said. "I think she deserves to win. Are we all agreed?"

"I believe we are, old thing."

As Martin spoke, Captain Pugwash's macaroni nose slid down the picture and on to the carpet. Anna let out a squeak, but it was too late as his hair, eyebrows and ears also fell in a rattling cascade to the floor.

"Damn," Ralph said, trying to catch the last pieces. "I need to display the winning painting in the shop window. Does anyone have any glue?"

They spent the next twenty minutes collecting the pasta together and trying to recreate little Laura Panter's picture, laughing and working in perfect harmony. Joe eventually sat back and watched his friends, trying to fix the memory in his mind. It was at times like this he struggled to remember why he was going to do what he had planned, and why he couldn't continue to build his life here. But this was when the image of Ruby would come back to him, in his arms in the kitchen of The Copper Kettle, and the feel of the kiss they had shared. He had sent her many text messages trying to explain how he felt, but silence was the only response. She had made her choice and he was left alone and exposed, never having truly expressed his feelings to anyone before.

As the others giggled and tried to stick the pasta back in place he slipped from the room, collected his bike from the shop and cycled back to his house by the beach.

Despite the cold air and freezing March temperatures he walked down the shingle to the edge of the sea with bare feet. To his right he could see the lights of Rye glowing softly against the deep grey sky, the dark expanse of water stretched away in front of him until it met the horizon that cradled a bright crescent moon. He took a deep breath and filled his lungs with the damp, salty air. He shivered as he looked into the gently rolling waves. He scrubbed his hands across his face and through his beard. Then with trembling fingers he unzipped his jacket, stripped off his shirt, unbuckled his trousers and threw all his clothes aside.

The cold water stung sharply. One step, two, then three, up to his knees already. A few more steps and the water lapped the top of his thighs. He took a last lungfull of air and launched himself up and forwards. His body broke through the wave that closed around him and covered him, as if he had never been there.

CHAPTER 32

*The bright Copper Kettle, Maltesers
and Judy goes solo.*

For opening day at The Copper Kettle, Anna had decided to base herself in the kitchen there, leaving Martin in charge at The Cookery. As things settled down in the new tearooms, they would swap and fall into a regular routine. As the clock ticked towards ten o'clock on Sunday morning, Anna was flying around the kitchen with armfuls of scones, teacakes and pots of clotted cream.

Fiona had bought a new outfit of black pencil skirt and black silk blouse, with smart shiny black shoes with a small heel and a gold buckle across the front. She checked her appearance in the mirror in the ladies loo for the third time, not quite believing it was her. She thought she looked elegant and had colour in her cheeks for the first time in an awfully long time - it felt good.

Anna's voice floated into the toilet, "Right, five

minutes to go, everyone! Doors to manual."

Fiona returned to the tearoom and Anna handed her a white lace cap and apron, "Here you go," she said. "Rosie, do you need a hand with your hat?"

Rosie was trying to stuff her hairband of daisies into the little cap.

"Perhaps it would be easier without the flowers?" Anna suggested.

"Leave it to me," Fiona said, moving Rosie into the toilet to stand her in front of the mirror while she sorted out her head gear.

"Thank you," Anna said. She took a deep breath and let it out slowly as she stood in the middle of the transformed tearoom.

The room was now bright and clean, but still had an air of its long history. The tables were covered in crisp white linen and each table had a vintage tin of syrup, treacle or condensed milk with a small spray of early spring flowers in them. Each napkin was rolled and held in place by a different vintage napkin ring supplied by Anna's friend, Jumble Jim.

Ralph's painting on the long wall lifted the room, with a rich copper kettle shining in the centre, surrounded by piles of sponge cakes, muffins, scones, jam jars and even a couple of cute looking mice nibbling on a piece of cheese at the bottom by the skirting board. Above the painting in a scrolling font was written *The peace of cake.*

Anna was hugely proud of what she had achieved with the help of her friends, but it had been her drive and her determination that had made it all happen. She glanced at the wall with Dew-drop Dobson's bird illustrations and smiled, "I hope you like it," she whispered.

"I also hope you know your daughter is safe now."

She was wiping away a tear when Fiona and Rosie re-appeared from the toilet, "Are you alright, Anna?"

"Yes, sorry, just having a moment," Anna said. "You two look great, very smart."

"I'm so excited," Fiona said. "And a bit nervous, I hope I don't let you down. I am not going to be as good as Irene."

"Now, enough of that, we are all going to be great. I am sure Irene is having a lovely time being in charge of The Cookery, she appeared this morning with a whistle, some new comfy trainers and a tabard her kids had bought her for Mother's Day. I had to confiscate the whistle." Anna checked the cup-cake shaped clock on the wall, "Right, troops, I have no idea how many people are coming, it's a soft opening, so we haven't really advertised. I'm hoping that as everywhere else is pretty much booked up for Mother's Day we will get a few people looking for somewhere they can just walk in and get a table. Rosie, do you want to put the music on?"

Rosie nodded, still fiddling with her cap, "OK, can I choose the music?"

"Not yet, Rosie, maybe one day. We'll have the Agatha Christie TV themes album for now and then we can decide where we go from there. Alright?"

Rosie floated off behind the cake counter and Fiona turned to Anna, "I hope you are very proud, Anna. When I suggested you bought this place, I hadn't really thought about what you would do with it. I saw it as a means to an end for me. But look at it, it's wonderful, better than I ever remember it with Dad."

"Thank you," Anna said, beaming. "It is exactly what I dreamed of and I never thought I could do it alone. Of course, I haven't done it alone, I've had all my friends around me, so how could I have failed? They wouldn't have let me. It's also a new beginning for your father's café and for you - he would be proud."

"Yes, I think he would. Of both of us."

"I'm not sure about that, but he'd definitely be proud of you," Anna said as she gave Fiona a hug.

"There's a man with his nose up against the window," Rosie said from behind them.

Anna let Fiona go and straightened her Miss Marple and the Gardens of St Mary Mead apron, "Then you had better go and let our first customer in then, Rosie."

* * *

Judy McMurray did up the poppers on the new blue boiler suit she had bought to begin her new job as manager of Let's Screw. Her sister, Janet, had embroidered her name on the top pocket, where she now tucked a new pen and pencil. She was ready to begin her first solo day without Joe. She had shadowed him for the previous four days and felt confident she could handle what would probably be a fairly quiet Sunday. On a clipboard she had the check list of daily tasks her friend Susan had laminated for her, but she wasn't worried, as Joe had promised to pop in during the morning to check she was alright and answer any last questions before he got ready to go to the airport - but by the end of trading there had been no sign of him.

* * *

Ralph arrived at Cinque as the streets of Rye were

starting to empty and the shops closed. He waited while Stanley finished licking the remains of an unseasonal ice cream from the edge of the pavement and then they went inside.

"Hi, Dawa," Ralph said. "Can I put Stanley in Sam's cupboard? I've brought a bone for him to tackle, which should keep him busy for a while. He likes it in there when it's nice and quiet."

"Be my guest," Dawa said from behind the bar, where he was relaxing with a tiny espresso.

"Busy day?" Ralph asked as he shut the door on Stanley.

Dawa sighed, "Yes, but there are still plenty of mothers with handbags stuffed dull off indigestion tablets to feed yet."

"Everything alright?"

"Was your mother obsessed with you getting married, Ralph?"

"Not really, I'm not sure she was too bothered either way."

"Excellent woman, would you like to swap? You can have Mama Singh."

Ralph smiled, "Do you like cruises?"

"I get seasick."

"I don't think it would work then."

"Shame."

Ralph leaned over the counter and whispered, "Has Jane been in touch with Sam?"

"Not that I know of, why?"

"Well, he texted me to come over when I closed. He made it sound really odd, like I had to come as soon as I could."

"Ah, I don't believe that is to do with his mother,

thank goodness. You will find him upstairs."

Ralph looked around, "Upstairs? I didn't even know there was an upstairs."

Dawa chuckled and led him back to a small door beside the large kitchen swing doors, "Here you go," he said.

"How come I've never seen this before?"

"We normally have some coat stands in front of it. We don't use the floor above, although it came with the deal Sam got for the building. Both floors are his, he had thought about expanding the dining room up there if things went well. Do go up," Dawa turned and headed back to the bar to make himself another strong coffee to see him through the rest of the evening.

Ralph made his way up the narrow staircase behind the door and saw that light was flooding down on him from above. As he reached the top of the stairs, there was a simple wooden balustrade separating him from an enormous open room with exposed brick walls, large metal framed windows and a dust covered timber floor. Sam had his back to him at the far side of the room, looking at some large sheets of paper pinned to the wall.

"What are you doing? It's a huge space, I had no idea it was even here."

"We all have our secrets," Sam said turning to him. "Now, I should really have carried you over the threshold, but you've been knocking back the Maltesers lately and I'm not sure my back would have taken it, so you'll have to hop over here on your own."

"You bought me the Maltesers! I knew you were a feeder," Ralph said as he limped across the room. "Bloody hell, this must be as big as the restaurant and kitchen combined."

Sam stood in the middle of the floor, looking nervous, "It is, but currently it's just a big empty room."

"I can see that, but what's it for?"

"I've never known what to do with it, but it's amazing. The light is fantastic," Sam led Ralph over to one of the huge windows, made up of dozens of square panes of glass held between metal frames, lumpy from layers of paint added over the years. He ran his hand along the exposed red bricks of the wall, dislodging dust and dried mortar. The floor was scuffed floorboards and the ceiling was exposed beams and joists. "It'd take some work to transform it, but it could be incredible."

Ralph smiled at him, "Are you ready to expand then?"

"Kind of. Do you like it?"

"I love it!"

"Thank heavens, because this is where we could live," Sam said, his green eyes shining.

"What?"

"Look, it's so big, we can turn the whole thing into the most amazing apartment. Come here, come on," Sam practically skipped over to the far wall. "The architect who worked with me to convert the restaurant downstairs has drawn up these plans for us. They are only very early ideas and obviously you can change what you want, but at least it shows what can be done. We've got room for a fabulous bedroom over here," he gestured to the corner of the room. "Then there'd be a bathroom there, then an open plan living room and kitchen. I mean, we could have two bedrooms if we wanted, but they'd be much smaller, so I thought maybe just one nice big one for us..." Sam ground to a halt as he saw Ralph standing still, his face slack with shock. "You're not saying anything."

Ralph swallowed, "Wow, this is quite a...you know. When did you...?"

Sam stepped closer to him and took both of Ralph's hands in his, "It started on Valentine's Day, the day of your accident. When I thought something really bad had happened to you, for a moment I knew what it would be like if you weren't there anymore and it was the worst feeling I had ever known. Then, when we each went to the wrong house, it seemed crazy we didn't live together. We stay a few nights in your place, a few nights in mine. Then all the stuff with my mother - how could I have survived without you at my side? And my habit of running off if I get scared...well, if we lived together I could only run to the bathroom, couldn't I? This makes sense; we can make something truly special out of it and we can be together. I've waited so long for you, I don't want to waste another minute. If you rent out your flat above The Bookery and I sell my house, we can do this. What do you think?"

Ralph looked into Sam's eyes, "I think I don't know what I'd do without you either. But...this is a surprise. I mean, I've only known you a few months...a few crazy months."

"I know this has all happened really quickly, but we are meant to be together, aren't we? Here, in Rye?"

"Yes, I think we are, but..."

"Please don't keep saying *but,* you're frightening me. I want us to start building a proper life together. I know I want nothing more than this...than you."

Ralph looked at Sam for a long moment, "What the hell, let's do it! Everything's been thrown up in the air so often, why not do it again?"

"Are you sure? I mean, you can think about it..."

"I've spent too long thinking about things and not doing them. I want to do *this*."

"This is amazing!" Sam laughed.

Ralph turned and looked at the room that would soon be his and Sam's home, "Alright. We're doing this... building a home together. Right. Good. Fine."

"Fine? Is that it?"

"I'm sorry...I...don't have the words. Oh, yes, I do...I have one condition I need you to agree to."

"Ok, what is it?" Sam said, warily.

"We have to make this a one-bedroom apartment, so your mother can never come and stay."

"That, Mr Bookseller, sounds like a deal." Sam pulled Ralph to him and held him tighter than he had ever held anyone in his life.

❊ ❊ ❊

Judy closed Let's Screw at the end of the day, carefully following her laminated check list on her clipboard. It had been an anxious day, but nothing major had gone wrong – except locking herself out of the till on one occasion when she'd been a bit overconfident with a few of the buttons. She would enjoy a nice glass of whiskey tonight with her coven of female friends and prepare herself to do it all again tomorrow. She switched off the lights and locked the door behind her, looking back to check the shop was dark and secure. As she walked home, she thought it was strange Joe had not called in to say goodbye and check she was alright, but she supposed he must have changed his plans.

CHAPTER 33

*The return of the gnomes, baba ganoush
and time to fly.*

Anna sat at one of the tearoom's tables watching the light fade outside, enjoying the warm glow of success. From the moment the first customer had stepped over the threshold Mother's Day had been a blur. They had faced a steady stream of customers - enough to test them, but not enough to be overwhelmed. The afternoon teas were a huge success, the Rye Tea was the most popular, including sandwiches made with local honey and fairy cakes topped with fondant seagulls. The Brighton Tea also proved popular, featuring meringues in the shape of the famous Regency Pavilion and little chunks of Brighton rock in the mint chocolate brownies.

She knew there was a lot of work still to do, but she was pretty sure things would be alright. Just as she was thinking about getting out of the chair a dark shadow appeared outside the tearoom door and she heard a soft knock.

"I'm afraid, we're closed," she called, but the knock came again. "Sorry, we aren't open now," she said more loudly as she made her way towards the door.

"It's me," a voice said through the glass.

"Who's me?"

"Your mother."

Anna halted, "Oh."

"Anna?"

Anna shook herself and opened the door, "I wasn't expecting anyone, that's all."

Ruby stood on the pavement with a large bunch of red and cream roses and a card in an envelope, "I wanted to bring you these on your opening day." She handed them to Anna and started to step back, "I won't stay."

"No, don't go. Come in," Anna said.

"I don't want to be a nuisance."

"Come in," Anna opened the door wide for Ruby. "Please, I've been so worried about you."

"I'm fine," Ruby said as she stepped inside and looked around. "Oh, Anna it's beautiful. Well done you. Have you had a successful day?"

"Yes, it's been great. People really seemed to like it," Anna laid the flowers and card on the table. "It should be me giving you flowers and a card today, shouldn't it? Not the other way around."

Ruby waved her hand at Anna, "Oh, don't worry, I'm quite used to not getting anything on Mother's Day," then her hand shot to her mouth as she realised what she had said. "That was awful, I didn't mean it like it sounded."

Anna smiled, "Yes, you did. You had a perfect right to

say it because it was the truth." She pulled out a chair next to the one she'd been sitting on, "Sit down, we need to talk."

Ruby tucked a stray piece of hair behind her ear, "Really?"

"Just sit, Mum."

Ruby sat carefully in the chair, holding her handbag tightly on her lap.

"I missed you," Anna said.

Ruby looked shocked, "Did you?"

"Yes, I was worried about you."

"I thought you needed some space away from me, so I went to visit your Great Auntie Beryl."

"Is she still alive?"

"Very much so. Still singing soprano with the church choir at full belt, making rock-hard sponge cakes for anyone she can."

"Good for her." Anna stared at her mother for a moment, "Who are you?"

"I don't understand."

Anna smiled, "I have no idea who you are, do I? Not really. Dad knew you when you were a girl and he liked you so much he married you. Auntie B was always telling me to get to know you, as if she knew you too."

"She was a good friend to me."

"Joe has seen the real you and appears to be completely...smitten. There's a word I don't use often. Smitten. I've never seen him so *smitten*. Anyway, the point is that I've realised the person who should know you best, your daughter, really doesn't know you at all."

"What child really knows who their mother is? They're simply Mum and that's enough."

"But we've tried that and it didn't go too well, did it?

I blame you for not being a very good mother and you blame yourself for the same thing. Right?"

Ruby laughed, relaxing her grip slightly on her bag, "That sums it up pretty well."

"Well, then, let's try something else. Tell me who Ruby is. Tell me all the things she did as a child, growing up – all those things a mother should never tell her daughter. Waking up in a skip with no idea how she got there, breaking laws, kissing boys, stealing make-up, screaming at boy bands. I want to know everything and anything about Ruby."

"I'll tell you about Ruby if you promise to tell me about Anna. The force of nature that is Anna."

"OK, but it won't all be pretty."

Ruby smiled, "I want to know it all." She leant forward and took Anna's face in her hands, "But first, listen to me, Anna, I'm sorry I didn't tell you about Joe. I should have done, he is a part of your tight circle, your Rooftop Club. But, you see, I felt happy and almost worthy of someone else wanting me and I got carried away. It was wrong and it will not happen again. You are my priority."

"Listen, if I have learnt anything – and Baba Ganoush knows I need to learn some things in a hurry!"

"Isn't babaganoush mashed aubergine?"

"Is it? I thought he was a god of something? Anyway, I was wrong and ridiculous and completely unfair to you. You have every right to be happy and you absolutely should feel wanted - we both should! If you want Joe and he wants you then you need to go get him. He's gorgeous and kind and sweet and…he's leaving."

"Leaving? Where is he going?" Ruby's heart started to beat a little faster. "Not Scotland?"

"No, Imogen is long gone. He's completely fallen for *you*. We've tried everything, I even offered to fling myself in the River Rother, but he's booked a ticket back to Canada. I know he doesn't want to go, but he's being bloody minded. The only person we think can change his mind is you."

Ruby held her breath, "Me?"

Anna nodded, "Absolutely, but unless you are serious about him too, we have to let him go. Wow, I can't believe I said that! Do you think I'm growing up?"

Ruby looked at her daughter, her beautiful open face and large kind eyes, "Maybe a little bit. Maybe we both are."

"Well, do you love him?" Anna asked.

"Love? I don't know yet and I'm pretty sure he doesn't either. But I do know there is a real connection between us and given time there may be love, one day. I know it's been awful hiding from him, convincing myself I didn't feel anything."

Anna jumped to her feet, "Then go get him. If you both feel that way, then you need to find out if it really is love. Now! Look at the time!" The cup-cake clock said it was nearly six o'clock.

"What's the rush? We still have so much to talk about. You wanted to know more about me…"

"Yes, yes, I know and I still do, but we can do it later over big non-alcoholic cocktails, with little umbrellas and disgusting cherries and stuff. You have to hurry; he's leaving for the airport soon. He didn't want a fuss, so he said he'd be gone before we'd all closed the shops. He's staying in one of the hotels at the airport overnight, as the flight is at the crack of doom in the morning. So, you have to go to his house – shit, shit,

shit - sorry, emergency language, but it might already be too late! So, if he's not there you have to go to Gatwick and try all the hotels. Put your foot down and with your driving you could still catch him," she pulled her mother up from the chair.

"But Anna, if he's made up his mind…" Ruby tried to say.

Anna opened the door and started pushing her through it, "He made up his mind without *you*. He thought you'd given him up, like alcohol. Once he knows you want him, he'll stay. Please, Mum, you have to go and find him - for both our sakes. I nearly ruined everything, but you can make it all alright."

Ruby stopped and looked at her daughter, "That's my job after all," she said. "That's what mother's do."

"Exactly," Anna smiled. "So, go get your man and bring my friend home. Two birds with one whatsit in the hand with a bushel. Go!"

Ruby ran to her car, struggling to get the keys out of her bag. She dropped them once then retrieved them and unlocked the door. She threw her handbag across to the passenger seat and snapped her seatbelt in place. She gripped the wheel hard and revved the engine, "Come on Ruby," she said to herself. "You can do this. It's just like racing along the back of Camber Sands in Auntie Beryl's Triumph Toledo."

The bright red car shot around the corner from the old marketplace, past The Copper Kettle where Anna stood waving a tea towel wildly in the air like a starting flag. Ruby bounced down the cobbles and screeched around the sharp left turn into the High Street, she put her foot down as she flew past The Cookery, then The Bookery and finally Let's Screw.

She slammed on the brakes, throwing herself against the seatbelt as the car slid and squealed to a sudden halt. She sat panting in the middle of the road, the engine noise roaring around her. Then a car horn honked from behind, so she indicated and pulled into the curb. Still out of breath, she got out of the car and ran back up the High Street.

Ruby didn't know whether it was instinct or something catching her eye that had made her stop, but as she arrived at Let's Screw she let out a small cry. Sitting in a deckchair in the window display with a gnome on his lap was Joe.

The streetlight barely lit him in his dark jacket and jeans, but something had told Ruby he was there. She watched him for a few moments, then knocked gently on the window. He had his eyes closed and didn't respond. She knocked louder and his eye lids flickered and opened. He took a moment to focus, as if he had been fast asleep, then his eyes locked on to hers and he smiled. Finding the shop door unlocked she stepped inside and carefully tiptoed through the gnomes and garden tools and sat on the other deckchair beside him.

"Hello," she said.

"Hi."

"Caught any fish lately?" she nodded at the lecherous little gnome with his fishing rod.

"Nope, neither of us."

"Why did the vegan go fishing?" she asked in a serious voice.

Joe frowned, "I don't know, why?"

"For the halibut!"

He shook his head, "I think you should leave the jokes to me."

"Good idea. That's the only one I know anyway."

They sat for a moment as the butterflies and birds on strings swung around their heads.

"I'm sorry I ran off again," Ruby said. "I didn't want to leave you. I loved kissing you."

"But you still ran."

"Yes, it was a mistake."

"Really?"

"Yes. Joe, I'm no Psychic Sue, and even though we shouldn't, somehow I think we fit together."

"Who's Psychic Sue?"

"Never mind. The point is that I don't want you to go. I want to spend more time with you and see what happens...with us. If that's something you want too then please stay in Rye."

Joe sat forward in his deckchair and put the gnome on the ground, "I went skinny dipping last night. Boy, it was cold. I lasted about thirty seconds, but it woke me up. It made me want to fight – fight to get out of the water, fight to get warm...fight for you, but I didn't know how."

Ruby reached forward and caressed his face, her hands trembled as the soft bristles of his beard tickled her skin, "So, you're not going to go?"

"I have to go."

"Why?"

"I have to face my family. I have a brother and a sister I haven't spoken to in more than ten years, and nieces and nephews I've never met. Look, you may as well know, I am not the cool guy you think I am...you do think I'm cool, don't you?"

Ruby smiled, "Yes, I think you're cool."

"You may change your mind, but I want you to know

the real me – be the first person to know the truth. When I left home as a teenager I was mad with my family, as lots of kids are, and I took off round the world. After I'd settled down here with Auntie B I began to see things differently, I realised they hadn't pushed me away because they didn't like me, but they'd wanted me to have a better, fuller life than them. It had been tough for my Mom and Pop to start with nothing in a new country and they'd had to fight for everything. Then my Pop died and later my Mom died of cancer, she hadn't told me she was ill because she didn't want me to stop having fun and disrupt my life. I went back for her funeral; Auntie B couldn't face coming with me so I went alone. But..." he took a few deep breaths. "Jeez, this is hard."

Ruby took his shaking hand and squeezed it, "You're doing really well. Her funeral must have been hard."

"That's just it...I didn't go. I landed in Canada, but I couldn't go. I couldn't face the rest of my family. I hadn't been there when Pop died and I hadn't been there for my Mom when she was sick."

"But you said she didn't tell you; she was trying to protect you, Joe."

"I know, but I failed them. There I was living this crazy life when they were going through all that without me. I stood outside the airport and I knew I didn't belong there, I didn't deserve to be a part of the family anymore. So, I spent a week hiding in a hotel and came back to the UK again. I never told Auntie B or anyone. I let my Mom down right at the end."

"No, no you didn't, Joe. You did exactly what she wanted – you were living your own life. If a mother truly loves her children, she wants them to be amazing people in their own right, doing their own thing, being free to be exactly who they want to be."

"You think?"

"Absolutely. Families are so complicated and there is no right way to navigate them, but if we turn out to be good people doing good things then I really think they can be nothing but proud of us. And I am sure she would be incredibly proud of you - you are a good man, Joe."

"You think so? I've spent so many years running - from home, from family, from making proper connections with people. Jumping from country to country, from girl to girl, from joke to joke. I never really felt like I belonged anywhere, even here. But now I want to. I want to commit, to stop, to come to rest. But before I can do that, I need to go back one more time and face what's in Canada, what's left of my family and show them who I am now."

"I see. Well, then you must go."

"But I'd rather not do it alone," he stood and pulled her up with him. "Ruby, you are the strongest person I know...you have changed everything about yourself, dealt with so many of your demons and right now I need some of your strength. I think we both need to let go of our pasts."

Ruby let out a small gasp and stepped away from him and leant against the window, "You just reminded me of something my Yogini, Sharon, said. She told me I should be more like a snake."

"Now, it may be because I'm foreign, but everything in that sentence needs explaining."

"Sharon is my life coach, she's a bit odd, but at the same time a lot of what she says makes sense. You see, a snake sheds its skin up to twelve times a year, just slips out of it and leaves it behind. Sharon believes we should be like that as we go through life. We all change as we grow and we all have to leave things behind, so maybe we should just shed the skin of who we were and move on with who we are now," Ruby looked embarrassed. "Well, that's her theory anyway."

"I think it's brilliant, that's exactly what we should do," Joe pulled Ruby into his arms again. "New you, new me. A fresh start for us both."

"Do you think we could?"

"I think we should give it our best shot. I'd like to find out who we really are...together," as he stared at Ruby's flushed face he smiled and slowly leant in, kissing her gently on the lips. Her tension melted as she kissed him back.

"So, what happens now?" she said.

"Well, I guess we have two options. We can either stay here and try and party with the gnomes..."

"Or?" she said, quickly.

"Point taken," Joe grinned. "Or we can get away from this place for a while, start with Canada and see what happens. I have a new shop manager on a six-month contract, so she'll look after the shop. Martin is going to live in the flat upstairs. So..."

"How can I go to Canada?"

"Easy, you call and see if they have a ticket for the same flight as me or the one after that. Then go home pack a bag, lock the house and leave."

"You make it sound so easy."

"It can be. Do you have anything else to do tomorrow?"

"Well, no."

"Do you have an empty bag at home?"

"Yes."

"Do you have stuff you can put in it?"

"Yes."

"Then let's go."

"But Anna and your friends…"

"Will all be here when we get back."

"They will, won't they? And I will come back to Rye, Joe, my daughter is here."

"I know, I'll be back too, Rye is my home. This is where I want to be."

"Oh, fuck it! Let's do it!"

Joe whooped and started to race around the shop collecting his bike and his keys, "Your bad habits are getting so much better! That is the best swearing I've ever heard you do. Right, we can go to your place then back to mine, I've got a taxi booked from there. There's a room in the airport hotel waiting for me…but I can get another one for you, if you like?"

Ruby smiled at him, "I think one room will be absolutely fine, Joe."

Joe put his arms around her, "Are we really going to do this, Ruby?"

"Yes, Joe, I think we are," and she kissed him long and hard.

Joe took a moment to enjoy the sensation and then frowned, "Are you ready? The last time anyone sat on the handlebars of one of my bikes I was in Bangkok wearing nothing but a paper butterfly and pair of flip-flops."

Ruby laughed with a freedom that seemed to rise up from deep inside her, "Now, everything in that sentence needs an explanation, but I think I will get in my car and meet you at yours in an hour. We may be starting our adventure together, but I do not intend to get there on the handlebars of your bike..."

CHAPTER 34

The last moments of Mother's Day.

As the church clock ticked silently towards midnight and the end of Mother's Day, Anna walked the silent streets of Rye bathed in the blues and greys of night. An unusual calm surrounded her as she thought back over the day; the thrill of hearing happy customers chatting and laughing their way through cakes and scones in her new tearooms, the clunk and ping of the till as she made the first sales in her new business. Not to mention, the pride she felt in seeing Fiona's flushed face serving tables all day, with a genuine smile that never once faltered.

Then she thought of the laughter in her mother's voice when she had rung to tell her she had found Joe and they were both in a taxi on their way to the airport! Her instant reaction had been horror - Ruby had not done what she had been asked and kept Joe in Rye, instead, she was leaving with him. But then she realised it was comforting that Joe was not going home alone to Canada to lay to rest whatever family demons awaited him there. She realised she was pleased that her mother could spread her wings and fly away from the confines of Rye to see if she could find happiness, and she knew she had to let them go – for now. She had wished them luck and told them to come home soon.

She approached Cinque as the last light was extinguished inside and the door opened ahead of her. Dawa stepped out and locked the door, only seeing her as he turned, "Anna? Is everything OK, you're out late?"

"Dawa, yes, I'm fine. Just blowing the cobwebs off after a busy day."

"I hope your launch went well?"

"It went really well, thank you," she stepped to one side to start to walk around him. "Goodnight, Dawa."

"Anna? Do you want to be alone?"

"I beg your pardon?"

"On your walk. I wondered if you might like a little company?" he said.

"Oh, yes, that would be nice, thank you."

He smiled at her, his beautiful teeth and strong jaw beneath his beard making Anna feel a little giddy, "I may need to take your arm, though," she said. "These cobbles are a nightmare with these clogs. They're from Holland and I don't know how they tiptoe through tulips in them when I can barely walk down the High Street."

He held out his arm to her, "I'd be delighted. Which way would you like to go?"

"Down to the quay, I think," Anna said, so they turned and walked down the road. "You have such good manners and shoes and teeth, why aren't you married?"

Dawa laughed, a sound Anna did not hear often from him, but she liked it…a lot.

"Have you been talking to Mama Singh?" he said.

"No, but I'd like to."

"And she would like talking to you Anna…a lot."

They chatted easily as they strolled away from the centre of town, so they didn't see Ralph walking Stanley in a different direction, too excited at the prospect of his new life and new home with Sam to sleep. They didn't see Stanley pull hard on his lead as he came to the top of the hill or hear Ralph say, "Not again, Stan, no pulling," as he brought him to heel. They didn't hear Stanley's bark as he passed The Copper Kettle or the whimpering that followed as Ralph kept on walking for home.

So, none of them, except Stanley, heard the crackle or saw the glow of orange flames growing stronger behind the ancient glass of the windows, or the thick, dark smoke drifting under the door of The Copper Kettle, up into the air and out over the roofs of Rye.

Thank You For Reading Book Two In The Rye Rooftop Club Series.

If you enjoyed this book, please review it on Amazon.co.uk so other readers can find their way to Rye and meet the Rooftop Club.

The Rooftop Club will return for new adventures in

The Rye Rooftop Club:

Summer Solstice

To keep up to date with news on further books in the series and more from author Mark Feakins, follow us on Facebook: **My Writing Life**

Acknowledgements

Thanks again to all of my friends and acquaintances who have had their names recycled for this second book. Although I have borrowed their names, I have not used any of their characteristics and any peculiarities of the characters named after them are entirely of my own creation.

Thanks also to my insightful team of early readers, Marie, Sue, Rosie, Gillian and Joanne for their continued enthusiasm and guidance.

Last, but by no means least, to Martin, who continues to laugh with me every day and ploughs through every version of each book putting me back on the straight and narrow. He is also my tireless comedy contributor - the highlight in this book being the title of Jane Scott's autobiography, *Whatever Happened to Jane, baby?*

About The Author

Mark Feakins grew up on the Sussex coast and has been a frequent visitor to Rye throughout his life. He moved to London to go to drama school and, after a brief time as an actor and running his own theatre company, he began working in theatres; as the Programmer for The Bloomsbury Theatre and the General Manager of the Young Vic. He then travelled further north as Executive Producer of Sheffield Theatres before creating his own photography business. He has a degree in Librarianship, danced around a maypole on BBC TV's Playschool and won Channel 4's Come Dine with Me in 2010. Mark now lives happily in the region of Valencia in Spain, with his husband Martin.

E: markfeakins@gmail.com
Facebook: My Writing Life

Books by Mark Feakins:

The Rye Series

#1 The Rye Rooftop Club
#2 The Rye Rooftop Club: Mother's Day

Printed in Great Britain
by Amazon